11/21

Rising Star

Rising Star

Book One in the Rise and Fall of Dani Truehart Series

MICHELE KWASNIEWSKI

RAND-SMITH PUBLISHING

RISING STAR: Book One in the Rise of Dani Truehart Series

Print ISBN: 978-1-950544-16-5 (paperback)
Digital ISBN: 978-1-950544-17-2

Registered with the Library of Congress

Rand-Smith Publishing
www.Rand-Smith.com
Ashland, VA

Printed in the USA

Contents

Dedication

For Craig & Liam.
  Love you both forever and a day.

Acknowledgements

I've dreamed about writing this page for years! This book was a long time in the making. Lots of starts and stops, but we finally made it. I say we because this was truly the product of a village! Thank you to all my family and friends for listening to me talk about my characters and story for hours, listening to me moan about querying and encouraging me not to give up.

Much love and appreciation to my wonderful agent, Diane Nine, and all the people at Nine Speakers whose time and energy made this dream come true. Diane, I know you're always going to tell it to me straight, and to me, honesty is as valuable as gold.

Many thanks the team at Rand-Smith for taking a chance on an unknown mom with a dream. Your insightful editorial notes really took my story to the next level, and I cannot thank you enough for all your hard work.

The best thing to come out of my job on a popular reality show is my friendship with Jack Owens. Thank you for recommending me to Diane and for all your help and support in getting my first book published. You blazed a trail for me into the world of publishing, and I am very grateful.

I would never have started writing without the encouragement of my dear friend, James Perez-Gillespie. You've read this book almost as many times as I have and your encouragement, love and support has been invaluable. Onward and upward!

My sister, Christina Dicker, whose cheerleading and endless reading helped me through many days of doubt and fear. Thanks for encouraging me not to give up. You're the best sister a girl could have, and I love you.

Debi Tarvin, who patiently corrected all my spelling and grammar issues only to be asked to do it all over again three weeks later after a massive edit. Thank you for loving Dani and Jodi as much as I do! No one I'd rather sit next to in choir than you.

A big thank you to all my good friends and readers who gave me wonderfully honest feedback: Andrea Saraffian, Heather Arnwine, Tatiana Crapporatta, Hillary Schwartz, Neena Williams (miss you every day), Elaine Kwasniewski, Eva, Dicker, Claire Dicker, Barbara Martin, Hannah Aalborg and Shay Arnett.

To my wonderful husband, Craig, and our son, Liam, I would never have been able to do this if it weren't for your love, support and patience. You put up with a messy house, my distracted mind, and ate countless leftovers around my kitchen table "office." If you hadn't believed in me, I wouldn't have been able to keep going. Thank you for giving me the space and time to see this through. I thank God every day for both of you and can't believe my good fortune to have you both in my life. Our family motto wins again!

My mother passed away right before this book came out, and the loss has been devastating. But one bright spot is knowing how excited she was for my book to be published. I like to think she's up in heaven, with the rest of our loved ones, cheering me on. Miss you so much, Mom. Love you.

Special thanks to my grandmother, Barbara Martin, for her love and support.

Thank you Trino Alvarez for my beautiful author photograph. And to everyone reading this: It's never too late to chase your dreams. Don't be scared to fail, and never stop trying.

Speaking of which, anyone know Adam Ant??

I

As I stand before the gym doors, my heart beats wildly. *I can't believe I'm actually walking into junior prom!* My light pink, shimmery gown floats to the floor; my hair is a mass of loose, dark curls with rhinestones tucked among the strands. The elastic band from my wrist corsage itches a little. As I rub my wrist, a scent from the cluster of tiny, pink roses is released. I know corsages are old-fashioned, but I've wanted one ever since I saw my mom's old prom photos. *How had Sean known? And where is he?*

I look around as a steady stream of people jostles past. *I barely know the kids I go to school with, though I've been classmates with most of them since first grade. It seems like I'm always rushing off to rehearsals or skipping school for competitions. Tonight, I'm finally going to get to know them and have some fun!*

The bass from the music pulses along with my heart as I start to walk inside.

A high-pitched "Dani!" comes from behind, and I'm almost tackled by my best friend, Lauren Hannon. "Can you believe we're here? Tonight's going to be epic!"

Lauren is a blur of blonde curls and teal tulle as she bearhugs me before tottering off in her high heels, like a baby deer learning to walk. "Hey, Dani," is all her boyfriend, Tom, can say as he chases after his hyper date.

Inside the gym, the lights are pink and purple with strings of twinkle lights hanging from anything standing still. Yards of fabric and crepe paper cover the entire gym and bubbles fill the air. It looks like a deranged pack of fairies threw up on the place, but I have to admit it makes the rank, old gym seem romantic and magical. *Jeez, I really am into this prom thing.*

Closing my eyes, I take a deep breath. As the smell of sweat and gym equipment mingle with the sweet smell of perfume and hairspray, a wave of utter freedom overtakes me. *I cannot remember the last time I felt so excited and unencumbered. Lately, I've started to feel like I'm thirty-five years old, worrying about my career, my diet, my future...*

The bass pounds louder, less subtle, and more high-pitched, and I open my eyes. *Who is picking this awful music?*

I turn and walking toward me is Sean Mitchell in a tux with a bow tie that matches my dress. His light, normally shaggy hair is cut and combed to perfection, his green eyes flash with love. A smile spreads across my face that is so big it feels like it will crack in two. He's popular, handsome, and most importantly, he's my boyfriend.

We've been inseparable ever since we bumped heads on the first day of kindergarten. How we made the transition from friends to a couple, I can't really remember. At some point, everyone just knew we were together and that was that.

Sean calls out something, but the bass line takes on a blaring, nagging quality, drowning out everything around me. I squint at Sean and shake my head; I can't hear what he's saying. I walk toward him, and he reaches out his hand and quietly says, "DAAAAAANNNNNIIII-IIIIIIIIIIIIIIIIIIIIIIIIII..."

***

Sean, the lights, and the gym quickly dissolve into my shrieking alarm clock and my equally grating mother yelling my name. I roll over groaning and blindly striking out for the clock, knocking odds and ends off the nightstand. A final violent swipe turns off the alarm. I pry open my eyes. It's 5:12 a.m.

"Danilynn Marie Truehart, get up this instant! Don't make me walk up those stairs and get you, girl."

I pause for a second, wondering what evil I've done in my past life to deserve such torment in this one. Jodi Truehart is her own special brand of torture. Some days it's all I can do not to either burst into tears or erupt in a tirade of swear words. My mother *never* stops. She is unrelenting, unforgiving, and utterly determined to make me into a star.

Sighing as I haul my bones out of bed, I remind myself that if I'm really that miserable, I could make the endless lessons and rehearsals stop. My mother is all about the bottom line. If there's any chance she won't receive a big payoff after all these years of pushing and spending, she'll cut her losses and turn her maniacal stage-mothering skills to some other money-making prospect. She'd probably just have another baby. I chuckle to myself...*third time's a charm, right?*

Grabbing the stack of workout wear on the dresser, I stumble down the hall to the bathroom. My father is shambling up the stairs from the kitchen, a steaming mug of coffee in hand.

"Sorry about all the noise, Dad. Guess I overslept."

He shakes his head. "No worries, Marie. I had an early meeting anyway." He blows me a kiss and continues down the hall to the master bedroom.

My dad is the only one who calls me Marie. I'm named after his mother, who used to visit us a lot when we were younger. We used to hang out at her house all the time, and she used to bake the best cakes ever. But there was some sort of falling out between her and my mom, and we stopped going to see her. No one ever mentions it, and I'm too scared to ask what happened. Though I haven't seen her in years, I always think of her when he calls me "Marie."

"Where's *my* apology, superstar?" Geena appears in the doorway of her darkened room, arms folded across her t-shirt, her blonde hair tousled. She smirks and gives me a playful slap on the butt as I pass. "Better get in that shower." Geena puts her hands on her hips and wags her finger at me in a perfect imitation of our mother's Texas twang, "Don't make her walk up those steps and get you, girl."

I groan. "God, you're lucky you're the smart one! If you'd been able to sing, maybe they'd have stopped at one kid, and I'd be blissfully unaware up in the stars somewhere."

"You make your own luck, sis, believe me." Geena winks at me and disappears into her room.

I skip showering, knowing I'll soon be drenched in sweat at practice. I brush my teeth, wash my face and dress. Grabbing my backpack, I head downstairs. My mom is shoveling a pathetic-looking egg concoction onto a plate.

"Well, finally! Eat up and let's hit the road." Mom is dressed, with a full face of makeup, and ready for the day. She's probably on her second cup of coffee. She bustles around the kitchen like a tiny Texan tornado, wiping down the counter and putting yogurt and fruit in a bowl.

I sigh. "Egg whites again?" The soggy mess on my plate makes me want to gag. I wish I had some toast to cover it with, but that's not in my diet plan. My mom seems to read my mind.

"Don't blame me if you didn't hit your numbers yesterday. You know how important every ounce is this week. I'm not going to have you bloated and gassy just because princess wants a piece of toast. Egg whites and kale is a healthy, low-carb meal."

"Yeah, you don't want to end up a fat ass like me," Geena chuckles as she plops herself in the chair across from me. Mom swats Geena on the back of her head as she slams the bowl of fruit and yogurt in front of her.

"Language, missy! You'd think with all that learning, you'd know more eloquent words. And you're not fat. You're just full-figured." She leans down and kisses the spot where she hit Geena. "Besides, you don't need to be skinny when you've got that big, fat brain of yours. You're going to show 'em all, baby."

Geena rolls her eyes. "Show what to whom? I study for myself, not you or anyone else, Mom."

My mom forces a smile and nods as she sits. "Right you are, Missy. You don't need to be smart for anyone but yourself. And for those people handing out scholarships. Your sister's ticket in life is her body and her voice. Yours is your brain. All I'm trying to do is help you two make the most of your gifts." My mom produces a nail buffer from nowhere and begins working on her nails. Never does she let a moment pass where she isn't being productive, a trait she feels neither of her children inherited.

Geena stares at Mom. I scarf down my disgusting food as Geena takes a deep breath.

"I don't know who you're kidding. You're not doing anything for Dani or me. Everything you're doing to us is for you and the life you've always wanted to lead."

Mom gets up and starts furiously wiping invisible crumbs off the table, shaking her head. "I don't know why you have to be so hateful, Geena. Just because you couldn't cut it in gymnastics doesn't mean you have to be so sour..."

I ease out of the kitchen. It's too early for this crap! My mom and sister get into it every few days. Sometimes I think that Geena creates a lot of the problems between herself and Mom. Isn't it just easier to ride the wave, like I do, rather than fight against Mom's wishes, like Geena does? It doesn't seem like it makes Geena any happier than I am.

Dad comes down the stairs, carrying his empty mug. "Are they at it again?" He gives me a sideways squeeze as he passes by. "You're going to knock 'em dead at that big audition of yours. Know when it is yet?"

I give my dad a tight hug. "Maybe we'll find out today."

"Into the fray I go," he says as enters the kitchen, female voices escalating. I overhear him fruitlessly tell them to knock it off. I shake my head as I climb the stairs to look for my history book. Back in my room, I find my book under the comforter; I fell asleep studying last night. I have an exam today after rehearsal. I've never really been a good student, probably because my mom never really encouraged me to study. But for the first time, I'm really enjoying a class. I'm looking forward to showing how much I've learned.

"Sorry, D." Geena pops her head in the door and looks sheepish. "I didn't mean to start a fight."

I wave her off and give her a smile. "You two are going to fight until the day you die. I don't think I really even notice it anymore." My smile fades. We both know I'm lying. I shrug, tossing my book on the bed, and sit down.

Geena leans against the doorjamb. "I wish I could just be like you...let Mom steer the ship and not put up a fight."

I shake my head and bend to pick up the alarm clock and other things scattered on the floor. "I never thought about fighting back. I just want everyone to be happy and get along, you know?" I arrange the things on the nightstand. "So if that means doing what Mom says, is it really that bad? I mean it's not like she's making me get tattoos and hold up grocery stores. I'm singing and dancing. How tough is that?"

Geena gives me a hard stare. "You know it isn't just singing and dancing, sis. She's got your whole future all planned out. And she's spent most of your childhood trying to make that happen."

I shrug and get up. "I just don't think about it that way. I trust Mom. Besides, if it pays off like she thinks it will, then everything will have been worth it, right?"

Geena looks at me with a smile I can't quite read; it's unsettling. "Sure, it will." Geena surprises me with a big hug. "I'm proud of you, Dani. No matter what happens, you're a star to me." We pull apart, staring at each other for a moment before we both fall down snorting and laughing. We gasp for air, rolling around in the doorway. "I think I just peed myself," Geena says through her giggles.

I laugh as I pull my sister up, "And with that phrase in my mind, I face my future. Thanks for keeping it classy, sis."

"DANNNNNNNIIIII," rings out from downstairs. We both flinch.

Geena hands me my history book and shoves me out of the room. "Fame is calling you," She cocks her head to one side. "Sounds different than you thought it would, doesn't it?"

I laugh. "Go change your underwear, G. Coming, Mom!" I gallop down the stairs.

Mom looks annoyed. "What took you so long?"

I wave my textbook at her. "I have my first test today. I think I'm going to ace it for once!" I stuff the book into my backpack.

Mom rolls her eyes, exasperated. "Oh, come on, Dani. You're not going to school today! This morning we're going to find out when your big audition is. I'm not wasting any prep time having you sit in class taking some stupid test. You've got rehearsal all day today and every day after school until your audition. I could kill Martin for not clearing the whole week for us, but no use crying about that now. I know this week will be hell, but then it's fame and fortune from here on out!" My mom spreads out her arms in an embarrassing grand sweeping motion more appropriate for a spastic five-year-old than a thirty-six-year-old mother of two.

I'm crushed. "But Mom, I really studied for this test. Can't I go to school just for this one class?"

Annoyed, my mom drops her arms and gathers her purse and keys. "Honestly, Dani! It's not like you're on the path to becoming a Rhodes Scholar. You've never expressed an interest in school, and today of all days you decide to be difficult. Just do as you're told and get in the car already."

Defeated, I drop my backpack onto the bench and take my workout bag from my mother's outstretched hand.

2

It's still dark as we pile into the car. Disappointment from my interrupted dream, the argument between Mom and Geena, more disappointment from missing my exam–I'm already exhausted, and we haven't even pulled out of the driveway. A heavy sigh escapes as I lean my head back against the car seat.

"Why don't you grab a cat nap."

I close my eyes as thoughts race through my mind. *Why am I so disappointed about missing that test? What if I freeze in my audition? What did Geena mean that Mom has my whole future planned out? I want to be a singer, so it's not like Mom is forcing me to do something I don't want to do. Right?*

Right?

That's the question that makes me want to jump out of the car and run in the opposite direction. It dawns on me that I've never actually thought about why I'm doing all the rehearsing, lessons, dieting, etc. I just always did it.

Do I want this? Duh! Of course, I do! I trust Mom–she isn't going to steer me down the wrong path. Geena's just angry with Mom and trying to get me on her side. I'm tired of those two trying to play me against each other. I need to focus on myself for once. This week is so crucial.

I pop in my headphones, drowning out my thoughts with the songs I'll sing in the audition. I let the music wash over me, happy to leave these unsettling thoughts behind.

***

Too soon, Mom nudges me awake as the car stops. The sun is up over Martin Fox's studio, which is in an industrial part of North Hollywood. I grab my bag and head inside, avoiding any conversation with my mom. The lights are on and coffee is brewing as I glide past the empty reception desk into the main dance studio.

The wooden floor, scarred and scuffed, creaks slightly as I drop my bag and inhale deeply. The dusty, sweaty smell both invigorate and relax me—making me feel more at home than I ever feel in the house I share with my family. I've been Martin's protégée for over three years now, and I feel like he's more of a driven big brother than a paid coach.

When my mom first suggested hiring Martin, I had no idea who he was. Until that point, I shuttled from voice coach to dance classes in different studios that specialized in hip-hop or ballet. I spent more time in the car than I did training. After seeing Martin on a "Where Are They Now?" segment in the local news, my mom tracked him down. Now, instead of driving all over creation, I commute from Santa Clarita to Martin's North Hollywood studio each morning before school to study voice and back again after school to study dance.

Martin was part of a popular boy band called REVOLUTION! in the '80s. Before I began my lessons with Martin, I scoured the Internet for information on his career. I couldn't wait to meet the tall, impossibly skinny teen with the high-top fade who strutted on the stage and gyrated in neon spandex. But once I stopped laughing at his teased hair and ridiculously tight pants, I became mesmerized by the timing and stamina in his dance routines and his incredibly crisp and commanding voice that could range from a deep baritone to an impressively high falsetto.

He's almost unrecognizable now from the teen star I watched online. He sports a small paunch that he disguises as best he can when he isn't dancing, with blazers, overcoats, and scarves. His luxuriantly teased hair is completely gone, and his bald, black head dazzles in the harsh light of the dance studio. A prominent soul patch decorates his chin, almost in homage of the long-lost brethren of the scalp.

This man is different from all my previous coaches and teachers. Martin is the only one to have actually lived the life I'm working so hard to achieve. I believe that if anyone can lead me to my dream, it will be him.

3

Martin pops his head into the studio while I'm taking off my shoes. "Morning, Sunshine! I'm just going to have a quick meeting with your mom. Why don't you start warming up? I'll be in as soon as I can."

Martin's speaking so fast I can barely understand him. He's got a totally different vibe about him this morning. Normally, he's playful and mellow, but today he's jumpy and a little intense, like he's had four gallons of coffee.

"Sure, Martin. You OK? You seem a little high-strung this morning."

Martin pauses a moment, concerned. "I do?" He takes a deep breath and shakes his head. "Yeah, I guess I *am* a little wound up this morning. I just need to run something past your mom before I lock things down. You know her...she can set a person on edge sometimes." His attempt at a carefree chuckle is pathetic.

"Is everything OK? There's no problem with the audition is there?"

Martin rolls his eyes and smiles. "Nothing you need to worry about. Just get warmed up and I'll be back in a bit."

He leaves the room before I can respond. That man has toured the world and performed in front of thousands of people. Why would a conversation with my mom make him so nervous?

***

I run through my stretches and decide to warm up with a piece I've been choreographing on my own. As the music plays, my body automatically flows through the movements and my mind wanders to my earlier conversation with Geena.

I know Mom pushes me relentlessly to become a star, but the truth is that I love singing and dancing more than anything in the world. There's nothing I want to do more than to perform. It's not about the audience, which freaks me out beyond words if I'm telling the truth. I hate being the center of attention. Totally weird, I know. And it's not the money...though that would be phenomenal, of course. I mean, who doesn't want to be rich?

But it's more than that. It's about this energy inside me. I love mastering a new song or dance routine. Hearing my voice hit those high notes and feeling myself nail a difficult dance move is more satisfying than anything. I know I'm not super book smart—Mom tells me that every chance she gets. But singing and dancing are my talents, and I've done everything I can to perfect them. It's hard to explain...I feel their energy vibrating inside me all the time, and it feels like a secret that I have to share with the world. Like if I don't, I'll explode. It's not like I can do that while I'm a banker or teacher. So while Mom is focused on money and fame, all I care about is doing what I'm meant to be doing every day, as often as I can. It's what keeps me going.

4

I spin in circles and wilt to the floor as the song comes to an end. Sweaty and satisfied, I'm resting my head on the floor when the door flies open.

"What in the hell was that crap...?"

My mom's harsh voice rips apart my peaceful moment. I'm slammed back into reality. I push myself off the floor and take a deep breath, trying to shake off the dreamy thoughts of the dance. I hadn't been practicing my routines for the audition and, *of course*, my mom had to walk in on *that* piece.

Martin quietly follows in behind my mom, clears his throat and cocks his head to the side. My mom stops her tirade mid-sentence. "I mean, glad you got a chance to, uh, blow off some steam, honey." She comes over and gives me an affectionate slap on the bottom.

"You'd better get your head straight, darlin'. Martin just sent your career into overdrive. You've got an audition with Jenner Redman on Friday. All our hard work is about to pay off!" My mom grabs me and gives me an uncharacteristically fierce hug. She pulls back and stares at me, squeezing my shoulders.

"I have to call your dad about something." She hurries out of the studio and her words finally sink in. I scream and hug Martin, almost knocking him over.

"Ohmigod, ohmigod. Martin, is it true?" I'm talking a mile a minute, shaking Martin and jumping up and down simultaneously.

"Calm down, girl! We can't risk you getting all broke up right before your big audition! Yes, it's true, Dani."

It's like a cold bucket of water got poured on my excitement. I find myself in a panic. "Oh my God, I am so not ready. How am I ever going to pull this off ?"

Martin gives me a big hug. He shushes quietly into my ear like I'm a spooked horse, which weirdly calms me down. After a few moments, he stops. "Sit down for a second."

I shake my head and start to get worked up again. "We don't have time! We've got so much to go over."

Martin guides me toward a couple of old metal chairs lined up against the wall. "We can't get anything done with you hysterical. We've been working on your routines for months. You can do this in your sleep. Just try to relax, baby girl. Remember, you're supposed to be enjoying this, right?"

I snort as I collapse into one of the uncomfortable metal chairs. "Yeah, right! Enjoy singing and dancing while my mom takes notes during my performance?" I hunch over, scrunching my face, pretending to hold a cigarette in one hand and a pad of paper in the other. In a grating voice and imitating a perfect Texas drawl, I'm transformed into my mother. "Dani, your gut was flapping out over your leggings every time you jumped. No more bread for you, Tubby. You were late coming in, and you were flat on the top note of the last verse. Bye-bye dairy!"

I relax and start to laugh, then I realize it's not really funny. Suddenly, the toe of my sneaker is too compelling for me to tear my eyes away, and I shrug. "Guess it isn't as funny as it sounded in my head."

Martin shakes his head quietly, "No, it's not funny at all. I'm sorry your mom is so hard on you, honey. She means well in her own way, but I know she ends up hurting you more than helping."

Watching as my toe draws circles on the battered wooden floor, I nod slowly, unwanted tears welling up. "I love performing but, honestly, I wish she'd just lay off me. I'm already nervous, and then she comes in and reminds me of the millions of ways I could mess things up." Looking up, I sniff, swiping at my eyes. "Sometimes I just want to quit so I can stop her from picking on me. But then I figure how much time I'd have to spend with her at home, and I realize that'd be a big mistake. God, can you imagine?"

Ugh! I just realize what I've said to Martin, and I look at him apologetically. "Oh my God, Martin. You know I'd never quit. All the work and time you've put into me. I wouldn't do that to you…"

He gives me a reassuring smile. "Honey, you could quit right now, and I'd still be your biggest fan. You aren't supposed to be doing this for me, your mom or anyone but yourself. I know we've been working together for years, training to be the next 'big thing.' But if this isn't what you want, you need to tell me. I won't be upset at all. And I'll help you talk to your mom."

Martin wipes away a tear that leaks from my eye. "It's really important that you're honest with me and honest with yourself. Being a pop star, especially when you're so young…it's more pressure than you can imagine. You've got so much independence. When you're famous, everyone is clamoring for your attention. All of a sudden, you find yourself responsible for so many adults who are depending on *your* success to pay *their* bills. It's nothing you can prepare for, really. And yes, the perks are amazing. But this will change your life and who you are forever. You can't do it because your mom wants you to. You have to make a conscious choice to go down this life-changing path with your eyes open. This business is a machine with only one product—success. It will mold you and shape you into whatever is sellable at the moment and abandon you the first moment you aren't profitable anymore. It's worse than the meanest bunch of girls at school, and you're about to enter the never-ending slumber party from hell. I don't want to scare you, but I want to be honest with you. Just a little advice from one 'has-been' to a 'might-be.'"

I sigh, overwhelmed. "All my mom keeps focusing on is the money we'll have once I make it. She plans on moving to Beverly Hills, buying a place in New York, and a jet to travel the globe. She's spending my money before I've even made any! I'm scared as hell of failing. But I'm also scared of making it, too. It sounds like so much pressure. And performing in front of a huge audience all the time…I don't know if I'm up for that part of it."

I think about it for a few minutes and what I want hits me like a punch in the gut, so much so that I exhale loudly. "But I have to try.

Not just for my mom, but for me." I look Martin in the eye intensely. "Do you think I'm good enough to make it?"

Martin nods and gives me a smile, moving a strand of hair behind my ear. "You are. You've got the talent, the drive and an appointment with the one man I know who can turn you into a star. I just need you to believe in you."

A smile spreads across my face and I nod. It feels good to have someone believe in me. I just hope I can put my mom's criticism aside and start believing in myself. Martin puts his arm around me, and we sit quietly together, each realizing this could be the last time we talk like this. The last time before we know...success or failure.

Martin clears his throat. "There's one more thing, and I'm worried that you might take this the wrong way...I know how much your mom gets to you. I'm afraid she's going to push you into some bad places if she's in charge of your career."

I must look confused because Martin takes a deep breath and continues. "I never had anyone looking out for me when I was young. My mom had to stay home and take care of my sister. I did whatever Redman demanded, including hiding my sexuality. He didn't make me feel ashamed to be gay, but he made it clear it wasn't profitable for the band. I lost a lot of money from his shady contracts and did some things that I wouldn't have chosen to do. So, to best protect you, I'm asking your mother and father to let me be your guardian until you're eighteen. I'm not adopting you; they're still your parents. But I know your mom is willing to do anything so you can make it, and your dad just seems to let her do what she wants. I want someone looking out for you and helping you make informed decisions. It's the only way I can move forward with this audition on Friday. If they decide against it, I can't set you up with Redman."

My mouth drops. I'm at a loss for words. I breathe for a few seconds, trying to get a grip. "I don't know what to say, Martin. I don't know if I should be grateful or creeped out."

Martin raises his hands. "I know. I can only imagine how creepy this sounds. I just want to protect you like I wish someone had protected me. I'd hate to see you shaking your ass in a G-string and sequined bra three months from now on MTV. You're still fifteen. I want to make sure no one exploits you or takes advantage of you. You've got *talent*, Dani. Your voice, your movement—you've got everything you need to be a star. Being half-naked on stage isn't going to make you more of a star or sustain your career the way the proper display of your talent will."

Tears come to my eyes. For the first time, I finally realize how much Martin truly cares for me. Unlike my mom, who seems to only care about me in terms of the type of payout her investment of time and money will yield. Or my dad, who loves me but can never seem to stand up to my mom. Martin is offering to protect me.

My head starts to spin, and doubt starts to creep in. *Is Martin being sincere about why he wants to be my guardian, or is he in it for the money too?* I shake my head and sigh. "You're going to be paid for this, right? I mean you're not working with me for three years out of the goodness of your heart?"

Martin quietly shakes his head. "No, I'm not, hon. The breakdown is this: Redman gets forty percent, you get forty percent in a trust fund, I get fifteen percent and the remaining five percent covers travel costs, etc. When I started, I got fifty thousand a year and Jenner got the rest. It didn't leave a lot for retirement."

The numbers jumble together in my head. I'm sure they probably add up, but things like math and deductive thinking that my friends are learning in school are a muddle in my mind. *I wish Sean was here to talk to...*I rub my forehead and sigh again. *I'm pretty sure Martin just wants to make sure I'm OK. And if I have to choose, I'd rather have Martin stealing my money—if that's what he's doing—than my mother. At least Martin will be nicer about it.*

"Well, I'd rather deal with you than my mom. I'm in." Martin slaps his knee and folds me into a hug.

***

Ten hours later, we're both drenched in sweat. We've run through my routines about twenty times each, tweaking foot placement, spins and vocals. I'm just finishing up a soulful love song as Geena enters the studio and sits next to Martin. They put their heads together and fall into a serious conversation.

When the last note of the song fades, it takes a minute for Geena and Martin to realize it. Eventually, Geena looks up and starts clapping. "That was amazing, sis! I definitely get what all the fuss is about." They walk over, and Martin hands me a towel. I wipe down my hair and neck.

"Thanks, G. What fuss?" I catch Geena and Martin sharing a look. "Seriously, what?"

As Martin and I sit down to change our shoes, Geena takes a deep breath. "Mom and Dad are having a huge blowout over Martin's guardianship. Dad doesn't want to sign the papers." Geena holds up her hands. "No offense, Martin. And Mom's in a full-blown tizzy over it. I swear, it's gone nuclear back at the old homestead."

Annoyed, I shake my head and begin shoving shoes, water bottles and towels into my dance bag. "I can't deal with this right now. I've been nauseous for weeks, thinking about this stupid audition. It'll either happen or it won't, depending upon what they decide." I look at them. "And let's face it, it *will* happen because Mom always gets her way." My lip starts to quiver for an instant as sadness washes over me, but I shake my head and get angry instead. "I mean, it's not like I want the audition to be canceled because they won't let you be my guardian, Martin. But for once I'd just like to see Dad grow a pair and stand up to Mom."

Geena and Martin are shocked, mouths agape. They've never heard me speak that way about anyone, especially my parents. I peel off my wet tank top, towel off my torso and shrug. "What? It's not like you weren't thinking it. I'm just really nervous right now, and I need to prepare for this audition like it's going to happen, which we all know it will. Dad will cave. Mom will rage, pout, and get her way. Why waste the next thirty-six hours worrying about it?"

Martin gives me a look. "Maybe you're more ready for this business than I thought."

I shake my head. "Maybe I'm just sick of my mom being such a head case and putting so much pressure on all of us. Give me five minutes to shower, sis, and we can go."

5

"Think it's safe to go inside?"

Geena and I are sitting in the car trying to gauge what's happening inside the house. She leans over the steering wheel and peers at the house. "It looks quiet, but let's give it a few more minutes just to be sure."

Everything looks normal. Lights are on and the TV is glowing in the front window. No yelling is heard when we crack open the car window. It's gotten cold since we left the studio, and the closed car windows are fogging up from our breath.

"Thanks for coming to get me, G. I'm sure Mom would have forgotten all about me."

Geena sits back in her seat, trying to get comfortable. "I did it as much for you as for me. If I weren't picking you up, I'd be stuck at ground zero trying to ignore World War III crashing down around me. And you know Mom would keep trying to involve me in the argument. Like it's somehow appropriate to involve your teenage daughter in a major parenting decision."

We both shake our heads and Geena giggles. "Remember the time Mom talked Dad out of taking that job in Bakersfield? She was convinced we'd never get anywhere if we didn't stay in L.A. She was practically unhinged!"

"Yeah!" I gasp. "I remember she woke me up and told me she'd get us a dog if I told Dad I didn't want to leave my home. I was so sleepy I didn't even make it downstairs. He found me curled up on the landing fast asleep. We ended up staying, and I never did get that dog!"

Geena shakes her head. "I just don't understand her. Half the time I can't tell if I'm lucky to have a mom who cares so much if I succeed or if I'm cursed to have an over-involved stage mom who's never happy with what I do. I wish she'd just love me for me, you know? Not what I can do."

I nod. "I know. I wonder what Mom will do if I don't make it. I mean, 'my career,'" I make air quotes and roll my eyes, "is like her full-time job. Everything she does revolves around my lessons, diet and paying for everything I need. What will happen if Jenner Redman decides I don't cut it?"

I take a deep breath and turn to Geena. "Do you think she'll stop loving me if I don't make it?"

"Look, Mom won't necessarily stop loving you. But—and I'm speaking from experience here—it'll change how she sees you. It's the disappointment. It'll be a part of how she views you. Remember when I gave up gymnastics?"

I nod. Geena continues, pulling her long sleeves over her fingers and folding her arms across her chest. "Well, I didn't just start gaining weight randomly. I hated my life. Mom ruled every aspect of my day —from the classes I took, to what I wore, to every piece of food I put in my mouth. I was desperate to end the cycle—the constant nagging, guilt trips and angry, tearful rants. I was twelve! I should never have had to deal with such a psycho. I saw Dad wasn't going to step in and save me, and I knew standing up to her would only make it worse, so I did the only thing I could do."

I finally connect the dots, and I'm stunned. "You gained weight on purpose?"

Geena nods and shifts in her seat. "I did. My friend Charlotte helped me. She snuck extra food from her house—peanut butter sandwiches, cookies...whatever had the most calories. I traded with kids from school. I did their math homework in exchange for their desserts. I had to hide in the bathroom to eat because Mom kept meeting with all my teachers to find out what was happening with my weight. Was I eating more than the lunch I brought from home? Had they noticed anything?"

"Oh my God, Geena, that's insane! I can't believe you did that to yourself."

Geena grimaces. "Gaining weight isn't the worst thing you could do..."

I shake my head, eyes going wide. "I didn't mean it that way, I just meant..."

Geena sighs. "I know." She hits the steering wheel in frustration. "Damn, I was in good shape back then! The things I could have done in gymnastics...I was on track for the Olympics." Geena shakes her head and stares off into the distance. She says softly, almost to herself, "I don't like to think about it too much."

I'm totally shocked and can't make sense of it. "Oh Geena, if you honestly feel that way, why did you throw it all away? Just to get back at Mom?"

Geena shudders a little and comes back to reality, tears in her eyes. "It had nothing to do with getting back at Mom. It had everything to do with saving myself. My hair was starting to fall out from the stress, and I was eating the barest minimum of calories just so I could maintain the weight Mom wanted me to be."

Geena turns to me. "I honestly don't think I'd have made the Olympics with Mom driving me into the ground like she did. Because I had started to think that I didn't want to keep living if I had to live with her constant criticism."

I clamp my hand over my mouth and just stare at my sister, tears welling up in my eyes. *How had I not known all this was happening?* I see Geena in a new way. Her attitude toward Mom totally makes sense now. "I wish you'd told me."

Geena reaches out and gives my hand a squeeze. "Aww, come on, sis. You were nine. What could you have done? You've done a much better job of it than I have. I'm proud of you."

We're quiet, looking at each other. We don't say anything, but we both know this is a big moment. Our relationship is taking a turn. Now that I know what Geena's been hiding from me, it feels like we're on more level ground, that we're equals now.

Geena continues. "I ended up telling Grandma. She picked me up from gymnastics one night. She had bought me a piece of chocolate cake as a treat and I burst into tears because I knew it was my calorie allotment for the entire day. After I calmed down, she took me out to Denny's. I told her everything while she stuffed me full of burgers, fries and shakes. And, of course, I ate the cake before we even got there. I was so damned *hungry*. Once Grandma gave me free rein to eat, I didn't want to stop. She was furious with the state I was in and waited until Mom got home. Grandma railed at Dad, but he stood by Mom, saying his wife knew what was best for his girls. He promised to feed me more, but he wouldn't change anything else unless Mom approved. Grandma was so angry at him for not protecting us."

I stare out the window, trying to process this new information. "So that's why Grandma never comes over anymore?"

"Yep. And why we could never talk about our visits to her house. Mom knew she was riding a fine line with the way she pushed us, but since Dad never objected, she kept it up. I don't think Grandma's ever forgiven Dad for letting us down."

Geena nods. "I started seeing her a lot after that. Once I stopped gymnastics, I'd go to her house after school instead of the gym. She'd make snacks and we'd talk while I did my homework. She did everything she could do to make me feel loved. To kind of make up for Mom."

"Because Mom changed how she treated you after that." It's a heavy statement, one I realize I've tried to avoid thinking about all these years.

Geena nods. "Yeah, she did. She didn't hate me and wasn't outright mean. It was more like she just couldn't be *bothered* anymore. I wasn't going to produce, so she wasn't going to expend any more energy on me. I don't know which is worse. Being criticized constantly to the point you hate yourself or being ignored as if you don't exist."

I stare out the window, guilt suddenly weighing me down. "I haven't seen Grandma in years. I had no idea you saw her so much. I went a few times the first few years with Dad, but I always seemed to have rehearsals when he went to visit." Another realization dawns on me and I turn to Geena. "Oh my gosh, do you think Mom did that on purpose?"

Geena nods slowly. "Totally. Mom holds a grudge like a pro.

Grandma didn't stand a chance with her after they fought. You've seen how hard Dad works just to keep his visits with his own mother a secret." Geena shakes her head, disgusted, "It's pathetic, the way he lets Mom dominate him like that."

I cover my mouth and start to tear up. "God, I feel so terrible. Who forgets their own grandmother?"

Geena reaches for my hand. "You just got caught in Mom's war with Grandma. She knows, believe me. She asks about you all the time."

Surprised, I look up. "She does? You see her a lot?"

Geena smiles and nods. "Yeah, as much as I can. Mom doesn't know. Of course, she'd freak if she did. But I'm not at the library every afternoon." She winks at me.

I exhale loudly, wiping my eyes with my sleeves. "Well, you must think I'm an idiot. I mean, why am I still putting up with Mom's crap? I should just stand up for myself!"

"The difference is that you love what you do. Besides, Mom learned something from her failure with me. She backed off on you just a bit. After all, she couldn't survive if both her pet projects imploded. I know you've got it hard, but trust me, she is far easier on you than she was on me."

I sigh, overwhelmed, absentmindedly playing with a strand of hair. "I feel as if I'm just waking up, seeing our family for the first time in an entirely new way. And I don't know how to feel about it." Tears well up. I swallow hard. "How can I go on and act like none of this happened?"

Geena awkwardly hugs me across the center console. "You can deal with Mom, Dad and Grandma later, after your audition. But I think Martin has the right idea. You need an advocate; someone to protect you. Martin's a good guy. He'll take care of you. Just focus on yourself and the audition right now. Our messed-up family will still be here for you once it's over. Don't let it ruin your big chance."

I nod and let out a shuddery sigh. The mountain of revelations seems a weight too much to bear. "I just want to go to bed. I'm exhausted."

Geena nods and we gather our things. As we get out of the car, I stop. "Will you tell Grandma that I'm sorry?"

Geena smiles as we walk toward the house. "I will, but there's no need. She's not mad. She's just waiting for you to reach out. Why don't you give her a call after the audition? We can go see her together if you want."

I smile and nod. "I'd love that."

We enter the house and see Mom asleep on the couch. Dad is nowhere to be seen.

"Guess they've called a truce for now," Geena says as she turns off the TV. "I'm sure we'll find out what's happening tomorrow."

It's all I can do to drag myself upstairs. I kick off my shoes, fall onto the bed, fully clothed, and sleep.

6

Waking up feels like I'm dragging myself up from the deepest, darkest seabed. My body aches and my head feels fuzzy. I feel physically affected by my talk with Geena last night. I look at the clock–6:59 a.m. I have to hurry, or I'll be late for school. In a haze, I get ready and stumble downstairs. My mom is doing her best June Cleaver impression, which is a sure sign that all is not normal.

"Morning, chickadee. I didn't want to wake you because I know how hard you worked yesterday with Martin. There's a note for school on the table. Here." She slides my favorite pink "My Little Pony" mug in front of me. "Some green tea to help you wake up. Breakfast will be ready in a minute. When you're finished, I'll drop you off at school."

I can barely follow her speedy chatter. I slump in the chair and sip the hot tea. The caffeine slowly breaks through the fog in my head.

"Where are Geena and Dad?" I ask, reaching for the fork as my mom sets down a plate of egg whites.

Mom bustles about the kitchen, cheerily washing the frying pan. A stranger would assume that my mom is a true domestic goddess for whom family and home are her greatest joy. I know it's just nervous activity while she waits for my dad to sign the papers. "She was gone before I woke up this morning. Left a note saying she had an early math lab. Your dad had to get down to the office for a big presentation. Just you and me this morning, chickadee."

"Is there anything you want to talk to me about?" I ask as I bite into the soggy eggs, watching my mom. The flurry of scrubbing pauses just enough for her to figure out a game plan.

"Well, as a matter of fact, there is, honey." She replies, as she rinses the pan and leaves it on the draining board. Wiping her hands with a dishtowel, she sits next to me at the table. "I didn't want to tell you about it until I knew what was happening. No reason for you to be upset. But since you asked…"

We look at each other as her sentence trails off. We're measuring the other, waiting to see what will be said, how much will be revealed. "Martin thinks it would be best if he's in charge of your career until you're eighteen. The legal term is 'guardian.' Of course, your dad and I will still be your parents." Mom reaches out and grasps my hand, which is still holding my fork. It's an awkward attempt at a heart-felt moment. "That will never change. But Martin thinks it would be easier if he were the one to make costume decisions, deal with your manager and tour with you. He has the impression that I might make you nervous or something."

My mom looks slightly green as she navigates this shaky explana-tion. She looks at me. "Do I? Make you nervous, I mean." She seems to gain some sort of momentum, a gleam appearing in her eye. I shake off her hand and she doesn't even notice. "Because if *you* were the one to tell Martin that you wanted me on tour with you, then there'd be no need to pay him all that money. We could keep it in the family. Just think of it, you and me on the road together, honey. I could han-dle everything you need. It would be a dream to work with you like that. I could be a regular 'Momager' like that Kardashian lady. What do you think?"

"You want to be like Kris Kardashian? Market me like she does her kids?"

Clearly, it isn't what my mom expects to hear. She starts to lose patience. "Well, not market you per se. I know you're not a can of beans. But I'd do what I could to promote your brand. Why stop at singing? Why not a clothing or perfume line or even a reality show? We could get the whole family involved!"

I can see my mom's mind shift into overdrive, which sends me over the edge. "And on the payroll, Mom. In fact, we could learn how to shoot and edit on our own footage so there wouldn't be any need to pay anyone else for anything with you in charge."

I glare at her as I push away from the table, dishes clattering. "Thanks for breakfast. I'll walk to school. And for the record, I agree with Martin one hundred percent. I think it would be best if he were the one looking out for me. *Not you.*"

My mom looks dumbfounded; I've never spoken to her like this before. *But I don't care! She's out of control and I feel like I'm going to scream. I need to get out of here.* Before she can even speak, I grab the note for the office, sling my backpack onto my shoulder and slam out of the house.

7

Walking to school is a big mistake. It only takes twenty minutes in the car, but after the fight with Mom and an evening of family skeleton finding, it's all I can do to put one foot in front of the other. I finally make it to campus by 9:00 a.m. I stop by the office of Valley Hills High School and hand the note to the secretary, who's seen dozens of such notes from my mom.

Finished at the office, I enter a hallway flooded with students changing classes. So much noise, so many people make me want to shrink into myself even more. I feel trapped inside my head, trying to figure out if I want to go through with this audition or if I'm tired of being my mom's pawn. I drift down the hall with the flow of bodies, brushing and bumping against other kids who don't seem to notice me. I look at the faces streaming past and wonder if anyone else has a family as messed up as mine.

"Nice of you to stop by, Truehart. Need me to show you where your locker is? I know it's hard to remember since you're so rarely here."

A tall, willowy blonde in a tight sweater and a miniskirt sneers at me as I pass. Zoe McFadden. Always perfectly dressed, with perfect grades; she's a cheerleader and a massively spoiled brat. She runs the school because all the boys are in love with her. So are the teachers. All the girls are either scared of her or want to be her. Her ego is as big as her daddy's bank account and there isn't anything she can't have, except Sean. Zoe has her heart set on him and can't believe he wastes his time on such an insignificant nobody like me. Zoe lives to taunt me, and she's the last person I want to see this morning.

"Dani!" Lauren rushes over from her locker and gives me a quick hug. "Buzz off, Zoe. Don't you have a freshman to torture or something?" Zoe snorts disgustedly and stalks down the hallway. She prefers to needle me one on one, lest Sean hears about it.

"God, she's such a bitch." Lauren turns back and punches me in the arm. "Where were you yesterday? You missed the history test. Miss Miller was furious. She made a big deal about how there were going to be 'no makeup exams.' What happened?"

I shake my head and start to tear up. Students continue to jostle around us. Lauren pulls us out of the flow of traffic and into a space next to a bank of lockers. "OMG, are you OK?"

I shrug and swipe at my eyes as Sean comes up. Before I can say hello, he wraps his arms around me and lifts me up into a long hug. I bury my face into his shirt, some of the tension melting away. I inhale deeply, taking in his clean, woodsy smell. He puts me down and kisses me.

"Hi." We stare into each other's eyes, the noise and people fading away.

Lauren clears her throat. "Um, hi. Dani, you were saying?"

Sean turns to Lauren as I continue to snuggle into him. "Hi, Lauren. Sorry about that. Just haven't seen Dani in a few days."

I turn to face Lauren. "Martin set up an audition with his old producer, Jenner Redman. He created all those boy bands in the '80s."

Lauren leans against the locker wall. "That's great!"

I nod. "Yeah, I mean I wish it were with a producer who had more current success, but beggars can't be choosers."

Sean reaches out and tugs on a lock of my hair. "So, who died then? This is what you've been working for, like, your whole life."

I sigh, staring off into the hallway. "Martin told my mom he won't go through with the audition unless my parents let him be my guardian. He thinks she puts too much pressure on me and might force me to do things I shouldn't be doing at my age."

Lauren pauses for a minute before she speaks. "OK, I don't want this to come off the wrong way, but isn't that great news? All we've heard for years is how your mom rides you all the time. She put you on a diet at ten years old! Who knows what she might do if millions of dollars are on the line?"

I sigh. "That's the thing. At first, I was upset because I felt like they'd just given me away for the chance to earn money. But now I see that maybe it's a good thing for me. It's just hard to wrap my head around it."

Sean puts his arm around me. "That's messed up, Dani." Lauren sharply inhales, "So does that mean that Martin is like your dad now?"

I snort. "No, just my guardian. You know, the one who signs off on my schedules, costumes and stuff like that 'til I'm eighteen. He'd also set up a trust fund so most of what I earn would be put away until I'm a certain age."

Lauren gives me a sidelong look. "So, your mom can't get it?"

I shrug and nod, looking away. Sean gives me a kiss on my head. Lauren runs her hands through her hair. "Holy crap. This is way bigger than the history test." Sean chuckles.

"Sure is. Never a dull moment when you're around, huh, Dani?"

I sigh. "I'm just waiting to see if my dad will agree to all this. Apparently, they had an epic fight about it last night. Part of me wants him to stand up to my mom for once and say no, someone else can't be my guardian because *they're* my parents. But then I'd be giving up this huge opportunity. I'm so confused." The halls are almost empty now. The bell for the next class rings.

Lauren grabs my hand and pulls me down the hall. "Come on, D, let's get to Art. We'll do some therapeutic painting or crap like that. Work out how you really feel by modeling clay."

Sean slowly lets me go, holding my hand as long as possible. "See you at lunch." I blow him a kiss and walk down the hall, linking arms with Lauren.

8

"God, that was the longest day ever!" Lauren's head is buried in her locker. "How are you not going crazy?" She finally appears, red-faced and with a handful of crumpled papers. "Hey! At least you won't have to worry about a stupid chem exam when you're on the road to fame." She flashes me a bright smile. I envy her carefree attitude.

"Believe it or not, I wish that chem test was my biggest worry right now." I give her a weak smile and hold up my hands like a scale. "I mean, on one side my parents give me up so I can get the audition. Or they say no, and I never get a chance to find out if my years of hard work would have paid off." I shift my hands as if weighing both prospects before dropping them, frustrated. Lauren gives me the millionth hug of the day.

I exhale loudly and smile. "Thanks, Laur. Sorry I've monopolized the day with my drama." We walk down the hall and push open the big metal doors that lead outside. A deluxe minivan pulls up and toots. Lauren waves at her mom.

"Want to come over? Decompress before you head home to hell? Mom's making tacos today."

Reluctantly, I sigh. "Man, I love your mom's tacos. But I'd better get to the studio."

Lauren gives me a fist bump. I shake my head. "If things go south, I'll be coming over to eat my weight in tacos. Be prepared."

Lauren laughs. "OK, so that'll be like two tacos, beanpole? I hope your parents give guardianship to Martin just so he can start feeding you! Good luck and keep me posted"

I wave as they drive off, then go to look for Geena so I can catch a ride to the studio.

***

Rehearsal is quick; Martin and I are both distracted. Forty-five minutes later, we're finished and sweating, packing to go home. As I leave with Geena, Martin gives me a big hug and wishes me luck.

At home, we walk into the house, unsure of what we'll find. Will Mom be hurling plates at the wall (*it's happened too many times to count*), crying (*ditto*), or will there be a stony silence hanging in the air? Instead, we're surprised to be greeted by delicious aromas coming from the kitchen and the sounds of country music. Mom is barefoot in the dining room, placing a pitcher of yellow daisies on the table. There's a cloth on the table, which only comes out on birthdays and special occasions, and Mom is dancing as she moves about the room. "Oh, hey y'all. I figured we could use a good home-cooked meal tonight."

"Did Dad sign the papers?" I ask, as Geena slides my bag off my shoulder and disappears upstairs with it.

Mom shakes her head slowly, turning to grab a pile of utensils on the sideboard. "Noooo, not yet." She places forks and knives by each plate. "I know how stressful it's been around here for everyone. I figured we could all use a nice family dinner together."

"Well, thanks, Mom. It smells great. Need any help?"

My mom smiles. "Naw, sugar. Your dad should be home any second. Oh, and honey? You've worked so hard. No matter what happens, I'm proud of you."

I feel like I've been hit by a bus. That is the *first time* my mom has ever said something like that to me. It *should* feel good—it's what I've always wanted—but it feels...awkward. "Um, thanks, Mom." I manage a weird smile and a shrug. "You've never said that before."

Mom nods seriously, "I know. I should have told you more. Your sister too. And your dad, come to think of it. Being emotional is kind of hard for me."

I roll my eyes, "OK, that's the biggest lie ever, Mom. You're famous for throwing dishes and crying at the drop of a hat. Why do you think the neighbors run into their houses every time they see you?"

She laughs. "Ranting and being angry is easy; it's healthy to vent! It's the love stuff I have a tough time with...telling the people I care about how I feel about them. My mother wasn't the most emotional person in history...I guess I never learned how to express myself."

My mom shakes her head and exhales loudly. "OK, no need to get so heavy in here. Go wash up. We'll eat as soon as Dad gets home."

As we wash for dinner, I fill in Geena on Mom's declaration of pride.

Geena splashes water on her face and all over the bathroom counter while she listens. "Wait, what?" She turns off the water and flails for a face towel.

I laugh, tossing her one. "I know; can you believe it? She said she was proud of me, you, and Dad, and that she needed to tell us more. I was so shocked. I didn't even know what to say."

"Is she drunk? It's not like Dad was there to hear it, so she wasn't going to gain anything," Geena muses as she towels off.

I shrug and fix my hair. "Maybe this whole situation has made her think about things. Signing me over to Martin might have gotten her to take a good look at herself."

Geena stares at me in the mirror. "Hmmm, maybe. It's nice she said it to you, but it's going to take more than a secondhand confession of pride on her part to get me onto Team Jodi. She could start by saying that to my face and then apologizing for being such a monster when I was younger."

Geena frowns, hanging up her soggy towel. "I'm not buying it. I'm glad you're happy, but I'm too pissed at Mom to be won over by some warm emotions and a home-cooked meal. Now if she'd let us have dessert, maybe I'd consider it." Geena elbows me and smiles. "Come on. Let's eat before she decides we don't need all those extra calories."

We're just sitting down at the table when Dad comes home. Mom emerges from the kitchen holding the pot roast on a platter, with roasted root veggies arranged stylishly around the perfectly browned meat. She's clearly trying to impress us. Without meaning too, even Geena oohs and aahs.

"Well, well, well," Dad says, taking his place at the head of the table. "Dinner looks delicious." He reaches out and gives Mom's arm a squeeze.

I look at Geena questioningly. Dad isn't his boisterous, happy self, but he isn't angry or sullen either. Mom sits down and puts her napkin on her lap.

"So, I guess you girls know what your mother and I have been discussing the past twenty-four hours?" Dad asked, placing his napkin on his lap. Geena and I exchange glances. *Here it comes...*

Without waiting for an answer, he proceeds. "At first, I was really angry. I'm not in the habit of handing my children over to people who are practically strangers."

I start to protest but Dad raises a hand, cutting me off. I sit back in my chair and take a deep breath. I'm on pins and needles; the wait is excruciating.

"I know Martin is practically family, but he's not your parent. However, I realized that by saying no, I'd be putting to waste all your years of hard work. I can't do that to you, Dani. I wish it didn't have to be this way, but I'll agree to have Martin act as your guardian."

I stare open-mouthed at my father, not believing what I've just heard. Geena gives a war-cry yelp and slams her fist onto the table, rattling the dishes.

"You just remember, Danilynn Marie Truehart, I am your father." He points to my mom. "*That* is your mother and no one, I mean *no one*, loves you as much as we do. If you decide this is too much for you, just tell us and you can quit at any time. We're always here for you."

I leap up and throw myself in my dad's arms, hugging him. Tears of joy are streaming down my face. "I know that, Daddy. Thank you so much. I won't forget, and I won't let you down." I pull back and smile at him. "Ohmigod, I have to call Martin!"

Dad squeezes me again, almost crushing the air out of me. He kisses the top of my head. "You could never, ever let me down, honey. Not in a million years." He lets me go, patting my arm. "I already called Martin. He'll be here at 10:00 on Friday to pick you up for the audition."

My mom beams but remains silent, knowing her victory needs no acknowledgment. Part of me is totally bugged by that smug look on her face, but I shake it off. *Not tonight. This is too big to get wrapped up in her crap.* Instead, I high-five Geena.

Dad reaches for the carving utensils. "OK, Trueharts, let's eat. Who knows when we'll all be able to sit as a family like this again? One last meal together before our little girl makes it big."

I laugh, bouncing in my seat like a toddler as we dive into the delicious meal.

9

For the first time in a long time, Mom isn't raging, Dad and Geena are smiling, and I'm so happy that everyone else is happy, I feel as if I could float right up to the sky. We spend a rare evening together watching a movie. It's the perfect ending to an amazing evening.

When the movie ends, I rush upstairs to call Lauren. I'm so excited that my words run together. "Lauren! DadsignedthepapersIgettoauditiontomorrow, ohmygodisittoolatetocallsorry!"

Lauren screams. "I've been waiting all night for your call! OMG! Tell me everything!"

I describe every detail of the evening, dreamily reliving each moment. Lauren laughs. "I'm so happy for you! I mean, not only that you can audition, but that your family really pulled together to support you."

I smile. "Me too. I just wish it was like this all the time." I sigh. "God, am I getting to be like my mom or what? Can't I just be happy that I had this one peaceful, perfect night without wishing I had more?"

"Dani, I hate to break it to you, but there's nothing wrong with wanting your family to get along. Feeling that way does *not* make you like your mom. And for that matter, can we not let your mom ruin the next few days? You need to focus on nailing that audition."

I flop on the bed, stretching out. "You're right. Moving on. I am *so* nervous about the audition."

"You've been prepping for this for years. You've got a killer voice, amazing moves and you know your routines backward and forward. Try not to overthink it." Lauren giggles, "I just realized that by this time on Friday, you'll have a signed contract."

"Oh God, Lauren, don't jinx me. We have no idea what Jenner Redman is looking for."

"Come on, Dani, if this guy doesn't sign you the minute you open your mouth then he's a total idiot and you know it. *This is happening!*

My best friend's going to be a superstar! You'd better not forget me when you make it big. Or I just might have to call *InTouch* magazine and tell them all your childhood secrets."

I laugh, playing along. "Lauren who? Who is this again? I'm too big to be answering the phone these days, please call back and speak to my assistant."

Lauren screams. "As *if*! You do that, I'll tell *Star* magazine all about the time you got so scared at dance camp listening to ghost stories that you wouldn't walk to the bathroom and you peed in your night-gown."

I gasp. "You swore you'd take that to the grave."

Lauren chuckles. "Well, don't test me, superstar. Remember to take my calls. I've got a lot of unfortunate pictures with braces, perms, and one very awkward Halloween pumpkin costume."

"OK, Hannon, you made your point. I'll take your calls no matter how rich and important I become."

My mom's howl bellows out from downstairs. "Daaaannni! Lights out!"

I cringe and sigh. "I gotta call Sean before the warden does bed check. Love you."

Lauren blows a kiss into the phone. "You too. Bye."

I dial furiously and Sean picks up on the first ring. "Well?" I clutch the phone, beaming, and whisper, "Dad said yes!" Sean whoops. "That's awesome, Dani. What happened?"

I start to explain but Sean cuts me off. "I can barely hear you. Why are you whispering?"

"Sorry. I'm supposed to be asleep right now, but I wanted to call you. We had such a wonderful night together as a family. I don't want to break the spell and have Mom switch back into her drill-sergeant self because I'm on the phone too late."

"Don't worry about it. We can talk at school."

I pause. "Um, I won't be in school for the next few days. Rehearsals, hair appointments, stuff like that. But I'll give you a call when I can." What I say feels totally inadequate because all I want to do is celebrate this moment with Sean. I'm just now realizing I can't see him for the next few days.

Frustrated, Sean sighs. "I get why you're so busy, but, man, it sucks! I just want to wish you good luck." After a long pause, Sean sighs. "If I can't see you, know I'm cheering for you all the way."

Tears come to my eyes and I exhale, relieved. "I do."

"Good. Now you better get going before you get in trouble. Sweet dreams."

10

Wednesday and Thursday pass in a blur. Between twice-daily rehearsals and generally trying not to panic, I try on an endless stream of clothing options, get my hair cut and sit for hours while my mom tries out different makeup and hairstyles.

My family does their best to make things go as smoothly as possible. The only spot of annoyance has been the constant needling from my mom. While she knows she's no longer in the driver's seat for my career, she's still hoping that she can somehow change that. She has been trying in many subtle ways to bring it to my attention, but, unfortunately, subtlety was never her strong suit. I've spent much of the past two days either ignoring my mother or directing her concerns to Martin. It's stress I just don't need.

Friday finally comes. I awake to light fingers touching my hair as my mom whispers, "Sugar, it's time to wake up."

She keeps smoothing my hair until I slowly open my eyes. I stretch and smile. "Morning, Mom."

My mom smiles as she sits on the bed. "Good morning." She holds out a steaming mug of green tea as I sit up in bed, rubbing the sleep from my eyes. "Here you go." I blow on the steam, taking a tentative sip of the strong tea. "Your father and sister are almost finished with the bathroom. Martin will be here in four hours, so you've got plenty of time to get ready."

I take a deep breath. "I can't believe it's today."

Mom smiles. "I know, sugar. This is the day we've been working so hard for. You're going to dazzle that Jenner Redman." She has a sad smile as she pats my arm. "I wish I could be there today to watch you shine. All this hard work, and I'm not even going to see the big pay-off!"

I sigh heavily and get out of bed. "Come on, Mom, don't start. You're not supposed to stress me out about this kind of stuff, remember? Especially not today!"

My mom pouts, just like a four-year-old trying to get her way. "Well, I'm not trying to stress you out, Miss Sensitive. I just want to be involved."

I shake my head and leave the room. "Today of all days, I can't worry about you, Mom."

I'm fuming as I stomp down the hall. Once again, my mom is making everything about her. I'm so angry, I'm seeing spots. I feel like I'm about to explode when I remember what Lauren said about my mom. I take a deep breath and exhale slowly, trying to slow my heartbeat. My shoulders start to relax. I look at myself in the mirror.

"Danilynn Marie Truehart, you are *not* going to let your mom get you all worked up. This is your day. Do *not* get caught up in her craziness." I stare at myself in the mirror. I feel empowered and a little heady from saying "no" to my mother for the first time.

I smile at my reflection. "Maybe having Martin as a guardian is already having positive effects on you, Danilynn. Less than forty-eight hours and you're already standing up to Mom!" I crank up the shower, hot steam immediately filling the bathroom. I hop in and enjoy an extremely long, relaxing shower.

II

After my shower, I work my way through my usual egg-white breakfast. The last thing I want to do is eat. All the nerves combined with a second cup of tea are making my stomach jump. But I need food to absorb all that caffeine. My mom spends an hour blowing out my hair, rolling it in hot rollers and teasing it to impossible heights. The amount of hairspray she uses probably burns another hole in the ozone layer. She spends another forty-five minutes applying my makeup.

My mom is just finishing up when the doorbell rings at 10:00. She places a final stroke of blush on each cheek and steps back to check her work. "Perfect timing. Our star is ready!" She gives my knee a squeeze and runs downstairs to answer the door.

I glance in the mirror and I don't recognize myself. I look like I'm twenty-five! Heavy eye makeup makes my eyes seem enormous. I have shimmery powder on my face that makes me look like I'm headed to a club rather than a daytime audition. My lips are outlined into a ridiculous pout. I mug in the mirror, making fish faces, horrified at the effect. And my hair! It's a mass of teased, curled horror. Hidden clips and pins form some kind of faux hawk that makes me so tall that I look like some futuristic amazon. *I can't go out looking like this!* I start to sweat and feel dizzy.

I turn around as Martin enters the room. Unwinding his gray scarf from his neck, Martin gasps. "Holy Gene Simmons! What the hell happened to you?" he whispers. You look like you should be working the pole at Juggernuts."

Just then my mom enters the room. "Ta-da! What do you think, Martin? Is she ready for her closeup or what?"

Martin calms himself and adjusts his leather jacket. "She suuuure is ready for somethin', Jodi," Martin says, plastering on a smile. Under his breath, he says, "Like your own street corner."

I snort and have to turn back to the mirror so my mom doesn't see me laugh. I start clearing up the makeup scattered on the counter, trying not to look at myself.

"Not too bad for an amateur, if I say so myself." My mom beams at her handiwork, oblivious of our horror.

"Wow, that sure is, uh, something, Jodi! I can't believe you did this all, uh, on your own. No prior beauty experience, you say?"

My mom proudly shakes her head and smiles. "Nope, just natural talent! Kind of makes you want to take me on the road with you, huh? You'd save a ton of money with me as her makeup artist." She rocks back on her heels, pleased as punch.

Martin gives me a tight smile and turns to my mom. "You know I would if I could, hon. But we have a deal. You're in charge of the home front and I've got the business side of things." He looks back to me, opens his eyes wide and smiles. "Well, this was such an unexpected surprise. I thought we'd have to do hair and makeup, but now you've saved us so much time. I guess we can head to the studio and walk through the numbers before we go."

Mom looks panicked. "Wait, Martin. If she dances, she might sweat off her makeup." Suddenly, she smiles excitedly. "Why don't I come with you? Then I can retouch her makeup and help her get dressed before you leave. I could even go with you and wait in the lobby, you know, in case she needs any last-minute touchups!" She starts grabbing things from the bathroom counter. "Just give me five minutes and I'll be ready to go."

Martin shakes his head and smiles. "That won't be necessary, Jodi. Dani won't be doing a full-paced run-through, just a slow walk-through. I don't want her to strain her voice or get injured. Absolutely no sweating scheduled. Besides, since today is the first official day of our agreement, it wouldn't do if I broke the rules by bringing you to the audition." He reaches out and puts his hand on my mom's shoulder, catching her eye in the mirror. "Let's just stick to the plan. We'll grab her clothes and then we'll get out of your hair."

My mom knows she's defeated and shrugs. "Whatever, Martin. I know the deal. I was only trying to help." She throws the items she's holding into a plastic makeup caddy. I'll just pack this up in case you need to touch up anything. Hope you can figure it out."

Martin squeezes my shoulder reassuringly. "Thank you, Jodi. You've done a great job getting her ready. I really appreciate it."

Mom smiles at the compliment and takes a deep breath. "You're welcome, Martin. All I want is for my baby to succeed, with or without me." She bends to close the caddy and I roll my eyes. "I've got her costumes already packed. I wasn't sure what you were looking for, so I gave you a few options. I'll leave them by the door. Dani, go get changed."

I scramble out of the bathroom, happy for any excuse to stop looking at this insane makeover. Trying to change my clothes is a nightmare. I had a cute outfit all picked out, but I can't put it on over my enormous hair. So, I have to settle for skinny jeans, the black tank top I'm already wearing and a crop faux leather jacket.

I come downstairs and immediately pick up on the tension between Martin and my mom. She has her arms crossed and is giving Martin a death stare. Martin's standing next to a pile of garment and duffel bags with a fake smile plastered to his face. Lord knows what my mom tried to pull while I was changing. I just want to get out of the house without a fight. "Everything OK, guys?" I try to be breezy as I cross the living room, slinging my old canvas dance bag over my shoulder, but my huge tower of hair is throwing off my balance. I move slowly and awkwardly, scared I'll fall over if I move my head too much.

Martin's big smile becomes more genuine when he sees me. "Just fine, hon. You ready to go?"

I nod and give my mother a peck on the cheek. I'm surprised when she almost knocks me over with a bear hug, practically squeezing the life out of me.

"This is it! Have a great audition and do everything like we discussed."

Martin pats my mom's shoulder as he gently pulls me from her grasp. "She will, Miss J. Thanks again for everything. We'll give you a call when we're finished." I'm almost free when my mom, still holding onto my hand, yanks me so hard I almost fall over.

"What in the world are you doing, Danilynn Truehart?" She yelps, "Why are you taking that ratty old dance bag to your audition? You are not going to impress Jenner Redman with a piece of junk like that hanging off your arm. Let me loan you my fake Louis Vuitton bag. It'll look better."

"God, Mom!" I groan as I rub my hand, finally free of her grip. Martin steps firmly between us, giving me a friendly push out the front door. He artfully blocks my mom from following us out the door by bending over to pick up the costume bags and reaching for the makeup caddy. "That's sweet, but not necessary. Jenner won't even see the bag, which will be left in the car. He's after talent, not accessories."

By the time Martin gathers everything, I'm already at the car. "We'll talk later. Ta!"

Martin, weighed down by bags, the caddy and his own little paunch, waddles as fast as he can away from the house, gray scarf flapping behind him. His bald head glistens with sweat by the time he reaches the car. He repeatedly hits the button on his key fob, making the ancient BMW unlock and beep madly.

"Get in, get in!" Martin whispers. He looks over his shoulder and sees my mom step out onto the front porch, waving. "Get in the car before she jumps in."

As I fold myself into the front seat, my faux hawk scraping the roof of the car, Martin whips open the back door, hanging the garment bags and depositing the other items on the floor before he slams the door. He gives my mom a final big wave and plastic smile over the top of the car and hops in. He locks the doors as he slams the key into the ignition.

I laugh. "It's like we're in a horror movie, and we're running for our lives." I wipe tears from my eyes and see my hand is smeared with makeup. "Oh dang."

Martin looks in the rearview mirror. "You know if your mom thought it would get her into that audition, she'd hop on top of this car wielding an ax as we drive away. She's one crazy mother!" Martin glances at me. "Oh God, look at you. You're melting!"

He rummages in the side door pocket and pulls out a wad of paper napkins. "Here. Don't worry, they're clean. What did that woman do to you?"

After a couple of tries, he finally gets the car started. Just as my mom is about to step off the porch and offer to drive us, he pops the clutch and peels out, making a clean getaway.

I smile and wave goodbye to my mom. "Well, you know she used to do the makeup for our pageants. I guess she just pulled out that bag of tricks today."

"You're looking like you're going to *turn* some tricks, if you know what I mean. This is an emergency."

Martin pulls out his flip phone and punches the keypad. "Pauline? Girl, you've got to drop everything and meet me at the studio STAT. I've got Tammy Faye Baker's sister from a different mister riding shotgun and only a few hours for a supreme make-under. You up for the challenge?"

I pull down the visor mirror and attempt to wipe my face. The makeup seems glued on.

"Dani's mom went full-blown pageant makeup on her and now my sweet-teen-pop-star-to-be looks like a forty-six-year-old lounge singer in Reno. Can you bring your supplies and a gallon of soap to the studio? You're a lifesaver, sis! See you there. Muah." Martin kisses the phone and hangs up.

I heave a sigh of relief as I snap the visor back into place, crumpling the soiled napkins. "That's awesome. I don't know what we'd do if Pauline wasn't available."

"If she wasn't free, I'd have gotten a stick of dynamite and a Brillo pad. We'll have you looking fresh-faced and subtly accented in no time." He gives my knee a squeeze and I close my eyes as Martin speeds to the studio. I'm nervous enough as it is. I don't need to see him bob and weave through traffic, barely missing pedestrians and forgetting to look before he changes lanes.

Martin keeps a running commentary all the way to the studio, complaining about the crazy drivers on the road (*oh, the irony!*), observing the questionable fashion choices of the pedestrians and telling me how excited he is that my parents finally decided to sign the contract. I think he's trying to keep me from focusing on how nervous I am. His comments wash over me and trying to follow the flow of his thoughts does keep my mind off my nerves.

We screech into a parking space outside the studio, Martin's old beater shimmying to a halt. I open my eyes and smile at Martin as I open the door. "I guess we can run through the routines one more time before Pauline gets here."

Martin gives me a serious look. "Give it a rest. You know this stuff backward and forward. I just told your mom that so we could get out of the house." He claps his hands excitedly. "Let's pick your outfit."

"Are you sure? We told my mom..."

Martin holds up a hand and interrupts me. "From now on, as long as I'm your guardian, you don't need to explain your performance choices or how much you practice. I order you not to feel guilty about me telling your mom you'd do a run-through. You know this stuff by heart, and relaxing is more important than second-guessing yourself."

I nod. "OK." Closing the door, I add, "And thanks for doing this. I know you're getting paid, if we get any money at all, that is. But I feel like I at least have a chance of enjoying this whole thing with you looking out for me."

"Me too, hon. OK, let's get these bags inside and see what your mom packed. If your makeup is any indication, we might be in big trouble." I groan and we heft the bags inside.

12

The glass door to the studio bangs shut behind us and Martin hollers, "Hi, Mama. We're here!"

Norma Fox, Martin's mother, pops out from the back room. "What in the world?" She grabs a tissue from the box on the counter, licks a corner and starts to wipe my cheek. "Is it painted on?"

Martin grimaces. "Pauline's on her way with reinforcements. Want to check out the costume choices Jodi sent?"

Norma shakes her head. "Lord, I can only imagine."

We bring the bags into the main studio, flicking on the overhead fluorescent lights as we enter. Norma appears a few minutes later, noisily wheeling in a clothing rack. Martin hangs the garment bags on the rack and begins pulling out clothes. I begin unpacking shoes from one bag while Norma pulls accessories from the other.

My mom sews as well as she applies makeup. She's taken ordinary jeans, shorts, tops and dresses and cut, customized and bedazzled them beyond recognition. Saucy cutouts, lace appliqués, grommets and sequins are on every piece. Hot pants, bra tops, mini dresses...no inappropriate attire has been omitted. It's perfect for a Las Vegas review or a night at the club, but hardly appropriate for an afternoon audition for a fifteen-year-old. We stand back and survey the clothes.

Martin walks up and down the rack, flicking through the clothes, hangers clattering back and forth. "Oh my God," he whispers, "We are *screwed!*"

Norma joins Martin, calmly pulling each piece off the rack, discarding the most outrageous pieces and rehanging a few of the plainer pieces. When she's finished, about eight items are hanging on the rack. She turns to face us.

"OK, here are the least offensive. Let's see what we can do." Norma shakes her head, holding up a tiny string bikini as if it were contaminated. "Why on earth did your mama pack a bikini? And what about these bustiers and brassieres? You're auditioning to sing, not model lingerie for Fredericks of Hollywood!"

I can only shrug. I'm mortified. My face glows red with shame. Norma throws the suit onto the pile of discarded clothes. "We'll make it work, Dani, don't you worry," she says, rubbing her hands together. "Martin, why don't you give us a few minutes."

Martin nods and hurries away, shutting the door behind him. Norma drags over an old-fashioned Japanese screen and sets it up in the corner. "Come on, honey." Norma pulls the pleather pants and red bodysuit off the rack and gently pushes me behind the screen. Forty minutes later, we've pieced together an outfit. We opted for tight jeans, the black tank that I was already wearing, a black belt that hangs loosely on my hips and the crop pleather jacket I wore from home. Martin is finally allowed into the room.

"Ta-da!" Norma trumpets. "What do you think, son? She's sassy, trendy and totally covered up."

I'm sweating bullets hoping we've pulled it off as Martin slowly walks around me, silently scrutinizing. I turn around for him once, arms out, and smile. He thoughtfully taps his lip. "I don't like it."

My heart sinks as Martin's face lights up. "I love it!" I heave a sigh of relief as Martin hugs Norma and me. "You're a miracle worker, Mama! It's just perfect." He gives his mom a big kiss. "Dani, you look young and edgy, but totally age-appropriate. I couldn't be happier." He scrubs his thumb on my chin. "Now we just need to scrape off all that makeup and get that rat's nest smoothed out."

As if on cue, the front door rattles in the reception area. "A little help over here!"

"Pauline, I'm coming!" Martin runs into reception, returning moments later with his sister. Pauline is tall and graceful like Martin, but slender as a willow. Her long hair is pulled back into a low, sleek ponytail. She's dressed in a chic black dress and boots, pulling a wheeled bag behind her. She looks as if she stepped out of a magazine.

"Good God, what happened to you?"

Pauline turns to Martin, who is dragging two more wheeled bags and carrying a makeup caddy. "How much time do we have, Martin?" "A little less than two hours. I want to give us at least an hour to drive over there. Can you do it?" Martin is sweating from the stress and looking desperate again.

"It'll be close, but I think we can." Pauline rummages through one of her bags and pulls out a bottle of cleanser, a wad of cotton pads and a headband. "Dani, honey," she hands me the items. "Get scrubbing." I nod and scoot toward the door.

"Oh, Dani," Martin calls out. I turn around, and I'm momentarily blinded by a flash of light. Martin chuckles. "I'm gonna want to remember this look for the future." He waves the undeveloped Polaroid picture as dark spots swim before my eyes. I stick my tongue out at him before I stomp out of the room.

Norma scrambles after me, grabbing one of the discarded, sequined tees and leggings from the floor. "Wait for me, girl. Change those clothes before they get covered in soap." She calls over her shoulder before she leaves the room. "Pauline, go grab that lighted makeup table and wheel it in."

"Great idea, Mama! On it!"

Fifteen minutes later and minus the top layer of my skin, I'm back in the studio, sitting in the makeup chair. Norma ended up scrubbing my face for me. My skin is sore from being tugged and scoured. I can only imagine what bath time had been like for Martin as a child!

Pauline turns to Martin, who is rummaging through the makeup table. "You, out. Now." Martin opens his mouth to protest while Norma grabs his elbow and drags him toward the lobby. "Pauline's right. Come have a cup of coffee. Or a tranquilizer."

Pauline smiles as they speed out of the room.

"Looks like you got all that makeup off and more! Your poor skin. Don't worry, sugar, we'll tackle that hair first and then finish with some nice, light makeup."

The next ninety minutes fly by. In the end, no amount of flat ironing and smoothing spray can tame the ratted mess my mom created.

Pauline has to dunk my head in the sink. After more blow-drying, hot rollers and brushing, it's finished. Perfectly styled into a long, shining sheet of dark hair hanging down my back with a subtle curl at the ends—I love it. A couple of rhinestone bobby pins pulls the hair up on one side, off my face. It's just perfect.

Makeup is next. Pauline carefully applies foundation, eyelashes, blush and a soft pink lip gloss. When she finally lets me look in the mirror, I don't look like I'm wearing makeup at all! I just look like a brighter, more perfected version of myself. It's miraculous!

"Pauline, you're amazing!" I leap up and give her a hug, practically knocking her over.

"Whoa, no sense in messing it all up just to give me a hug." Pauline laughs as she disentangles herself, checking to make sure no damage has been done. "Sweetie, I'm happy I could help." She places a hand under my chin and looks me straight in the eye. "Jenner Redman's not going to know what hit him." She winks. "Let's get you dressed." It's quite a process to change into my audition clothes while making sure my hair and makeup don't get mussed. When we're finished, I walk to the mirror. The transformation since I left my house is stunning. I *cannot believe this is me!*

Pauline watches me and smiles. "Now, let's put my brother out of his misery. Martin!"

The studio door opens, and Martin runs in with Norma trailing behind. I turn and face them, beaming. Martin heaves a loud sigh of relief and shouts, "Yes!" He grabs Pauline and spins her around. "You are a miracle worker, sis! Goodbye, Tammy Faye Baker!" He excitedly puts Pauline down and reaches for my hands. "Just what I imagined for your big day." He looks over at Pauline, who has her arm around Norma, smiling proudly at her handiwork. "Sheer perfection, sis. I owe you big time."

"How could I not succeed when I've got such a gorgeous subject? And yes, you do owe me, bro. But don't worry, I'll collect someday." She grins at Martin.

The lovefest is interrupted when the dance company's phone starts ringing. Norma answers the studio extension, "Martin Fox. Hello, Sean. Yes, she's right here. Looking gorgeous, I might add."

My heart leaps, and I run across the studio, grabbing the phone from Norma, who chuckles and steps out of the way.

"I'm so happy you called!" I gush. "How'd you know I was here?"

"Lauren told me you were headed to the studio before the audition." I lean against the wall, tightly gripping the phone. Sean's mellow voice is like a soothing balm, instantly calming my nerves. "I only have a few minutes in between classes, but I wanted to wish you good luck. I'm so proud of you!"

I smile into the phone and everyone else in the room seems to disappear. "Thanks. You should have seen me earlier today. My mom did my hair and makeup, and it was a total disaster. Luckily, Martin's sister came and gave me a make-under and now I feel great. God, Sean, I'm so nervous, but excited too, you know? Like all these years of hard work are about to pay off."

"I know! I just wish I could see you kill it. I bet you look amazing." The school bell rings and Sean sighs. "Damn. I'd better go. I can't be late for history again." It's hard to hear his voice as the mad scramble of kids rushing to class fills the background. "Knock 'em dead, Dani. Lauren says good luck too. She wanted to call, but there wasn't enough time for both of us to talk." The bell rings again in the background. "Ugh, I gotta run. Good luck."

"Bye." I happily shrug my shoulders, smiling into the phone as I slowly hang up. I look up to see Martin, Norma and Pauline staring at me and grinning.

"What?" I look from one to the other as they beam at me.

Martin shrugs his shoulders and shakes his head. "It's just you two are so stinking cute together I can't stand it."

I roll my eyes and hold up a hand. "OK, I'm so not discussing my love life with you guys right now. But I'm glad he called. Now I feel ready to go!"

Martin snaps his fingers. "Well then, let's go!" We spend a few minutes bagging the discarded costumes and packing up Pauline's supplies. Norma leaves the room and returns with a small cooler and a thermos. "I packed you some snacks. And here's some hot tea for your throat."

I give her a huge hug, taking the cooler and thermos. "Thanks, Mrs. Fox. I completely forgot to bring any food. I'd be lost without you."

Norma pats my back. "You're ready for this, sugar. Just do what you do best and let Martin handle the rest. You got this, girl."

Pauline comes over and hugs me. "I gotta run or I'll be late for work. You look fabulous, Dani. I can't wait to hear how you dazzled that fool Redman. He doesn't deserve someone as good as you!"

Martin kindly shoves Pauline along. "Yes, well, thanks for the sentiment, sis. But I think we need Redman just as much as he needs us at this point. I know he's been a bit of a question mark in the past..."

"A question mark?" Norma and Pauline shout simultaneously. Norma puts her hands on her hips. "Have you forgotten..."

Martin holds up his hands, "I have forgotten nothing, ladies, believe me. I know better than you what Jenner's done in the past and what he's capable of. But he's hungry for a comeback, and Dani's just the one to give it to him." Martin looks proudly at me. "She has the potential to be bigger than any act he's ever managed. And don't you believe for a second that I don't know it. I intend to see that he makes good on all his past mistakes by signing her. He's no fool, and these days, neither am I."

Norma harrumphs, looking away, swallowing her anger. She nods once, realizing it isn't Martin she was angry with. "Well, you're right on that, baby. You give that jackass hell and tell him how it's gonna be."

Martin gives his mother a hug and kisses the top of her head. "I will, Mama. I learned from the best, remember?" He looks down at her and catches her eye.

She grudgingly smiles and nods. "That you did, son, that you did."

Pauline stoops down to pick up the handles of her rolling bags. "All right, big brother, I know you've got this handled. Call me and let me know how much you stick Redman for." She kisses his cheek. "Love you."

She blows air kisses at me. "Love you too, sweetie. I packed extra lip gloss and powder in your bag for touchups. Taaaa!" Pauline wiggles her fingers at us over her shoulder as she wheels herself out of the studio.

13

Moments later, we're speeding down the street in Martin's old BMW. I grip the door handle as we fly past buildings and cars. "Can you drive at any other speed besides supersonic?" I plead. "I don't want to sweat off all this lovely makeup your sister spent hours applying."

Martin groans, taking his foot off the gas. "If it wasn't your big day, I'd tell you to shut up and stop nagging like my mama. But since it *is* your big day, I'll concede to driving like an *old lady* just so you don't stress-sweat away all Pauline's hard work." He gives me a slight bow. I just shake my head, marveling at how much time Martin spends *not* looking at the road. Between his phone, changing the radio and trying to read street signs, it's a wonder he even knows what's happening in front of him.

We get on the clogged freeway and slow to a crawl. Martin groans again, glaring at me like it's somehow my fault. "Happy now, princess? Babies are crawling faster than we're moving." He bangs his head on the headrest behind him. "This is torture. The biggest day of your career, and we're stuck in traffic. Just what our nerves needed."

I pull out my headphones and make a show of popping them into my ears. "We have plenty of time to get there, Martin. Take some deep breaths and try not to have a heart attack." I pat his arm. "Remember, you're the one who's supposed to be calming *me* down."

Martin's eyes bulge out of his head, as he turns to me. "Oh *my God*, you're right! I'm the worst guardian ever. You have my word from now on, I'll keep it together instead of acting like a spaz." He clears his throat and takes a deep breath. In his most soothing voice, he smiles and says, "Now, why don't you rest your eyes and let me concentrate on driving."

I roll my eyes and laugh. "Better. Look, this is my first audition for a big producer, and it's your first time managing a superstar. Let's just both be honest and patient with each other, and I think we'll be OK." Martin smiles. "Me too. Rest up. I'll wake you when we get there."

I turn on my music, put my head back and close my eyes. The slow traffic lulls me to sleep and the songs—*my* songs—wash over me. In my mind's eye, I see myself dancing the routines I've rehearsed hundreds of times. I completely forget I'm stuck on a crowded freeway, slowly inching forward. Over and over again, I listen to my songs on a loop, smiling as I see myself belting out the words, moving my body in time, telling a story with my entire person.

I jump when Martin touches my hand. "We're here, Dani.'"

I open my eyes, smile lazily, and yawn. "It's the craziest thing, Martin. I was just listening to my songs and it's like this car, the traffic and you just disappeared. I didn't feel like I was asleep; I felt like was dancing and singing. It was so surreal." Unable to explain what I've just experienced, my words trail off. I look at Martin with a puzzled smile on my face.

Martin smiles. "I remember moments like that. It's like the routines were ingrained in my body. But it was more than that..." He looks away and smiles to himself. "...it was the love of performing." He turns back to me. "We'd get new music or a new routine, and it was like an obsession for me. All I could do was work and work until I had everything down by heart. The other guys used to make fun of me for it, but I didn't care. It was so satisfying to flawlessly perform a song or dance routine, nailing every note or move. It was better than anything I can think of." He squeezes my hand.

I squeeze back. "You never talk much about your time in REVOLUTION! I mean, you make jokes and stuff, but I always felt it was kind of off-limits. So, you'd do it all over again if you had the chance, even all the stuff with Redman?" I absentmindedly chew on my lower lip.

"In a heartbeat, darlin'. Even with all the crap Redman pulled, I'd do it all over again every time. It was the best time of my life. I wouldn't be who I am today without that amazing experience." He puts one hand on his heart and holds the other hand up. "I am openly proud and lucky to be an '80s has-been." He laughs and then gets serious.

"And don't you worry. I'm here to make sure that what happened to me does *not* happen to you. You worry about performing. I'll make sure you retire at whatever age you want with a trust fund full of money and the best memories we can make."

I smile and nod. "I'm so glad to hear that. I wasn't sure how you felt. I know you don't have the best memories of Redman, but the fact that you called him must mean it wasn't all bad for you."

Martin snorts. "The fact that I called Redman means that I feel confident that you're good enough to interest him, he's desperate enough for a comeback and just guilty enough about what he did to REVOLUTION! to give you a chance."

I shrug. "I don't care. I'll take it."

Martin smiles. "Good! Now let's warm up those pipes and head inside. Time to get your career started!"

***

I've never been inside such a fancy hotel before. A uniformed doorman opens the lobby door for us. A woman in a suit is waiting in the lobby. She introduces herself as Caroline and escorts us to the elevator.

Marble floors, high ceilings, carved wooden walls polished until they glowed adorn the lobby; this is much fancier than the Hampton Inn where we usually stay. Martin doesn't seem fazed by any of this and keeps walking with the woman, making polite conversation. My nerves start to jitter.

We step into the elevator and Caroline presses a button. "You will find Mr. Redman in the penthouse. Should you require anything, just dial zero and ask for me. Mr. Redman wants to make sure you are completely taken care of." The elevator zips up.

Martin thanks her, and I give her a nervous smile. I take a deep breath and start going over my songs in my head. If I don't nail this audition, I'll probably never get a chance to walk through a hotel like this again, let alone stay in one. I tune out Martin and Caroline's idle chatter and breathe deeply.

Less than a minute later, we exit the elevator and are standing outside the penthouse. Martin gives me a reassuring nod. "You've got this, darlin."

I nod and smile shakily, giving Martin a thumbs-up. Martin faces the door, squares his shoulders, and firmly knocks twice.

14

The door opens into the first penthouse I've ever seen in real life. It's just like on TV. A doughy, weasel-faced man in his twenties introduces himself as Carlton, Mr. Redman's assistant. He gives us an ingratiating smile as he shows us into an enormous room with elegant furnishings and a table laden with food and drinks. A flash of terror overtakes me as I spy a gleaming piano and guitar in the corner. *Does Redman expect me to play music, too?* I've spent years singing and dancing, but I've never had time for formal music lessons. Sure, I know my way around the instruments, but I can't play well enough to impress a professional. I'm too embarrassed to ask Martin in front of Redman. I'm beginning to feel as if the train has left the station and I'm clinging onto the caboose with nothing to do but hang on until it stops.

Carlton walks toward a man sitting in an armchair, reading the paper. "Mr. Redman, Mr. Fox and Miss Truehart have arrived."

Redman looks up and smiles, folding his paper as he stands. He's perfectly dressed and looks powerful in a tailored suit and tinted glasses. "Martin! Good to see you again." He drops the paper onto his chair and walks forward with open arms. Martin already has his hand extended, as they share a hug that is awkward on Martin's part and warm on Redman's part. They step back and look at one another. They both break into smiles.

"Looks like we're both letting it shine these days, huh, Martin?" Redman says pointing at his bald head. "I still expected you to walk through that door with your high-top. Guess we're just a couple of geezers now."

Martin snorts. "Speak for yourself, old man. Just remember you've got almost twenty years on me. I may be shiny on top, but I've still got it going on."

Martin does a little hip twist and Redman chuckles, slapping his shoulder. "Yes, you do, Martin." Redman turns and smiles at me. I've heard such bad things about this man for so long, I keep expecting him to sprout fangs and attack. "So, is this the young woman you wanted me to meet?"

I smile nervously, not sure what to say. Martin puts his arm around me and gives me a squeeze. "Redman, this is Dani Truehart. She's the only reason on earth why I'd even think about giving you a call after all this time." He smiles to show he's sort of kidding. Redman good-naturedly ignores the dig. "Dani, please meet Jenner Redman, agent and producer extraordinaire."

Redman smiles even wider, reaching out and shaking my hand with both of his. "It's lovely to meet you, Dani. Martin's told me that you're quite an amazing young woman." He lets my hand go and motions to the sofa. "Let's have a seat. Before we begin, would you like some water? Coffee? Maybe something to eat?"

Martin puts his hand on my back as we move toward the sofa. I'm grateful to have Martin literally steer me through this meeting. I have no idea how to act or what to do. *How have we not discussed this part?* My head is spinning with all the other details Martin might have forgotten to mention. I nervously pick at a hangnail.

We sit on the couch and I try to look as casual as possible. Martin smiles at me. "No, thank you, Jenner. I think we'll wait until after Dani sings."

"Well, I hope you don't mind if I have a cup of coffee." Redman turns to Carlton, who is hovering beside his chair.

While they whisper, Martin lays a calming hand on my fidgety fingers and gives them a squeeze. "Breathe, hon," he whispers before Redman turns back to us.

"Well, welcome again, both of you. What can I help you with today?" Redman asks, sitting back in his armchair, one knee crossed over the other while holding his cup and saucer.

"I've been working with Dani for years, watching her develop into a fine young woman as well as an extremely talented performer. Compared to all my other students, I don't think I'm exaggerating when I say there's something rare about Dani that I think needs to be shared. She can sing like an angel and dance anything from ballet to hip-hop."

My cheeks burn with embarrassment. *This is so awkward!* I've never heard anyone praise me the way Martin is now. I have no idea where to look or what to do. I end up plastering what I hope is a winning smile on my face as I stare at the ground.

"But there's something else about her, Jenner. I think she's got *it*. I think she's going to be the next big thing. Girls are going to want to be her and boys are going to want to date her."

What? I panic. "But Martin, I have a boyfriend! I..."

Martin smiles and pats my hand. "I know, darlin', and Sean's a great guy. I'm not talking about you actually *dating* anyone, but part of being a success as a pop star is having mass appeal."

My confusion must show because Martin tries to explain again. "You're so friendly and outgoing. It's not a quality everyone has, but it is extremely helpful when you're building a fan base."

Redman chimes in. "Martin's right, Dani. The more kids that like you as well as your music, well, the easier it is to keep your popularity going. You are attractive and approachable. Meaning, someone can see you as a friend if you met them at the mall or at school. That helps attract and keep fans. In the business, we call that someone who has 'the whole package.' Talent and personality."

It makes sense. I realize that I've always wanted to meet and hang out with certain singers because I've always thought they were cool. I just assumed being cool was part of how they made it. I never thought it might just be manufactured by their managers. There seems to be a lot more at work here than just singing after all.

"So, Dani"—Redman gives me another smile, but it doesn't scare me this time. He's uncrossed his legs, placed his coffee cup on the table and is leaning forward—"Martin says you sing and dance very well. What else do you like to do in your spare time? Do you play an instrument?"

I smile and shake my head. "I play a little guitar and piano, but not so well that I'd play for you today. I'm just picking it up as I go."

Redman nods and smiles. "That's OK, Dani, I didn't expect you to play today. In fact, I brought Clint here to play whatever you need."

He turns around and indicates to a tall man holding a plate of food by the buffet who stops eating long enough to wave. I give him a small wave and immediately feel stupid. *What am I, six years old?*

Redman nods encouragingly. I try to relax a little. He opens his hands and smiles. "What do you say we get the hard stuff out of the way and get the songs over with?"

I exhale loudly and try to smile. "Sure." I stand up, wiping my sweaty hands on my jeans as Martin reaches for his messenger bag. "I brought sheet music as well as a recording. Which would you prefer?"

Redman moves to a new armchair by the window, facing the piano. "Let's try it with the piano first." He looks at me. "Is that alright with you?"

I nod. "Yes, Mr. Redman, that's fine."

Clint reluctantly puts down his plate of food and wipes his hands. He takes the music from Martin and sits at the piano.

Redman smiles and nods. "All right then, whenever you're ready." As Martin confers with Clint, I nervously sip a glass of water that Carlton hands me, my tongue suddenly feeling too big and dry for my mouth. I look around for a place to put the glass and Carlton silently creeps up, taking it away for me. It's flustering how he's everywhere at once, silent like a lizard. My stomach burns. I feel like I'm about to throw up. My skin feels prickly. All of my senses are on overdrive as the minutes drag on.

Finally, Martin finishes speaking with Clint. He comes over, takes my hands and squeezes, looking right into my eyes. "You've got this, Dani. This is the easiest part because you know these songs inside and out. Just try to have some fun." He gives me a hug and I lean in, seeking safety.

I try to get my tongue working. "What about the dancing?" I ask, nervously.

Martin looks around. "Jenner. I don't think there's enough space for the dance numbers we rehearsed."

Redman waves his hand. "No worries, Martin. From what you say, I don't doubt that she can dance. Right now, I just want to hear her sing."

Martin nods. "Alright then, darlin'. Knock 'em dead." He gives me a final squeeze and sits on the couch.

Carlton presses a button on a small recording device on the side table.

Clint clears his throat. "Ready?" I nod, feeling the pressure of the moment weigh down on me.

He smiles. "I'll count you in on three. Three, two, one."

I begin with a ballad by Whitney Houston from the '80s. Martin strategically chose this song because he knew it would not only show off my vocal range but also because it would strike Redman's nostalgia. It had come out at the same time Redman was at the top of his game in the music business. Redman smiles as he hears the first few notes.

I'm so nervous when Clint counts me in that I almost convince myself I've forgotten the words and in the brief moment before the music starts, I'm positive I'll fail. But as the music starts, the words bubble to the surface of my memory, pushing all fears and worries aside. Unbelievably, I relax and close my eyes, letting the music wash over me as the song springs from my lips.

I even start to enjoy myself about halfway through the song as the tempo of the piece picks up and the notes become more challenging. I spontaneously move to the music, swaying and using my arms to express the emotions pouring out of me. My throat opens up, allowing the soaring high notes to flow out with ease, filling the room.

As I sing the last line of the song, I open my eyes and relax completely for the first time since I entered the room. I see tears in Martin's eyes and that Redman is frozen with what I can only describe as a look of awe on his face. As the last notes melt away, the room falls silent. Martin beams at me and I grin back, feeling confident. As Redman comes back to reality, I catch him reeling in his smile and nodding, trying not to look too impressed.

Carlton drops his clipboard and applauds loudly. I can't help but laugh. It feels good to get some of my nervous energy out.

Redman laughs too, clapping his hands as well. "Dani, that was brilliant." He smiles, turning to Martin. "Nice touch, Martin. I can't believe you remembered I love that song."

Martin, still smiling, shrugs innocently. "I have no idea what you're talking about, Jenner. It just happens to be one of Dani's favorite songs." He winks at me and does a small fist-pump when Redman turns away.

The room is filled with new energy. Redman settles back into his chair. Martin nods for me to continue. I look back at Clint, who smiles and counts me in again.

The next song is a quick-tempo pop song that I sing perfectly. I feel my confidence coming through in my performance. As I dance around the room, I feel as if I'm mesmerizing Redman, Martin and Carlton. I can tell that my energy is infectious; it's enveloping them just as much as the music is.

The song closes with a fancy piano flourish and I spin just for the hell of it. I grin at the room, which erupts in applause. I take a bow and smile at Martin. I'm so amped up I feel like I could fly! Carlton steps forward with glasses of water for me and Clint.

Redman finishes clapping and looks at me. "You are one amazing girl! I'm really impressed." He looks to Clint. "Well done to you too, Clint. What do you say you sit this last one out and let's give Dani a chance to sing a cappella?"

Clint shrugs and gets up. He gives me a smile and a quiet, "Great job," on his way to the buffet for a fresh plate.

Immediately, my high is over and anxiety starts to set in. We haven't talked about the possibility of an a cappella number. Martin nods encouragingly and I say, less confidently than I feel, "Sure, I think that'll be fine."

Redman signals to Carlton who steps forward with sheets of music and takes my empty glass. My panic starts to rise. I look to Martin for help. He approaches Redman.

"Jenner, we already have a third song prepared. Maybe Dani can sing that one a cappella?"

Redman remains in his seat and looks up at Martin. "I'd prefer she sings the song I've provided. I want to see how she reads music, performs new material, deals with a last-minute change, that sort of thing. You know stuff like this happens all the time when you're performing live." He looks at me reassuringly. "You've already shown me you're a very talented girl. I'm just trying to learn as much about you as I can in the short time we have together."

Martin comes over while I just stare at Redman. I feel Martin's hands on my shoulder and slowly pull my gaze away to concentrate on his face. "He's right, sweetie. Lots of times your music is lost, a special request is made or something stressful happens right before you go on. You still have to perform regardless. You can do this, Dani. You know how to read music, and you have a killer ear. Just take a few minutes to review the song."

I take some deep breaths and nod. It makes sense, but it doesn't make it any easier to do. Martin calls Clint over to go over the music with me before taking a seat on the couch.

We put our heads together for a few minutes while I hum the song, make a few notes on the sheet, and confirm some thoughts on the music. I'm grateful to be able to bounce ideas off of Clint.

"All set, Dani?" Martin calls out and I nod. Clint gives me an encouraging pat on the shoulder and returns to the buffet.

"I'm ready." I close my eyes for a moment. I've been riding an emotional roller coaster for the past week. I'm at the point where I'm so tired of being nervous that my body just can't process the emotion anymore. After this song, I won't be living in limbo any longer. I'll either be on my way to a successful singing career or back to school and a lifetime of rebuke from my disappointed mother. I'm relieved to finally have an answer in sight. I take a deep breath and start to sing, but what comes out is a dry creaking croak. I clamp my mouth shut and shake my head. *Oh my God! That was awful!* I break out in a cold sweat. Carlton races forward with more water and I take a sip, hands shaking wildly.

Jenner gives me a pitying smile. "It's OK, Dani. Singing a capella can be hard for some people. Just take a minute and try again."

I try to smile but fail miserably as I nod my head and take a breath. I can just feel the door slamming shut on this opportunity, and I'm freaking out.

Eyebrows raised, Martin looks a little panicked, too. "You OK, Dani?" He gets up to come over, but I wave him off.

"Yeah, let me try it again." I take another sip of water and step over to the piano and put the music down. My hands are shaking too much to hold it. Finally, I start again; still shaky, but at least I'm singing rather than croaking.

My first few lines are so rocky flat and off tempo that I almost give up again. But the thought of having to tell my mom I blew it keeps me going. The longer I sing, the more comfortable I feel. I stop focusing on everyone in the room and just concentrate on the song. It's a song I've never heard before, a long-ago ballad of a love unrequited, sad and slow. The length of the notes and lack of music puts everything on the table. Any flat notes or wrong keys can't be overlooked or disguised, but the more I sing the stronger my voice gets, and by the end, I'm owning that song! Redman sits, transfixed. Carlton and Clint stand by the buffet, mouths open.

I concentrate as much on the words as the melody. Even though I haven't heard this song before, I have a feeling for how the music flows and my nerves begin to loosen, freeing my vocal cords. Something about the combination of the drawn-out notes and the heartbreaking story touches my innermost soul. The strangest part is I feel as if this tale is my own.

As the last note wavers into silence, Martin jumps up and gives me a big, long hug. I'm shaking. I realize I must have been crying during the song because Martin wipes away my tears as he lets me go. Carlton slithers up again, with a handkerchief and water, which I gratefully take. My hands are shaking so much I spill some water on Martin. "Oh gosh, I'm sorry, Martin. I don't know what's wrong with me."

Martin chuckles as he brushes away the water. "You were out of this world, Dani." He leans in and whispers, "I gotta admit, I was a little worried–you started out kinda ugly on that one. But, at the end, I've never heard you *sing* that way before." He looks at me with astonishment. He gives me another fierce hug. "Girl, you are full of surprises!"

Redman clears his throat as he stands and opens his hands. "I gotta say, Dani, I didn't expect that at all. I thought I was throwing you a curveball by giving you that song. You almost fell for it, but you pulled it together in the end and blew it away. You *are* everything Martin promised and more." He takes a step forward, hands pressed together and smiles. "I would like to formally offer you a contract with Redman Enterprises." Redman snaps his fingers. Carlton obediently jumps forward and places a large, sealed envelope in Redman's open hand. Redman presents me the envelope, which I accept with shaking hands.

I just stare at the envelope, stunned. *This is my future, everything I have spent my whole life working for.*

Martin gives Redman a quick and firm handshake. "Outstanding, Redman. I'm sure the contract is as we discussed. We'd be delighted to sign with Redman Enterprises." Redman nods and reaches into his suit pocket for a cigar. Martin turned to me. "That is, if that's OK with you."

I feel like I've been having some sort of out-of-body experience while this short exchange happens. I just keep staring at the manila envelope in my hands. I can't believe the words I'm hearing. Once Martin turns to address me, I snap back into myself and jump up and down, screaming.

"Ooooooowwweeeeeeee! Yes! Yess! Yessssssss!" I soak everyone with the glass of water I'm still holding while I jump up and down.

Martin and Redman just laugh before they both give me a hearty hug. Martin takes the envelope and shakes off the water.

Redman steps back and looks at me. I beam back at him, unable to wipe the ridiculously big smile off my face. "We are on the brink of something very big and life-changing for all of us." He shakes his head. "Martin, I can't thank you enough for giving me this chance. I am going to work very hard to make this happen."

Martin nods. "Thanks for taking my call, Jenner. I'll let you know once everything is signed."

"Very good. I can't wait to get started." He reaches out and puts his hand on my shoulder. "The world has *got* to meet you!"

15

Leaving the suite and the hotel is a blur. I finally come down to earth when we reach the car. We scream and dance in the parking lot until security comes out and gives us "the look." Martin smiles, waves at the approaching guard and unlocks the car doors.

Once we're inside, Martin gives me an awkward bear hug across the center console. I scream into his shoulder, stomping my feet. "We did it, Martin! I can't believe it! We did it!"

Martin pulls back from the hug and points his index finger at me. "No, baby girl, *you* did it!" He holds up his hand and counts off on his fingers. "You listened, practiced your butt off, fended off your crazy mama and gave it everything you got. It was all you, sweetheart. I am so excited for you."

I can't stop grinning. "You mean, for us! We're a team!"

Martin laughs again. "I'm on your team as long as you want me. But this is your show now. You're on your way to becoming a star!"

I stare off into the distance and sigh. "I can't believe it, Martin. It doesn't even *feel real*. I've been working for this for so long. I have no idea what to expect now that I've got a contract."

My elation slowly fades, and panic starts to creep in. "Oh my God, Martin," I say looking at him, dead serious. "Do you realize that my entire life has been the same routine since I've been six years old? I wake up, practice before school, go to class and then more practice or lessons after school. What's my life going to look like now? How am I going to have time for school? What if today was a fluke, and I'm a total failure..."

Martin grabs my hands as tears blur my vision. "Take a deep breath, baby girl. You're OK. I went through something similar right after I signed with Redman. I went from pure joy to utter panic in the span of a few minutes. I pretty much swung between those two emotions until our first show. Here's the deal: You're entering the big leagues now. Your daily schedule will change. Hell, it'll be erratic sometimes. That's a lot to handle when you're so young and everything is usually pretty much laid out for you until college."

I nod, listening intently. Martin squeezes my hands.

"I discussed the contract and your schedule with Redman when I called to book this audition. I'll go over everything with you and your parents. Even though I'm your guardian, it's up to you to agree to the terms of the contract. And I want you to know I would never expect you to decide something this big without your dad and mom being involved."

I nod slowly.

"Now, I want you to really listen to what I'm going to say because this is going to be one of the most important things you'll ever hear from me."

Martin puts his finger under my chin and gently raises my face to look at him. "When you're in the spotlight, you're always taking a risk, putting yourself out there and hoping to entertain others. Some people will love you. Others will hate you, and some just won't care. This comes with the career you're choosing, and it's something you need to be prepared for."

What he's saying sounds horrible and it must show on my face. Martin gently brushes some strands of hair behind my ear. "It sounds awful, I know. But if you have confidence in yourself, work hard and believe in the product you are selling —namely, your songs —you cannot go wrong. Don't let strangers dictate your life and critics rule your mood. That can be very dangerous."

I consider and nod. "Kinda like how I couldn't take the pageant judges too seriously when I read their critiques after a pageant."

Martin snaps his fingers and points at me. "Exactly! But there's something else. It's just as dangerous believing your own hype. You can't even imagine how much press there'll be about you. Every gossip rag and talk show will be running a story on you. Praising you, bashing you; whatever it takes to sell their story. Just remember, the truth lies somewhere in the middle of all the hype and the dissing.

If you start believing that you're as amazing as folks keep saying you are, you stop trying. You start thinking you're better than other people, that you can do no wrong or the rules don't apply to you. And that's when you start making some really bad choices. Believe me."

Martin stares off into the distance and sighs, lost in memories. After a few moments, he snaps out of it and shakes his head. "But that's way down the road. And hopefully, your road won't turn that way." He reaches over and pats my knee. "Let's get out of here! We've got to go celebrate, and I know just where to go." Martin starts the car. "I hope you're hungry."

My head is buzzing with everything Martin's brought up—it's a lot to take in. Happy to shake off the heavy conversation, I nod enthusiastically. "I'm starving!"

Martin looks behind him and backs out the car. "Well, buckle up, buttercup! This celebratory dinner is on me!"

16

A few minutes later, Martin pulls up to a dinky little food stand with a kitschy hot dog sign that reads, "Pink's." It has bright-pink canvas banners proudly celebrating seventy-nine years of business, hand-painted wooden menus nailed above the order windows and a line of waiting customers.

"Martin, I thought you were taking me somewhere special to celebrate?"

Martin turns off the car and gives me a knowing smile. "Well, Miss Thing, I know for a fact that your mama hasn't let you have a carb in weeks. You just had a killer audition for a legendary music producer who's itching for a comeback. What better way to celebrate your impending success than with the most iconic Hollywood hot dog?"

I glance doubtfully at the shabby food stand. "It's not what I was expecting, but if anyone knows good food, it's you." I shrug. "I'm in." We get in line, and I study a paper menu. Burgers, hot dogs twenty different ways, fries...the scent of grilled meat, spicy chili and onions wafts out, making my mouth water. Overwhelmed with hunger and excitement, I hand Martin the menu. "Can you order for me? You know what I like, and I'm sure you've tried everything."

Martin smiles. "More than once. When we were in L.A., we had a limo driver on standby just to do a late-night run to Pink's. It's not the fanciest place I could have picked, but much like your audition today, this place will change your life!"

Twenty minutes later, Martin carries a tray overflowing with sodas, chili dogs and fries to a table on the back patio, and we dive into the food. Aside from some groans of delight and vigorous head nodding, neither of us speak for a full five minutes. Coming up for a sip of soda, I let out an unexpected belch, and we both giggle.

"This *rocks*! Chili dogs are my new favorite food."

Martin smiles, wiping a dollop of chili off his chin. "I've wanted to bring you here for years, but I knew your mama would kill me if she found out. Now that she doesn't have a say in your diet, I figured it was time to let you in on this little culinary secret."

We both stop eating and stare at each other, horrified. "OMG!" we say in unison.

"My mother!"

"Your mother!"

I guiltily drop my hot dog, my stomach burning. "I can't believe I didn't even think to call her! She's going to kill me. I feel sick."

Martin wipes his hands and turns on his phone. "If she really wanted to get in touch with you, she'd have let you have a cell phone by now. Besides, your mama is officially my problem now, you hear?" Martin's ancient flip phone finally boots up and immediately starts buzzing with missed calls and texts. He rolls his eyes.

I chew on a thumbnail, trying not to throw up. "Well...?"

Martin stops scrolling on his device and looks up. "Twenty-seven texts and eleven missed calls. Kind of a pleasant surprise. Jodi must be losing her touch." Another buzz makes Martin snort. "Ahh, ten voicemails. Your mama hasn't changed so much after all."

I throw my crumpled napkin on top of my food. An old feeling of frustration creeps over me. God, my mother can ruin a moment even when she's not even here. I was actually enjoying a meal for once without feeling guilty and here she comes, stalking and controlling from miles away. I look out at the parking lot, feeling like I want to cry and scream at the same time.

Martin moves my napkin and nudges my plate. "As your guardian, I demand you finish that delicious dog." He winks at me. "We could be in a very important meeting for all she knows. Excuse me while I handle this." Martin types furiously for a few seconds and turns off his phone again. I eye him warily as he picks up his third chili dog and takes a huge, noisy bite.

"What are you doing?"

"I just told her that we're in a very important meeting after a very successful audition and can't talk now. Feel better?"

Strangely enough, I do. Normally there's no one to defend me from my mother's wrath. So, whenever my mom says, "Jump!" that's exactly what I do. I never thought there was another choice. It only recently started to bother me, especially with Geena always pointing out how controlling my mother is.

I slowly nod and look at Martin. "I do. Thanks for taking care of her."

Martin waves his hot dog at me. "I've wanted to do that for years. Taking care of you is my job now, sweetheart. I suppose I could have told her that we already had a contract and we're out celebrating...but how many times has your mama tortured me over the years? Time for a little payback. She can wait on pins and needles 'til you get home." He winks at me. "Now eat up. We've still got milkshakes to order."

I smile and happily dig back into my hot dog.

17

I fall asleep almost as soon as Martin starts the car. The roller coaster of emotions followed by a great meal has finally taken its toll. I wake up as Martin parks in front of my house. Still rubbing my eyes, I see the front door fling open. My mom, wringing her hands, runs out the front door, shouting, "Well?"

Martin looks at me and I nod, grinning. He gets out of the car and gives my mom two thumbs up. "She did it, Jodi!"

My mom starts screaming. Not a celebratory, happy scream, but a crazy, hysterical banshee wail that causes the neighbors to open their doors to see who's being murdered. My dad and Geena run outside. Dad helps Mom up. Although she's stopped screaming, she's fallen onto the ground, crying. Geena calls to the curious neighbors, "It's OK, Dani just signed a recording contract!" as she runs down to hug me. Neighbors shout their congratulations and Martin follows us up the walk with my bags as we all file into the house, laughing and shouting.

***

It's an unforgettable night. We're all giddy with excitement, talking over each other, everyone reveling in the part they think they've played that led up to this wonderful event. It's truly an achievement the whole family takes pride in, and my heart is bursting. I've always imagined this moment, and it's exceeding my wildest dreams.

Mom surprises everyone with a star-shaped cake and champagne. Martin and I almost throw up when she proudly carries out the cake covered in candles. But we force ourselves to eat a slice, not wanting to insult my mom when she's made such a sincere effort to celebrate.

Geena and I are each allowed a small glass of champagne. I don't care for it; it tastes dry and it makes me fuzzy-headed. Geena happily gulps down her glass and mine, sneaking sips from the others' unattended glasses when she can.

We sit around the kitchen table, imagining what my future will be like, thumbing through the contract, dreaming of the big mansion we'll live in and traveling the globe in my private jet. Amid all the chatter, I see my mom pick up the contract and start to read urgently.

Quick as a flash, Martin goes over and lays a hand on her shoulder, plucking it away, and slipping it into the envelope. "How about I get here around ten tomorrow? I can bring you copies, and we can go over all the details on this contract. It's too complicated to read with all this celebrating."

Mom looks irked. "I have a right to know what my daughter's signing. I'm not just going to let her get into a binding legal contract without reading it first."

Martin nods, "Of course. I wouldn't ask you to. But we need to take time to focus and discuss this. I think tomorrow would be better."

Mom looks to Dad for support. He nods, "I think Martin's right. Tomorrow is better."

The clock strikes midnight and seems to close the discussion, reminding us all of the late hour. I can barely keep my eyes open. After many hugs and kisses, Martin leaves, and I head upstairs to bed.

18

The sun is shining when I wake up. I yawn and stretch before finally opening my eyes. I can't remember the last time I woke up without an alarm or my mom shouting at me. I roll over and look at the clock. I do a double-take and sit up. 11:30 a.m.? In my entire life, I've never slept past 7:00. I hop out of bed, my body and mind sluggish from so much sleep.

I shuffle down the hall and smell bacon wafting up from the kitchen. That's also a first—my mom has *never* given the family bacon. *Things really are changing for me!* I smile and go downstairs to find everyone in their pajamas, eating breakfast.

"Well, good morning, superstar!" Mom gives me a big hug and pushes me into my chair. "We thought we'd let you sleep in today. You really earned it!"

She piles my plate with scrambled eggs, pancakes and bacon while Dad slides the syrup toward me. Geena giggles.

"Dig in, sis! Bacon and pancakes don't come to the Truehart household very often."

We all laugh, even Mom. I dive into my breakfast and for the second time in twenty-four hours, I eat until I almost burst. I carry my plate to the sink. "That was great, Mom. Thanks."

"My pleasure, sweetheart. Now we should get dressed. Martin was supposed to come by at noon, but you were still sleeping, so your dad called him and moved it to 2:00 p.m."

It's like Christmas morning, only without the presents. No one rushing, no arguments. We lazily troop upstairs to shower and dress.

I've just finished drying my hair when Geena bangs on my bedroom door. "Sean's on the phone."

For a second, my heart drops realizing that in all the excitement I've forgotten to call Sean yesterday. I'm mortified. "Oh my God, I forgot to call Sean!"

Geena hands me the phone. "Don't worry. He called last night. We told him about Martin's text. He knows you were tied up in a meeting after the audition. He's fine." I heave a sigh of relief. Geena smirks. "Or he thinks you've gone bigtime and have already started blowing off all the little people in your life." I throw a pillow, but Geena dodges it and sticks out her tongue as she closes the bedroom door.

"How's my rock star girlfriend doing? I knew you could do it!"

I flop onto the bed and melt at the sound of Sean's voice. I wish he was here, his arms wrapped around me. I smile. "I can't believe it, Sean. It's really happening! I was so scared. I mean, you should have seen this hotel. We were in the penthouse; can you believe it? It was so surreal."

The words pour out of me as I tell Sean about every second of the audition.

When I finally finish, he says, "I wish I'd been there to see you. I can totally picture you blowing that producer's mind. I know we've been talking about this forever, but I can't believe it's finally happening. What's next?"

I sigh and stare at the ceiling, my excitement ebbing. "To be honest, I don't really know. Martin's coming over this afternoon to go over the contract. Once I sign, I'm not sure what's next."

Sean pauses. "You'll come back to school, right? Or do you have to work during the day? I mean, we never really discussed what happens once you actually get a contract."

There's an edge to his voice that makes me sit up. "I don't know. I'm a kid, so don't I still have to go to school? But then again, I need to record an album and rehearse, so I guess maybe they would do that around my class schedule?" I shake my head, trying to clear these nagging thoughts. "I don't know. I have to ask Martin."

There's an awkward silence as we both realize how much might change for us because of this. I feel guilty for doing this to us. *How could I not have thought this through?*

I continue to stare into space, not focused on anything. "Martin started talking yesterday after the audition about how I should expect everything to change for me now that I have a contract, but I didn't think he meant I had to quit school, like, right now."

Sean groans, frustrated. "I guess we really didn't think about what would happen after you got a contract. This totally sucks!" Just as I start to tear up, Sean exhales loudly. I'm scared to say anything else, afraid to upset him even more. "But look, I'm on your side no matter what. Whether you go to school or not, you're still my girl as long as you want to be."

A wave of relief washes over me and I wipe my eyes. "Of course I want to be, Sean! More than anything. I didn't realize this would be so complicated. We already barely see each other as it is. Now if I'm not at school, how will this work?"

Sean exhales loudly again and says with forced cheer, "We'll just make it work. We'll call between classes and I'll visit after school. Hell, I'll carry your luggage around if I have to. No matter what happens, if it's important to us, we'll be together. And it's important to me."

I take a shuddery breath and smile. "Me too. You mean everything to me."

"Good." I can hear a smile in Sean's voice. "Hopefully you can find out more after you talk with Martin. And maybe you can finally join the twenty-first century and get a cell phone now that you're on your way to being a big star."

I laugh. "Oh God, yes! That'll be my first diva demand."

"Good. I'm so proud of you, Dani. We'll figure it out. Don't worry."

I feel better. "OK. Oh, can you do me a favor and call Lauren and tell her I'll call her tonight? I have to get ready for my meeting. I feel awful that I didn't call her yesterday either."

Sean laughs. "Sure. You're not even famous and you're already forgetting about us."

It's a throwaway comment, but it hits me hard in a way I don't expect. I inhale sharply. "Don't even joke about that, Sean. You know I'd never..."

"Hey, it was *just* a joke. A bad one, I guess. I know you wouldn't do that."

I nod into the phone, weary from our conversation. "OK, sorry. Bye."

"Bye."

I hang up with an uneasy feeling. I hadn't realized the enormity of the changes about to take place, even though Martin tried to warn me. Sean's joke struck a chord. *Will I lose track of people like Sean and Lauren in the whirlwind of my new life?* The idea seems impossible...but then again, everything that's happening had seemed impossible just twenty-four hours earlier.

I hear the doorbell ring and drag myself off the bed to finish getting dressed.

19

I hear voices as I clomp down the stairs. In the living room, the coffee table is laid out with mugs, plates, and napkins. My mom is hanging Martin's jacket on the coat rack while my dad pumps Martin's hand and leads him into the living room. Geena is perched on the arm of the sofa.

"There she is!" Martin beams when he sees me, opening his arms. I skip down the last few steps and into his arms for a hug. "How'd our pop princess sleep last night?"

Mom and Dad slip into the kitchen.

"Like a rock! First time in ages I've had nothing to worry about." I smile and quickly look away, realizing how much I've started worrying since I talked to Sean. I plop down on the couch near Geena.

"Why worry when you've got a team of experts paid to worry for you, sis? Nothing to bother your pretty little head from now on." She reaches out to tousle my hair, but her comment reminds me of Sean's joke. I move out of her reach and glare at her.

"Sorry. I didn't mean anything by it." Geena shrugs, bewildered that I'm so touchy. "Just a little joke."

I catch Martin's surprised look, but before he can say anything, Mom enters the room, carrying a tray of beverages. Dad follows with a fruit and cheese platter.

"I thought we could use a snack while we went over everything. I have coffee, green tea and water here. I can get you something stronger if you'd prefer."

Martin shakes his head and raises a hand. "No, coffee's fine for me. Thanks, Jodi."

She pours a cup of coffee and hands it to Martin. "Help yourself to cream and sugar." I help myself to a steaming cup of green tea. Geena fixes herself a plate of snacks when she catches Mom's eye. "Geena, honey, once you've grabbed a snack, why don't you take it upstairs and study for that algebra test. We have some business to discuss."

Geena rolls her eyes and pops a cube of cheese into her mouth. "Yeah, right, Mom. It's Saturday. And besides, like you guys really need your privacy." She laughs and looks from Dad to Mom, neither of whom is laughing. She looks at Martin who meekly shrugs his shoulders. I can feel her gaze fall on me, but I'm looking at my mug like it's the most interesting thing on the planet. I'm still peeved at her earlier comment, though I haven't had time to figure out why.

"Seriously? What are you going to discuss that I can't hear?"

I know it's a crappy thing to not make eye contact, but I really don't want to listen to her snarky comments for the next few hours. Finally, I sigh and shrug. "She can stay if she wants. It doesn't matter to me."

Geena gives me a hard look and slowly stands up. "No, it's fine. I don't have to stay. I can see this has nothing to do with me." Martin starts to protest, but Geena stomps upstairs before he can finish his sentence. Now my annoyance is replaced with guilt.

Dad stands up to go, but Mom yanks him back down to the couch. "Don't worry about her, Don. I think all the attention being focused on Dani for the past twenty-four hours has made her older sister a bit jealous. She'll be fine." She pats Dad's leg and hands him a small plate.

Mom gives Martin a big smile and elbows Dad, who's staring after Geena. Through gritted teeth, Mom insists, "She's *fine*. We can check on her after the meeting."

Martin clears his throat. "Well, if you're sure it's OK to get started..."

Mom leans forward on the couch, eager. "Oh, we're ready to go. Where do we sign?"

Martin opens his briefcase, pulls out a stack of papers and distributes copies of the contract to each of us. He then hands out pencils and highlighters.

"Aren't you the prepared one? If you're trying to prove to us you can take care of Dani, you're off to a great start!" My mom laughs at her own joke. I roll my eyes, embarrassed.

Martin taps his contract with his index finger, barely containing his annoyance. "There's a lot of information here, and it's very important that we're all in agreement about what's in this contract before Dani signs it. I didn't have anyone to go over my contract with me, and that's how I ended up losing millions to Redman."

Mom stares at Martin, surprised at his intensity. Dad puts a hand on her shoulder to keep her from speaking. Martin puts down his contract, rubs his face with both hands and exhales. "And yes, I am trying to prove to you, but more importantly to Dani, that I'm capable of taking care of her until she's able to take care of herself. This is a cutthroat business and no place for a teenage girl with no experience and no one to look out for her. It might seem excessive, but I intend to go over this contract line by line so that everyone in this room agrees on what it says and what it means for Dani. Is that OK with everyone?"

Mom, Dad, and I look at one another and nod silently.

"Sure, Martin," Mom answers. "I'll keep my smart-ass jokes to myself from now on. I'm sorry. I didn't mean anything by it."

Martin nods. "I know. I'm sorry. I didn't realize how much this contract has me concerned. I know how Redman operates. I didn't have time to review this last night and only had enough time this morning to make the copies. I want to make sure he's put together a contract that doesn't just favor his bottom line. Let's get started, shall we?"

It takes hours to go over the contract line by line, page by page. It gets pretty heated because my mom ruthlessly interrogates Martin, repeatedly asking for me to be paid bigger percentages or larger fees. However, items such as song lyrics, costumes, nudity, morality clauses, etc. don't raise any questions from her. She unsuccessfully tries every angle possible to reap some monetary benefit from my future career. She balks when she discovers the entirety of my earnings will be deposited in a legal trust monitored by a lawyer until I'm twenty-one.

Try as she might, my mom can't get Martin to make her executor of my financial affairs. I'm grateful he's pushing back so hard for me.

The longer I listen to my mom scheme and argue about my earnings, the quieter I get. I don't know whether I want to cry or throw my shoe at her. The more she talks, the clearer it becomes that she doesn't really care what happens to me. All she really cares about is her share of the money. It's crazy that she feels entitled to the money I haven't even earned yet, and that she cares more that my money will be kept in a trust rather than how scanty my costumes will be. Finally, I see what Geena has been warning me about the past few months.

It's getting dark, and Dad switches on the lights in the living room. Geena hasn't emerged from her room all afternoon. The only proof that she's still at home is the dull thumping of bass from her stereo.

"OK, so there's just one more area we need to review. I'm afraid, Jodi and Don, that you aren't going to like it much." I've been laying across the couch doodling on my contract, tuning out Mom's attempted money grab, but this catches my attention. I look up, curious.

Mom and Dad both lean forward, concerned. "What is it?"

Martin reviews the last few paragraphs as my parents scramble for their contracts and begin to flip through them. "Well, Redman likes to fully immerse his acts into their performance—all music and dance for an intense period with no distractions. He calls it 'boot camp', and it's usually conducted at his compound."

My mom looked incredulous. "This man has a compound? Like the Kennedys?"

Martin nods, "He does. It has dance and recording studios, a stage, gym, gourmet kitchen and a schoolroom. It has satellite broadcasting technology...in short, everything you need to create an album without ever leaving the house."

"Where's this compound?" Dad asks.

"On ten prime acres in north Malibu. Close enough to the Ventura County line to ensure that the Malibu party life isn't a distraction."

"Malibu!" I sit up like a shot. So far, the conversation seemed so nebulous—trust funds and song rights—that it didn't really feel like it affected me. But going to Malibu every day? That really caught my attention.

"Malibu? We can't drive Dani back and forth every day to Malibu. I hope this guy is providing a car for her." My mom snorts, and I give her a dirty look. *Of course, it's all about how she's going to be affected,* I think. Everything about her bothers me right now.

Martin takes a breath. "Well, that's the thing with a total immersion boot camp. Dani won't be traveling back and forth every day because she'll be living there."

My head feels like it's about to explode. It's been all I can do to put up with my mom negotiating with Martin for the past three hours. Now I find out I have to leave everyone behind and move into Jenner's house? It's so wild I can't even comprehend what I'm hearing.

Mom jumps up. "Living there? With some strange old guy we've never met? Oh, *hell* no!" She throws down her contract.

Martin holds out both hands to calm my mom down. "Yes, living there. I had to live there back when we were training for REVOLU-TION!" He looks at me, my mouth hanging open. "Though he assures me he's updated the house since then." He turns back to my parents. "And she won't be living alone with Jenner. She and I will have one wing of the house. Jenner lives in another wing. His full-time staff also lives there."

My dad perks up. "I feel better at least knowing that you'll be there, Martin."

My mom snorts. "Don't be stupid, Don. We have no idea who this producer is and now we're just supposed to hand him our daughter and cross our fingers that he's not a pervert? Not likely!"

Martin loses it and throws up his hands. "Really, Jodi? Look, you either want this thing to work or you don't. Redman has no history of inappropriate behavior with any of his previous acts. I'll be living in the compound with Dani. I think we can all agree that Dani's virtue is safe with me since I'm gay. Jenner's already agreed to a background check because I told him you'd be concerned. It's being processed as we speak. Barring anything coming through on that report, I think you need to decide if you're really on board, or if you'd like to continue to create drama where none exists. I agree, Dani moving into the compound is not ideal because she's so young. But if you want her to have a career with Jenner Redman, this is how he works."

With that, Martin gathers his papers and stands up. I start to panic because it feels like Martin is on the verge of walking away from this whole thing. "You should discuss this among yourselves as a family. I would never force you to make a decision like this. Let me remind you that you've already signed over legal guardianship to me. Once this contract is signed, I need you to back off and give me room to make the decisions I need to make to get Dani's career on track." Martin walks to the front door and grabs his jacket. I scramble after him. "I'll send over the background report as soon as I receive it, and I'll call you to find out your final decision. We can sign the contract tomorrow evening if you're still on board."

Martin gives me a quick hug and whispers. "Don't worry, sugar, everything'll be fine." Relief floods through me when I see him wink at me. He nods at my parents. "I hope I was able to answer all of your questions. Please let me know if you think of anything else. Good night."

I open the door and Martin sails outside. I walk back to the couch, sit down and stare at my parents. I feel like I've aged a lifetime in the hours I've listened to my mom haggle over every contract detail like I'm a piece of meat at the butcher. "Mom, I've been working for this my whole life. Stop causing problems and let Martin do his job. You can't threaten to stop me now after you've already given guardianship to Martin. Acting like a concerned parent this late in the game isn't going to work. If you really wanted to protect me, you would have never handed me over to Martin."

I shake my head and narrow my eyes at my mom, so furious I can barely speak. "I'm sorry that the money I make isn't going directly into your pockets like you'd hoped. I promise the first thing I'll do is to pay you and Dad back for all the lessons you've given me. You deserve some return on your investment. But if the past few hours have shown me anything, it's why you really pushed me to do this all these years. I'm sorry that you won't be getting the big payday you'd hoped for."

My parents just sit there, stunned. Tears stream down my face as I get up to leave. I'm a mess of anger and sadness, and I just want to be alone. Dad grabs my hand as I leave. "Honey, your mom and I love you. We don't care about the money. We thought giving guardianship to Martin was what you wanted."

I groan loudly confused by the sadness and anger swirling in my chest, "I did too, but now that it's happening it feels like...". I grasp for the right words, "like...you're just throwing me away. Like you don't care."

I turn to him, but I can barely look him in the eyes. I'm so bitterly disappointed in him, and I'm just now realizing it after a lifetime of deluding myself. "Come on, Dad. You never stood up for me. Or Geena. You've always let Mom do and say whatever she wanted. You're just as bad as she is."

He lets go of my hand and it feels like he's letting go of so much more—it's just another feeling of loss thrown into the hole that's forming in my chest. I shake my head and turn away.

My mom jumps up and reacts the only way she knows how. "Don't you speak to your father that way. You haven't even signed the contract yet and you're acting like an uppity diva. I'm going to call Martin right now and tell him the deal's off. It's not worth it if it's going to change you into a disrespectful brat like this."

I walk toward the stairs. "Give it a rest, Mom. Yelling or calling me names isn't going to make what I said untrue."

I leave the room, my head spinning at the disastrous changes our relationships have taken in the past few minutes. I wish I could turn back the clock and take back everything I've heard and said. But somewhere in the back of my mind, I know that there's no going back. It's clear that we've reached a new crossroads in our relationship and I have no idea where we will go from here.

I pass Geena who's sitting at the top of the steps, eavesdropping.

"Damn, Dani, that took guts." She grabs my passing hand and gives it a squeeze. "Sorry about earlier."

I squeeze her hand back before dropping it. "Me too, G."

I trail down the hall feeling hollow; my bedroom seems miles away. I collapse onto my bed. I lie there for hours, going over every detail of how my mom acted all afternoon, what I said to my parents and what might happen in the future. I can't get over how my entire life has changed in the past twenty-four hours. Everything feels different and weird. I start to cry all over again, wondering if anything will ever feel normal again and if all these changes are worth what's to come. My mind goes in circles until I fall into a fitful sleep.

20

It's just getting light when I wake up the next morning. I'm still in my clothes, and my head is pounding from all the crying. I try to lie still to avoid moving my aching head but after a few minutes, I realize I need some aspirin to get rid of the pain. I stumble down the hall and rummage through the medicine cabinet. I down two aspirins, gulping cold water straight from the tap. I squint at myself in the mirror and cringe as I take in my swollen eyes, puffy face and tangled hair.

I creep down to the kitchen and quietly make a mug of green tea, hoping the combination of caffeine and aspirin will stop the throbbing in my head. Back upstairs, I put on my pajamas and slip into bed. I watch the sun slowly light the room as I sip my tea, trying to avoid thinking about anything in particular.

An hour or so later, I hear the house begin to stir and feign sleep in case my parents want to continue last night's conversation. What I really want to do is talk with Lauren and Sean and try to sort through this mess. I hope they'll be able to shed some light on what I should do. I flinch when I remember the look in my father's eyes when I called him out for not protecting Geena and me from our mother all these years. While I still feel that way, I really wish I'd phrased it better. After all, although he didn't do much to help us, he always told me how much he loved and supported me. I know that no matter what, even after I said such horrible things to him, he still loves me.

I'm not so sure about my mom. The more I think about it, the more I'm beginning to believe Geena's opinion that Mom's love is tied to my ability to earn money. *What will happen now that Mom's discovered she'll gain nothing from my success?* The thought is so devastating that I shove it out of my mind.

I fall asleep despite my pounding head. When I wake again, the house is quiet. I get dressed and tiptoe downstairs. I find a note on the kitchen table:

Dear Dani,

Mom & I are running errands today. We called Martin & let him know you can sign the contract tonight.

Leave us a note if you go anywhere & let us know when you'll be back. Love,

Dad

I'm relieved! I quickly call Lauren and invite myself over. I scribble a note underneath the one Dad left, promising to be back by 8:00. I hear Geena's bedroom door open as I dash out the front door. I don't want to get into a heavy discussion with her at the moment.

21

The walk to Lauren's house is just what I need. The fresh air clears up the last of my headache. Before my finger leaves the doorbell, Lauren whips the front door open and screams, jumping up and down. "I can't believe I'm best friends with a rock star!" She pulls me into a jumping hug and continues to scream into my ear. Laughing, I finally pull away.

"If you don't knock it off, I'm going to be a deaf rock star." Lauren's mom appears in the doorway. "Dogs are starting to gather on the front lawn, dear. Can you please stop that high-pitched wailing?" Mrs. Hannon gives me a hug. "Congratulations! You must be over the moon. Bill and I are so proud of you! Your parents must be ecstatic."

I give her a big squeeze back, allowing the love to wash over me. "Thanks, Mrs. H. Yeah, you could say that emotions are running high back at home." I nod slowly, trying to figure out what to say as I step out of the hug. I run my hands through my hair. "It's kind of a lot at the moment."

Mrs. Hannon gives my arm a squeeze. "Well, I'm sure everything will work out. Lauren says that you've got Martin acting as your guardian. He seems to have a good head on his shoulders. Remember, we're always here if you need anything."

I smile. "Thanks, Mrs. H."

Mrs. Hannon smiles. "In honor of your very big news, I made all your favorites. I know you've been watching your diet lately."

Lauren giggles. "You mean, like, since birth." I swat Lauren's arm as we head into the kitchen.

Mrs. Hannon continues, "Scott and Bill are out, so you've got the run of the place. I'll be in the office, paying bills. Let me know if you need anything. Enjoy!"

Lauren's mom has outdone herself! Chocolate chip pancakes,

sausages and cheesy egg casserole crowd the kitchen table. We load our plates and pour big mugs of steaming cocoa from a carafe.

Through a mouthful of food, I say, "This is the fourth outrageous celebratory meal I've had since my audition. I'm going to be as big as a whale if people don't stop celebrating with food!" I lick syrup from my chin and shove another forkful of pancakes into my mouth.

Lauren laughs. "Puh-lease! Girl, your mom has been starving you since you were five years old. You're the only kid who had carrot cake and sorbet at their birthday parties. Stuff your face! Besides, once you start traveling the globe, who knows when you'll get to taste my mom's pancakes again?!"

I stop eating and stare at Lauren. "Travel the globe! My God, every time I talk to someone, I realize something new that's going to happen. I get to travel! As part of my job! Man, the more I think about this, the more I realize I never thought about anything other than getting a contract. Oh my gosh, I have so much to tell you. I mean, forget about the audition."

"I *will not*," interrupts Lauren. "I still have yet to hear every detail! You've been a horrible best friend since Friday. You owe me details. Lots and lots of details."

I nod sheepishly and grab Lauren's hand. "I know, I'm the worst. I'm sorry. I just got wrapped up in this downhill-rolling snowball from hell that's been my life since the audition." I hold up my right hand, still clutching my sticky fork and place my left hand on the heaping pile of pancakes in front of me. "I hereby pledge on this stack of delicious pancakes to never again leave my best friend in the dark when life-changing things happen to me."

We both laugh, and I lick the syrup off my fingers as I start to fill Lauren in. By the time the carafe of cocoa is empty and the last pancake has been eaten, Lauren is up to speed on everything.

Lauren crumples her napkin and throws it onto the table, pushing her plate out of the way. "Wow." She stares ahead and shakes her head. "That's a whole lot to take in."

I nod, feeling slightly sick from the huge meal. "Now you see how I feel." I look plaintively at my best friend. "What am I going to do?" We sit in silence for a few minutes, lost in our own thoughts.

Finally, Lauren leans forward and puts her elbows on the table. "Let's break this down. First off, moving into the compound will be a little strange, yeah. But you gotta admit, you need space from your mom or you two are going to end up killing each other. Martin will be there to look out for you and," Lauren grins, "you get to live at the beach! How cool is that! I wish I could come!"

I perk up. "Oh gosh, that would be so amazing. We could be roomies!"

Lauren shakes her head wistfully. "I know, but it sounds like this Redman guy is pretty serious about removing all distractions. I highly doubt he'd like you to bring your own slumber party."

I sigh. "You're probably right. What do you think that means for me and Sean?"

Lauren chews on her lip. "Well, if I'm a distraction, that means Sean's, like, a huge distraction, right? I can pretty much guess that Redman will insist that you put the brakes on dating while you're at the compound. Not total radio silence or anything, but your schedule will probably be pretty packed. I don't imagine he'll let you out for daily romantic walks on the beach. It'll be hard, but you two are rock solid. Your mom has done similar things to you two in the past and you made it through."

"And if I get a cell phone, he and I can Snapchat and FaceTime. That'll be an improvement."

Lauren nods, "Right! As for your mom and dad, well, that pretty much sucks." She reaches for my hand and gives it a squeeze. "I'm sorry, I don't have any better way to say it. As far as I can see, it can be one of two things. One, your mom was temporarily blindsided by the thought of all that money. I mean, for years she's been scraping by trying to pay for your lessons, and she finally saw a huge payout and lost her head a little, right? Let's call it temporary insanity. Maybe when you see her tonight, she'll apologize for how she acted and that'll be the end of it."

We both know that sounds nothing like my mom. She's never apologized to me in my entire life.

"And option number two?" I ask, somewhat doubtfully.

Lauren grimaces and closes her eyes. "Option number two is that you've just glimpsed what your mom is really like." Lauren puts her chin on her hand and thinks. "Which would suck."

I nod and start to tear up. "I just want to go home and hide under the covers. But even then, I don't think I could forget the things she said yesterday. What if she only loves me because of what I could do for her? What if she knows she won't earn millions off of me, and she just stops loving me?"

I start to cry. Lauren leans over and hugs me. We sit that way until I'm out of tears. Lauren hands me a napkin so I can blow my nose. "God, Dan, I wish I had the answers." She shakes her head. "Let's try and forget about all this stuff for a while. Hey, we're just kids, remember?" I laugh at her statement in spite of myself. "Let's give Sean and Tom a call and spend a lazy Sunday afternoon watching movies. You don't have to be home anytime soon, right?"

I exhale and shake my head. "Not 'til 8:00. I'm supposed to sign the contract today, but I'm not sure when. I guess I should call Martin."

Lauren shakes her head. "Absolutely not! Your parents know where you are. When Martin calls, they'll tell him when you'll be home, and you can sign it then. Instead, let's take a break from all the heavy topics and lose ourselves in mindless entertainment."

I get up to call Sean while Lauren clears the table, and he says he'll be right over. Tom's still helping his dad and can't make it. By the time we're finished cleaning, the doorbell rings.

22

I've never been so happy to see Sean in my life. I fall into his arms and start to cry as I begin to tell him about the argument with my parents. The thought of rehashing it all is overwhelming, so Lauren comes to my rescue and fills Sean in on the details while I sit quietly on the couch with his arms around me. Being in Sean's arms makes me feel extremely safe, and I cherish that feeling right now. Everything would be all right if I could just stay like this forever with Sean and Lauren.

When Lauren finishes, Sean gives me a squeeze and assures me that he'll always stand by me no matter what. But I notice he avoids saying anything else on the topic by suggesting we relax and start a movie. It's not like him to be so quiet. I wonder what he's not saying...

***

Hours later, we're sprawled in the Hannon family room, finishing our third movie. Lauren clicks off the TV as the credits began to roll. She's draped on an armchair. "Stick a fork in me folks, I'm done. Food coma and movie marathon are the perfect nap inducers! I've never been so tired from doing nothing." She yawns and stretches, pulling a blanket up to her chin. "You guys don't mind if I fall asleep, right? Don't you two have some canoodling to do somewhere else before you're due back home?"

Sean plants a quiet kiss on my head and rubs my arm. We're lying together on the couch, and I'm dozing with my head on his chest.

"Wake up, sleepyhead. Let's take a drive before I take you home."

I slowly open my eyes and stretch. "Hmmm, how long was I asleep?"

Lauren laughs. "You were sawing logs before the opening credits were finished!"

I yawn and sit up. "I guess I really needed it." I smile at Sean. "Yeah, let's go for a drive. It's been ages since we've been alone."

Lauren huffs and grumbles, "Not to make you feel like a third wheel or anything, Lauren. Thanks for letting us make out all over your couch today," Sean says.

I blush, embarrassed. "Sorry, Lauren. You know we love you." Lauren makes a face. "Blah, blah, blah. I'm going to call my boyfriend and give him hell for working in the yard with his dad and leaving me alone with you two all day." She smiles and throws a pillow at us as we put on our shoes.

We get up and give Lauren a hug. "Thanks for having us over, Laur. You're the best! And thank your mom for that killer breakfast. Say hi to Tom."

Lauren smiles. "I will, rock star. Keep me posted on what's happening."

Hand-in-hand, we stroll to Sean's car. We end up driving to park at our favorite spot. As we drive, Sean fills me in on his family, telling me that his grandfather recently moved in. He finally stops on a long mountain road in an exclusive but rural part of town that looks down into the valley below. Sean parks the car and slides his arm around me, and we gaze at the lights below.

"We haven't been here in months!" I sigh, feeling peaceful.

"I know. It's been hard to get any time alone with your audition looming over us. I'm glad we're here. I guess now with you moving to Malibu, we won't be seeing much of each other."

My peaceful feeling evaporates, replaced with anxiety. I turn to Sean and start talking a mile a minute.

"Well, I'm going to get a cell phone like we talked about. And I'm going to talk to Martin and make sure we can see each other in person at least once a week. I mean, Redman can't work me 24/7, right?"

"God, I hope not! Man, school's going to suck without you. But if we can see each other once a week, that's at least something. And, hopefully, once this boot camp thing is over, you'll have more time." Sean pauses, looking out the window. "I wonder if you'll come back to school..."

I shrug and lean my head back. "I don't know. I guess it depends on how well my music does. If it's a success, won't I tour or something?" I wrinkle my nose. "God, it would be a bummer if this didn't work and I actually had to start going to school regularly. What would I do if I actually had to graduate? I'm so far behind!" My thoughts are running a mile a minute, one chasing the next. I try to grab them as they pass, but it's impossible.

"OK, you need to stop worrying about if your album fails and how you'll graduate high school," Sean says. "You're always jumping five steps ahead! Just enjoy what's happening now: we're together, we had a great day with Lauren, and you've got an amazing chance to start a music career that you've been dreaming about your whole life. Can't you just leave it at that?"

I shake my head and try to smile. "I'll try." My mind slows and one nagging thought takes over. I take a deep breath and turn to Sean. "I noticed you didn't say too much after Lauren told you about what happened yesterday. What do you really think?"

Sean's eyes bug out for a second; he knows he's been caught. "Well," he considers, "let's start off with something easy. You know your dad loves you. He'd do anything for you."

"Except stand up to my mom!" I almost shout.

Sean holds up a hand. "I'm not the bad guy here, Dan. You know what a bulldozer your mom is. Every time anyone disagrees with her, she pitches a fit until she gets her way. Should he have stood up to her a lot more for you two? Absolutely! But you *also* usually take the path of least resistance with your mom just to avoid a fight. You and your dad are like two peas in a pod. He probably thought he was keeping the peace."

I sulk for a moment, thinking it over. "I guess I never thought about it like that before," I say quietly, "And what about things with my mom?"

Sean exhales loudly and taps the steering wheel with his hands. "Well, I think your relationship with her is going to change because you finally stood up to her. The power dynamic has shifted between you two. She isn't your legal guardian anymore. Martin's calling the shots now. Then you're eighteen and you can call your own shots. She's put all this hard work into giving you a chance at a career, and now it's just been taken out of her hands."

My burst of anger is electric. I bang the dashboard. "It wasn't taken! She gave it away. She gave me away! They both did. How can I get over that?"

Sean runs his hands through his hair, thinking. He's never seen me like this before, and I don't think he knows what to do. "It can seem that way, and maybe in a few years, we might actually realize it *is* that way. But do you want to live in a world thinking that your mom trained you up like a horse and sold you to the highest bidder?" Sean takes my hand. "Look, Dan, all I'm saying is that, yes, it looks bad. But I think, for the sake of your sanity, you have to give your mom the benefit of the doubt. She and your dad gave Martin legal guardianship, but only because it's the only way for you to pursue this dream you've had all your life. You know she gets defensive when she's cornered. And you're too hurt to listen to anything she might have to say, anyway. I think all you can do at this point is focus on boot camp and let some time pass. Maybe you two can talk when things calm down."

His eyes soften, and he reaches out to caress my cheek. I rest my face in his hand. "Look, I can't even imagine what you're going through. But as crazy as it must feel, Martin being your guardian is probably the best thing that could have happened to you. You're finally getting out from under your mom's thumb."

I sit quietly, absorbing everything Sean's said. "God, it's so scary. Who am I if I don't have my mother making all of my decisions and dominating every moment of my day? I don't think I do or say anything without obsessing about how she'll react."

Sean smiles. "You're going to get to start making some of your own decisions now. It's going to be scary, but I bet it's going to be pretty cool, too."

I look at him. "My family is really messed up. I can't believe you stick around and deal with it."

Sean nods. "I'm not going to lie; your family is whack." He smiles and brushes the hair out of my eyes. "But you are so totally worth it."

23

I wave goodbye to Sean as I open the front door. After our conversation, we spent the rest of our precious time alone together making up for the time we'll be apart. My lips are raw. I quickly run my fingers through my tousled hair, hoping I don't look like I've spent the last hour in a parked car with my boyfriend. Everything's quiet except for the low murmur of voices coming from the television in the family room. I see Mom and Dad sprawled on the couch watching a football game. I do a double-take because my parents aren't the type of people who watch a game together.

My dad smiles at me. "Did you have a good time at Lauren's?"

I nod. "Yeah, it was nice. Sean came over and we watched a movie." I wait for my mom to chime in with a snarky comment, but she remains silent, eyes glued to the screen.

"That's nice, honey. Are they excited for you?"

I nod again. "Yeah, they are. Mrs. H. made us a huge breakfast to celebrate. It was awesome." In my mind, I'm shouting, "*Say something! Aren't we going to talk about this?*" My eyes flick to my mom, who is still staring at the television way too intently for a woman who can't stand sports.

"I bet they are. Martin called, and he'll bring the contract by tomorrow. Why don't you give him a ring before it gets too late?"

"OK." I just stand there. My dad smiles again and glances back at the game. I keep looking at my parents until the silence becomes overwhelming, the muted yelling of the fans highlighting the brutal quiet in the room.

Finally, my mother looks up briefly, as if she can't bear having her attention diverted from this most crucial game. "Good night, Dani." She turns back to the game, dismissing me after the barest minimum of acknowledgment.

There it is, then. I've been through this a million times before. If my mom had remained silent the entire time, I'd have known that she was beyond nuclear angry and I needed to grovel STAT. But this slight acknowledgment means that my mom, while still royally pissed, knows deep down she bears some responsibility for the argument. While she'll never actually say the words, "I'm sorry," I know this is a turning point. My mom will take a few days to thaw and within a week, things will be back to normal. I'm just happy it isn't another yelling match. In fact, I can use a few days of being ignored by my mom to get my head straight.

I shrug and turn toward the stairs. "Night."

"Good night, honey," Dad calls. I trudge up the stairs, grateful to hear the water running in the bathtub. Geena will be occupied for at least thirty minutes before she comes out to dissect what went down last night. It's an inevitable conversation, and I dread it.

I flop onto the bed, reach for the phone and dial Martin's number. "Hey, Dani! How's my star doing?"

I smile despite my low mood. "Well, I don't feel much like a star today."

Martin sighs. "I know, sugar. Your dad filled me in when I called. I'm so sorry. You should be reveling in this amazing moment, not dealing with some tired family drama."

"So much has happened in the past few days. Everything is changing *except* for the fact that my mom cannot stop making everything about herself. I feel horrible because I said some terrible things to them. But I gotta be honest, Martin. I really meant what I said. I just wish...I don't know..."

"That you'd said it differently?" I nod at the phone. "Yeah."

"Aww, sugar, your mom and dad are always going to love you. Every family is messed up, so don't go feeling like yours is the only one. Everyone has some sort of crap they're dealing with at home. You just happen to have an extra special amount of it."

I snort. "Well, now I feel so much better."

Martin chuckles. "You're dealing with a bunch of uncomfortable stuff, sweetie. But deal with it now, or deal with it later. Family issues don't go away on their own. If you can try to wrap your head around it now, you'll be better off in the long run."

I groan. "Ahhhh! That's exactly the opposite of the advice Sean gave me! He said I shouldn't do anything right now because I'm too upset."

Martin's quiet for a moment. "You know I love Sean, but I think I know a thing or two more than a sixteen-year-old. I can't tell you how to handle your parents, but I do know from experience that sweeping things under the rug never makes them go away. Eventually, you'll have to address what happened last night."

I take a deep breath. "Martin, I *am* moving on. My mom said, 'Good night,' to me just now. And because of my vast experience with her, it tells me she'll get over things in a few days. You're in charge of things from now on, and since we've already reviewed the contract, she and I don't have to bring it up again. Hey, didn't I have to sign that tonight?"

"Sounds an awful lot like sweeping it under the rug to me, but I'm your guardian, not your therapist, so sweep away. And no, I called Redman this morning. We'll sign first thing tomorrow. He's getting our rooms ready. We'll move in this week if that's OK with you."

I sit up. "That's so quick! I thought I had more time."

"Sorry, babe, this train has left the station. Once that contract is signed, we're full steam ahead. Jump on board or get run over."

I let it sink in. "Wow." I look around my small room, crowded with posters, stuffed animals and a million things I've collected. "What should I pack?"

"Well, obvs, clothes. Workout gear, dancewear and whatever you normally wear when you're not doing those two things. Bathing suit—there's the beach and the pool when you're not in the studios working. And then whatever you need to feel at home—photos, books, your pillow. You can bring anything."

I wish I could tip my entire room into a giant box and take it with me. "This is so weird."

"Yeah, it is, darlin'. And it's only going to get weirder. But it's exciting, too. I mean, come on, don't you feel it?"

Underneath the overwhelmingly strange feeling of moving out, I *do* feel it. A tingle lingering behind the lump in my throat. Never before has my life been so uncharted. Usually, thanks to my mom, I know what I'm doing every minute of the day for months on end. Now, every day seems like an unending mystery. There's a quiet knock at the door.

"Yeah, I do, Martin. I feel it. Look, I've gotta go."

"Ok, darlin'. I'll be by tomorrow at 9:00 with the contract and some boxes. We'll get it signed, and then I'll help you pack."

"Sounds good. Good night."

"'Night." I hang up as Geena knocks again. "Come in!"

She peeks in. "I just wanted to see how you are. You've been gone all day."

"I just needed to get out of the house after last night. I hung out at Lauren's with Sean."

Geena nods as she stands at the foot of the bed. "Sounds like fun." She tilts her head toward the door. "How'd it go when you came in?"

I reach for a worn-out, stuffed rabbit, hugging it close. "Dad was fine. Super chatty and happy to see me. Mom was, of course, extremely absorbed in the football game"—I roll my eyes—"and couldn't be bothered to chat, but she did say good night."

Geena crosses her arms. "Well then, by the Jodi Truehart barometer, looks like a few days of snit with a chill in the air that should eventually thaw out. No apologies in the forecast, but some subconscious acknowledgment that she's not totally innocent. I'd say a victory for you, all things considered."

I shake my head. "She's so messed up. I just got off the phone with Martin. We sign the contract tomorrow, and then we pack up. Looks like I'm out of here sometime this week."

Geena sits down hard on the bed. "So soon?" She stares off into the distance. "It's going to be so different around here without you." A look of horror spreads across her face. "Oh my *God!* What am I going to do about Mom when you're not around? She's going to be a total nightmare with only *me* to focus on! Holy crap!"

I nod. "It's going to be totally weird not having you down the hall. And I'm so *sorry* I'm leaving you alone with her. It's going to suck." I reach out and hug Geena. "But I promise I'll make it up to you in a very big way once I make my first million."

Geena squeezes me tight, and we both start to cry. "You'd better! I can't believe you're leaving me alone with her! I'm really taking one for the team."

We laugh through our tears, hugging each other harder. Muffled in the hug, I say, "You know I couldn't have asked for a better sister, right?"

Geena pulls back. "You know you're not dying, right? Just moving out?" She tries to laugh but tears up again. "You're the best little sister ever. I'm so proud of you for not giving up on your dream."

Geena looks down and sighs. We both know that she's thinking about how she's given up on her gymnastics dreams. After a few minutes, I reach out and squeeze her hand. She stares at it as tears continue to roll down her cheek. Eventually, she nods and sniffs loudly.

"OK, enough. This is about *you* and your amazing accomplishment. When I get home from school tomorrow, I'll help you pack."

Geena stands up and wipes her eyes. "'Night."

For the second night in a row, I'm too exhausted to change out of my clothes. As I drift off to sleep, I try to memorize every detail of my room.

24

I awake to the sound of my sister's bedroom door slamming and feet pounding down the stairs. "Hurry or you'll be late, G!" My mom's voice bellows up from the kitchen, making it almost feel like an ordinary day in the Truehart household. Except if this were an ordinary day, I wouldn't be lying in bed. I'd have pounded down the stairs hours before my sister. I roll over and see it's 7:30. I head to the bathroom for a quick shower, throw on some clothes and go into the kitchen.

"You're awake," is all my mom says as she turns back to the stove. My dad rustles the paper he's reading. "Morning, Dani. Martin will be here in a bit."

I nod as my mom comes over with a plate of egg whites and a steaming cup of tea. "Sorry I won't be able to stay and help pack," She says. "I have some errands to run before work."

I sit down. "That's OK. Thanks for breakfast."

"Sure," Mom says. She cuts off any chance of conversation by turning on the sink and noisily washing the dishes.

I eat quickly while my dad makes safe comments about the articles in the paper. When I've finished, I bring my dishes to the sink. My mom silently takes them, and I say to no one in particular, "Thanks for breakfast. I'm going to start getting things organized in my room." I hustle upstairs, happy to escape. It's a good sign that Mom even made me breakfast. Many a morning, I've had to fend for myself when she's been angry about something. While it's uncomfortable, I think I can stand the chill from my mom over the next few days before I move out. At least we won't be talking to each other enough to argue again.

By the time Martin rings the doorbell, my room looks like it's been hit by a tornado. What had started as an effort to organize my stuff for packing has turned into a full-blown riot of things thrown everywhere. The room is a perfect reflection of the chaos in my head.

I'm only too happy to shut the door on the mess when Dad calls me downstairs.

Everyone is in the dining room. Martin introduces me to a notary public who will witness us signing the contract. It gets super uncomfortable when the notary starts explaining the signature process to my mother, who storms into the kitchen. Luckily, Martin and my dad swoop in to do damage control, and we're able to sign the contracts with minimal fuss after that. I keep pinching myself throughout the whole process. I can't believe I'm actually signing a recording contract. *Everything I've dreamed of and worked for is coming true!* Even my mom's temper tantrum can't spoil this moment!

After the notary leaves with the signed contracts, Martin lets out a celebratory whoop. "You're on your way, Dani!" I beam at Martin, my excitement making it hard to sit still.

My mom, still sullen, manages a strained, "Yes, congratulations, Dani," before she bangs back into the kitchen.

Dad jumps across the room and catches me in a bear hug. "Ignore your mother. We're both very excited for you. She just needs a little time."

I snuggle into my dad. "Thanks, Dad."

Martin comes over and hugs us both. "I don't mean to crash this tender moment, but we've got to get crackin' on that packin', girl!" He lets us go. "I'm going to get those boxes from my car."

Dad heads for the front door. "Have fun, you two. I'm off to work." We hear the back door close. "I think your mom just left, too. Stay for dinner tonight, Martin?"

Martin smiles. "No, thanks. I've got to get myself packed up. Lots to do before we're locked away at boot camp."

Dad nods. "Alright then. Bye now."

I head upstairs. When he reaches my bedroom door, he drops everything. Rolls of packing tape fly off his arms as he throws his hands on top of his head. "What the hell, Dani?!?"

I'm embarrassed. "I tried to get organized this morning and it just kinda backfired."

"I'll say! Luckily, you're working with the master. Not only am I a washed-up '80s has-been, but I'm also a packing maven. Years of touring have honed my skills. Bet I can get this room organized in three hours or less!"

I laugh. "Three hours? That's impossible!"

Martin rubs his hands together. "That sounds like a challenge to me!"

"You're on!"

Martin dives in. While he works his magic, I fill boxes with photos, books and clothes. Although it takes closer to four hours, my room is spotless in the end. Clothes are neatly sorted for packing, laundry is spinning in the washer and a pile of clothes has been sorted for donation. We're lounging on the floor taking a break when Geena walks in.

"You two don't waste any time! I was all ready to help you pack..." Martin gets up and stretches. "Fame waits for no one, Geena. Your sister has many talents, but packing is clearly not one of them. I had to jump in or she'd never have time to record an album."

He blows me a kiss and gives Geena a hug. "As much as I'd like to stay and witness the uncomfortable silence at dinner tonight, I have to jet. I've got to get myself packed *and* get my mom and Pauline up to speed. They're taking over the studio while I'm away."

I stand up. "No way! What about Pauline's job?"

Martin nods. "I know. Pauline loves managing the MAC store. But what can I do? They both depend on the income we bring in from the studio. If I'm not there, *someone* has to step up. Mom is great running the front office, and Pauline will be a smash with teaching. Bet you didn't know it, but she used to train with me back in the day. It was the only way we could hang out growing up."

"Your family is so awesome. I love that they're dropping everything to be there for you."

Martin smiles. "They *are* pretty great. But they're investors as well, so if they don't step up, buh-bye business! We'll make it work. It's only for a couple of years until you can handle things on your own." He steps toward the door. "Good luck at dinner, girls. And, Geena, make sure your sister doesn't mess with my hard work. Just place those final things in that box and walk away. *Don't start rummaging for anything.*"

He blows another kiss and leaves.

"This makes it even more real!" Geena says as she flops onto the bed, knocking over a pile of neatly folded clothes. She giggles. "Shh! Don't tell Martin." She gets up, drags an empty box toward the bed and begins filling it. "How'd it go today?"

I shrug. "Could have been better, could have been worse. Mom sulked while we signed the contract. But I had a nice talk with Dad, and we're cool now, which is a relief. They both left right after we signed. Martin's been helping me pack all day."

Geena clears the bed and tapes the box shut. "Sounds like you deserve a break. Come on."

We spend the rest of the day sprawled on the couch, snacking and making fun of daytime talk shows.

25

For the first time in my life, I have no set schedule, no school and no rehearsals. Yet the days are seamlessly filled with endless activity and preparation. I spend every spare moment I have with Geena, Lauren, and Sean. It's decided that I should clean out my school locker since it's unclear when or if I'll return. I stop by before classes let out for lunch on Wednesday. I have just finished dialing in my locker combo for what might be the final time when I hear an unmistakable snotty voice behind me.

"*Oh my God!* Valley Hills High's very own Future Has-Been." I sigh and open my locker without turning around. Behind me, Zoe chuckles sarcastically and continues, "Oh look, girls, she's ignoring me. I guess she's too big a star to acknowledge the *little* people like us." Zoe's cohorts guffaw hysterically.

There's no good way to deal with Zoe and her minions. Ignoring them angers them but talking back only provokes them more. I silently scream for Sean to walk by and rescue me. He's the only one who can stop Zoe's taunting. Since she's still trying to snag Sean for herself, she's always on her best behavior when he's around. I start grabbing items from my locker and shoving them into my bag.

"While you're busy dropping out of school and chasing your pathetic little dream, I'll be here maintaining my perfect GPA and building a real future. Oh, and don't worry about Sean. I'll make sure he won't be lonely while you're gone."

I'm so pissed that I drop a binder I've been trying to fit into my overstuffed backpack. Papers spill everywhere. I throw the bag onto the ground and start gathering the scattered pages while Zoe laughs. "God, what a klutz! You're planning on dancing for a living? Good luck with *that!*"

"Need any help?" I hadn't even heard Sean approach, but there he is, kneeling to grab the loose papers. He glances up at Zoe and her girls, and they immediately fall silent. "Oh hi, ladies. Wishing Dani luck? I'm so proud of her!" He gives Zoe a dazzling smile. "Can you hand me those pages by your feet?" Sean holds out a hand. Zoe and her girls fall to the ground, wildly grabbing papers.

Zoe immediately switches gears from bitch to sickeningly sweet, and I fume even more. "Sure, Sean! Happy to help, aren't we, girls?" While they're preoccupied grasping for papers, Sean gives me a wink, making my temper disappear. I'm relieved he isn't fooled by Zoe.

Once everything is picked up, Zoe magnanimously hands the stack to me and glances at my messy locker. "Here you go, superstar! I bet you're going to be here a while cleaning up that mess. No wonder academics weren't your thing. You can't find anything in that locker!" She shoots me a plastic smile. "We're really going to miss you around here. Poor Sean's not going to know what to do with himself without you tagging along everywhere." She gives Sean what can only be described as a hungry once-over. "But don't worry. I'll make sure he doesn't get too lonely."

Before I can speak, Sean wraps an arm around my shoulder and gives me a squeeze. "Aww, that's sweet Zo. But I'll be spending all my free time with D in Malibu. Did you hear that she's living there for the next few months?"

Zoe, at a loss for words, decides to retreat. "That sounds amazing. Good luck, Dani." To Sean, she says in a low, husky voice, "See you around school."

Before she's even finished speaking, Sean kisses me. Zoe huffs as her girls titter behind her. Then she stomps off down the hall with her minions trailing after her.

"God, I hate that girl. *Hate her!*" I fume. "This sucks! She totally has her sights set on you. With me gone, she's going to be relentless until she gets her hands on you. She's like one of those snakes who won't unclamp their jaws unless you use a crowbar."

Sean laughs. "Oh yeah, your life sucks. You have a recording contract, you get to leave school, live in Malibu, and you have an incredibly devoted boyfriend who worships the ground you walk on. Yup, your life is total crap."

I start to laugh, my anger evaporating. "Well, yeah, when you put like that...but you know that Zoe's just waiting to pounce on you the minute I'm gone like some feral cat on an unsuspecting mouse."

"OK, that's not insulting or anything. I'm not an entirely weak male whose life is dictated by the whim of the major general."

I give Sean a sideways look, "The major general...?"

Sean smiles and looks sheepish. "You know...I don't think with my pants."

I nod, blushing.

Sean continues. "I know what Zoe's after, and if I were interested in someone like her, I wouldn't be with someone like you. Simple as that." He puts his hand on his heart. "I'm immune to her charms."

It's my turn to smile sheepishly. "I'm sorry. I just get so jealous sometimes. It feels really strange that you're going to be here at school without me. What if you get tired of doing things without me?"

"I'm not going to *replace* you! Look, I'm feeling the same way about you. The only difference is that you already know what my days are like. I have no idea what your world will be like, who you'll be spending time with or what you will be doing. It's scary as hell."

I put my hand on Sean's shoulder. "I'm sorry, I didn't think about it from your point of view. Sorry I got so wrapped up in me. You know I'm going to miss you every day." I stand on tiptoes and give him a kiss.

We draw apart and Sean smiles. "Zoe was right about one thing, though."

I get serious. "What?"

Sean nods toward my locker and smiles. "Your locker's a total mess! It's lucky you got talent, baby, because housekeeping clearly ain't your thing!"

I playfully punch Sean in the arm. "Guess you'd better show me how it's done." I hand him an empty tote bag. "Enlighten me."

26

Sunday finally arrives—MOVING DAY! Martin comes over early to help my parents load their car. Dad insists that the four of us drive together since it will be the last activity we do as a family for the foreseeable future. Tired of watching my parents bicker about how to pack the car, I go inside and head upstairs.

My bedroom looks bare without my favorite things scattered about. Sighing, I flip off the light and shut the door, feeling like I'm shutting a door on part of my life. *Who knows what will happen to me before I next see this room?* It's sad and scary to think about, but there's something exciting about what lies ahead. *I'm ready to get to Jenner's and start my future!*

"Danilynn Truehart! Let's go!" I sigh as my mother bellows from outside. *Another thoughtful moment ruined by my mom.*

Martin looks as ready as I am to leave the Truehart family behind as he hops into his car. Once we're all squeezed into the family car, we slowly make our way from Santa Clarita to Malibu. Mom maintains her chilly demeanor toward me, which is more apparent in the close confines of the car. She barely says a word, preferring to stare out the window. Dad does his best to fill the silence. Geena just reaches out and holds my hand on the seat between us. I wish I were driving with Martin so I could skip this awkward car ride with my family! But then I feel guilty for wanting to leave my dad and Geena. It's really my mom who is making it uncomfortable. As usual.

Traffic eases as we make our way from the freeway to one of the canyon roads that connect the valley to the beach. The congestion of the freeway gives way to a shady, twisted road that's populated by horse properties and quirky houses. I roll down the window and smell the salt air as we descend the canyon road and come out to a glorious view of the Pacific.

It's around 10:00 by the time we pull up to a wrought-iron gate. In front of us, Martin presses the intercom buzzer. A great stone wall extends from either side of the driveway, behind which huge palm and shade trees wave in the ocean breeze. While most of the house is obscured, the rooftop is visible and the size of it is staggering.

"Are you kidding me, sis? This is where you're staying?" Geena whispers, in awe.

I whisper back, "I guess."

Dad chimes in. "It's like a resort! Can you believe this, Jodi? We must have done something right if our little girl gets to live here!"

Mom looks out her window. "Bet you won't have to wait to use the bathroom in this place."

Dad chuckles. "I'll say!"

The front gate finally opens, and I'm relieved as we follow Martin's car inside. I'm ready to get out of the car and away from this awkward family dynamic.

Inside the gate, a winding stone driveway leads us through immaculately manicured lawns and gardens to an immense Mediterranean-style villa. We park in the U-shaped driveway, and as we get out of the cars, Jenner bursts out the front door in a billowing Tommy Bahama shirt, tan cargo shorts and sunglasses perched atop his shiny head. He's all smiles as he walks down the steps, arms open.

"Welcome to *Pedazo de Cielo*, which means, 'Little Piece of Heaven.'" He gives me a hug. "I hope you'll think of this as your piece of heaven, too." Jenner makes his way through the group, shaking hands and introducing himself to my family while we stare at his mansion.

He claps Martin on the shoulder. "Martin. Welcome back! We've made some changes since you were last here."

"I'll say." Martin turns to me. "This used to be one of the wonders of '80s architecture. Featured in tons of magazines and even made it onto that show, 'Lifestyles of the Rich and Famous.' Glass brick, metal siding, polished concrete. A real statement to look at, but not so comfortable to live in. But now," he turns to Jenner, "it's a proper home. Well done, Jenner."

Jenner nods and chuckles. "I can't believe I lived with all that junk for so long. I did a complete gut in the '90s. I think this is much more timeless, don't you?" We all nod in agreement.

Jenner rubs his hands together. "OK, let me show you around. Don't worry about your bags. Anatoli will get them for you later."

Martin looks surprised. "Anatoli's still here? I can't believe it!" He grabs my hand and leads me toward steps. "Anatoli was just a kid when I was here. His mom, Magda, ran the house for Jenner. She was the cook, housekeeper and all-around den mother.' He turns back to Jenner. "Is she still here too?"

Jenner nods, "Yes, she is, and she can't wait to see you. They're inside getting lunch ready. Let's get the tour started, then we can enjoy lunch on the terrace." Jenner shoos us up the wide front steps like a mother hen.

27

More than an hour later, we sit down to lunch on a large terrace overlooking the grounds below. We've toured the main house, which contains a gourmet kitchen, a living room, a screening room, a formal dining room, a library, Jenner's office, and an array of smaller rooms and nooks. Almost every room has at least one wall of windows that look out onto the ocean. They are all elegantly decorated with plush rugs, fragrant flowers and masterpieces of art; furnished with over-stuffed sofas and chairs arranged to either encourage conversation or to give one privacy. Mementos from Jenner's music career are discreetly scattered throughout the house: gold and platinum records hang next to Picassos, autographed guitars, photos with musicians. We bypass the east wing that holds Jenner's private quarters.

The west wing is where Martin and I will stay. I'm over the moon when I walk into my enormous room. It's painted a delicate periwinkle blue and furnished with a sparkling chandelier, a king-sized bed with a white suede headboard, a white sofa, a mirrored dresser, a white desk and a cozy, two-person lounge chair. A luxurious white shag rug lies over the weathered, gray, wooden floors, and the walls are hung with framed starfish, sand dollars and various ocean-themed art. A huge flat-screen hangs on one wall above a fireplace with a large mantle holding assorted seashells. The walk-in closet is bigger than my bedroom back home, and the bathroom is the size of our kitchen! Geena looks thrilled for me as our mom pouts. In fact, the more we see of the compound, the quieter Mom becomes, her jealousy building as she sees me being handed the life she's always wanted for herself.

Below the main house, the land slopes down to the pool and a spa that also has a cabana, a sauna and a grotto with a waterfall. Farther down are the gym and the dance and recording studios. There are two guesthouses, a house for the servants, a koi pond and a steep wooden staircase that leads to a private beach. We tour the property on two golf carts that are parked outside of Jenner's ten-car garage. It's a lot to absorb as we sit down to lunch overlooking the pool. The waves crash faintly in the distance and a salty breeze stirs in the trees.

Dad peppers Jenner with a million questions regarding the design and upkeep of the compound. Jenner revels in the attention and magnanimously answers every question. They're deep in conversation when the glass door from the dining room slides open and a warm, heavy, Eastern European-accented voice says, "Martin, is that you? Mr. Redmond said you come here, but I don't see my beautiful Martin. Just this bald, chubby man at the table. I say to myself, could this really be you?"

Martin slaps the table and jumps up, almost knocking over his iced tea. "Magda, you old battle-ax! Still busting my chops after all these years!"

He runs over and lifts Magda into the air, which is no small feat because she is as wide as she is tall. He twirls her around which elicits girlish shrieks from the sixtyish-year-old woman. Her silvery-brown hair slips from her neat bun as he finally settles her down on her sturdy orthopedic loafers. She beams at him and stands on the tips of her toes to give him a kiss on the cheek.

"Oh, my little Martin! How you've changed. What happened to your beautiful hair?" Magda turns to the table and laughs, reaching up to push stray strands of hair behind her ears. "This one all the time in front of the mirror, primping and preening like a rooster, working to get his hair just so...I cannot believe it." She turns back to Martin, smiling. "You teased it so much it just ran away!"

Martin rubs his shiny head and laughs. "Well, my dear, I think my hair went the way of your waistline! Time really has done a number on us both, Magda, but you will always be beautiful to me." Martin clasps his hands together, begging. "Now, *please* tell me you made some of those Hungarian fried potatoes you know I love."

She laughs and rubs his paunch. "Of course, I did, Martin. You were the skinniest kid, but you ate like three men! I made special potatoes just for you. Never in my life have I enjoyed feeding someone more than you. You were a good, good boy, and I am very happy to see you back."

They beam at each other, and Magda turns to the table. "Mr. Redman, lunch is ready. May I serve?"

Redman smiles. "Absolutely, Magda. Thank you."

Redman turns to my mom. "Magda has been talking for weeks about Martin coming back to *Pedazo*. Of all the people who've roamed these halls, Martin is the only one she's ever missed. He and Anatoli became great friends and Martin, being the youngest singer we've ever had, looked up to Magda as a mother figure. It's nice to see them reunited."

Mom gives a half smile and reaches for her water. "It must be hard for kids to be ripped from their families at such a young age and sent to live with strangers. I'm glad they have someone to comfort them when they're lonely."

Redman's demeanor changes immediately, and he speaks in a stony voice. "Every singer who has entered this compound has come of their own free will *with* the support of their families. No one has ever been forced to stay at *Pedazo*. I hope I've misunderstood what you've said."

Mom avoids his eyes and sips her water as Dad hurriedly jumps in. "Please excuse my wife, Mr. Redmond. I think she's just a little emotional with the idea of Dani leaving home. We are very excited and grateful for the opportunity you are giving our daughter."

Jenner drags his eyes away from Mom and turns to Dad and gives him a curt nod. "Good to hear. As long as we're all on the same page." The table is uncomfortably silent as Magda carries out a large bowl of salad. Martin jumps up to help bring in the rest of the dishes. I'm jealous that he has a chance to escape the tension. Dad, Jenner and Geena attempt superficial chatter, but the carefree mood of the tour is broken. I sit back and ponder what I've just seen. I'm uneasy with the way Jenner's mood went from happy to frightening in a matter of seconds. I'd hoped to leave that kind of mercurial personality behind at home.

Jenner stands up once the food is on the table. "I'm going to let you dine together as a family. Tomorrow, Dani will be immersed in her training. In about four weeks, we can schedule a visit." He looks pointedly at my mom. "Thank you again for entrusting me with your daughter. I have very high hopes for her. I believe we can launch her into an extremely successful career by this time next year." He smiles at Martin and me. "You two spend the rest of the day getting settled. We'll start first thing tomorrow. Enjoy yourselves and welcome home."

With a final nod, Jenner exits the terrace and an uncomfortable lunch ensues. While Mom sulks and picks at her food, everyone else tries to overcompensate for her negative attitude. We're all exhausted by the time we finish dessert. With no food left to eat and nothing left to say, Dad stands up. "Well, I guess we should help you unpack."

By this time, I have a headache from all the tension. I feel like I could cry. *I can't stand another few hours of this.* Geena jumps in to save me. "Think we'd better hit the road. Traffic is going to be a nightmare and I have that physics test I need to study for. Dani has a staff to help her unpack. She'll be fine."

I throw Geena a grateful glance and she winks back. Mom, staring off at the ocean, shrugs. "That's fine with me. I'm kind of tired anyway."

Dad sighs "OK. Since no one else wants to stay, I guess we'll hit the road."

Geena and I walk arm and arm and stop next to the family car. I give her a long hug, starting to tear up. "I'm going to miss you, G. I don't want you to go."

Geena squeezes back. "OK, then it's settled, I'll just move into your closet!" She gives me an encouraging smile. "Dani, you're going to be fine. Go for it, sis!"

As Geena opens her door, Dad scoops me up in a hug. "I can't believe we're leaving you here, Marie. Home isn't going to be the same without you." He puts me down and smiles. "You're going to be amazing. No matter what you do, we couldn't be prouder of you than we are right now." He glances back at Mom, who is kicking the stone drive with her toe. "This is really hard for your mom—your leaving home, getting chances she never got. I know she isn't handling this well but try and go easy on her."

I know how important it is to my dad that Mom and I get along. So, I bite back my words and nod. "I'll try, Dad. I love you."

"Love you too." He tousles my hair one last time and gets into the car. Martin retreats toward the steps as my mom clears her throat, finally acknowledging me. "Well, good luck, honey. I'm sure you'll do fine. We'll see you in a month." Her forced smile only makes the lack of emotion behind her words more apparent. "Love you, Dani."

It's like those last three words make my mom finally realize she's leaving me behind. All her anger and pettiness seem to melt away. She draws in her breath and looks somewhat shocked at the realization. We stand there for a few seconds. I'm not sure what my mom will do or say, and it looks like she feels the same way. There is so much to say, but she cannot put all her love, hopes and regrets into words. With tears welling up in her eyes, Mom hugs me fiercely and whispers, "I'm sorry. I tried my best, and I messed up. You deserve better."

She pulls away and stares at me through her tears. I feel that so many opportunities have been wasted up to this point —I wonder if she feels it, too. All the moments that could have been encouraging and loving have been lost in arguments and miscommunication. It feels like we're on the edge of some precipice, a jumping-off point to change things. It's a very hopeful moment.

I nod. "Love you, Mom. Thanks."

Mom sniffs loudly and swipes at her eyes. She slowly slips back into her old self, instantly regretting her loss of control and raw emotion. She nods and gets into the car; business as usual.

I'm crushed.

Those few seconds of hope for a new relationship with my mother sink into an ocean of resentment and old patterns in which we're both trapped. Nothing will change, not at this moment anyway, and it hits me hard.

Martin comes down and puts his arm around me as Dad starts the car and rolls down all the windows. Everyone waves and blows kisses as the car drives away. Martin gives me a squeeze.

"I wish I had something to say to make you feel better right now, sweetie. But just know they'll always be your family, and they'll always love you, each in their own way."

He steps in front of me so we're facing each other. He wipes the tears that stream down my face. "And now, it's time to put *your* dreams in motion. Dry your tears and let's unpack. We have a lot of work to do."

I exhale and nod. We turn and enter the house.

28

The wave of sadness that overtook me when my family left dissolves when I open the door to my suite and take in the ocean view. All my tension vanishes, and I get excited. Rather than taking a nap like I'd planned all I want to do now is to settle in and make this my home.

I rummage in my purse and pull out a CD that Lauren made as a going-away gift and a silver-framed photo that Sean gave me yesterday. I'm a little sad as I stare at the picture of us smiling at the camera. I pop the CD into the stereo. As music pours from the speakers, I can't help but smile and bob my head to the beat of our favorite song. I place the photo prominently on my nightstand, grab a box and start unpacking.

By the time the CD is finished, my clothes are put away and all of my photos, stuffed animals and cherished trinkets are placed decoratively around the room. Now I feel that this is *my* room—my piece of home here at the compound. I'm just stretching out on the sofa when there's a knock at the door.

"Come in!" I call, too lazy to get up.

Martin, holding a small wrapped box, opens the door and whistles. "You've been busy, girl! I can't believe you got all your stuff unpacked already. Me? I'm *old*. I took a much-needed nap." Martin put a hand dramatically to his forehead. "I don't know about you, but that lunch nearly did me in! I needed time to recover."

Martin plops on the other side of the couch and stretches out his legs.

I exhale. "Yeah, it was pretty awful. I figured I'd better use my energy while I had it and get settled. But now I'm pooped." I shake my head and look at Martin. "Can you believe my mom? Do you think Jenner is pissed?"

Martin smiles and shrugs. "While this might be the one time that Jenner has done everything by the book, he certainly deserves to be called out for his past behavior. His feathers were a little ruffled, but he'll get over it. I just think he was surprised to find your mom wasn't as enamored by him as he thought she should be."

I nod and lean my head back onto the couch, thinking about today. Eventually, Martin pokes my outstretched foot. "Hey, you OK?"

I stare intently out the window as tears well up. "Saying goodbye to my dad and Geena was hard. I'm really going to miss them. But my mom..."

My voice quivers and my chin starts to wobble as I glance at Martin. "My mom's so *difficult*, you know?" I shrug and try to smile through my tears which only makes me start to cry. "There was a moment when she said goodbye, where she apologized for everything and told me she loved me. Oh God, Martin, at that moment, I honestly felt that things might change." Martin just listens.

"But then she took a deep breath, wiped away her tears, and it was business as usual. It was like the moment slipped away and she seemed more embarrassed by her feelings than anything else. She acted like she'd been caught farting or something."

Martin guffaws loudly and it's like a slap in the face. I flinch. Martin holds up his hand, still laughing. "I'm sorry, baby. I know it's not funny. But part of me will always be a fourteen-year-old boy who has to laugh at the word 'fart.'"

I giggle despite my tears and then shudder as my crying subsides. "Everyone else's parents just love their kids. Why is my mom so messed up?"

Martin sighs. "I wish she was a normal mama, but, honestly, a normal mama wouldn't have put you through what she did to get you here. So, the sooner you come to accept the fact that without her you wouldn't be here, achieving your dream, the better."

I never thought of it that way before.

He continues, "Stay focused on you and don't let your mom's antics distract you now when you're so close. You've only got one shot to do this right. Just know that she loves you in her way, even if it isn't the way you want her to love you." Martin reaches over and hugs me.

"Thanks, Martin." I sniffle as I wipe my eyes.

Martin hands me the wrapped box with a knowing smile. "For my second official act as your guardian, I hereby bring you into the twenty-first century."

I take the box, puzzled for a moment. Then I realize what it is and rip the paper off, like a happy five-year-old on Christmas morning. A shiny, silver iPhone gleams in the box. I scream with delight.

"Carlton put numbers in for Sean, Lauren and your parents. It's all charged up so you can use it right away. I told Jenner how important it is for you to stay in contact with everyone, and he had this waiting when we arrived today."

I leap across the couch and hug Martin. "You're the best guardian ever! Thank you!"

Martin hugs me back and stands up. "My pleasure, honey. And don't forget to thank Jenner when you see him. OK, now here's what I want you to do: get your swimsuit on and meet me at the pool in five minutes. We're going to swim and relax, and I'll have Magda rustle up some burgers and sundaes for dinner. I know it sounds crazy, but that Hungarian woman makes the best cheeseburgers on this planet! After tonight it will be full-on training and meal plans, so let's pig out while we can and rest up for tomorrow!"

I laugh and wipe my eyes again, feeling one hundred percent better than five minutes ago. "Yes, sir! If that's what my guardian wants, then that's what I'll do."

29

Martin had alerted Magda to our plans; the pool and spa are heated to bathtub temperatures and there's a tray of snacks and iced tea waiting poolside, just like at a fancy resort. Music pumps from hidden outdoor speakers. We swim and splash around until our fingers prune up. We snap endless selfies on my new phone, sing along to the music and imagine the famous neighbors Jenner might have. As gas tiki torches flicker on while the sun sets, we wrap ourselves in the thick terry cloth robes Magda left for us. Once it's dark, we head indoors and change into our sweats.

We eat dinner in front of a huge television in one of the many first-floor great rooms. We pop on one of Martin's favorite movies from the '80s, stuffing ourselves with cheeseburgers, homemade fries, and heaping ice cream sundaes. Martin was right: Magda makes the best cheeseburger I've ever eaten!

One more movie finds Martin and me sprawled on opposite ends of the oversized sectional with aching bellies and tired eyes. Martin is snoring softly. When the movie ends, I nudge Martin awake.

"OK, movie's over, sleeping beauty. Do you know how to turn this thing off?"

Yawning, Martin fumbles with several remotes before finally turning off the television. He gets up and stretches.

"Man, am I ready for bed!" He rubs his belly in a satisfied manner. "Oh, how I've dreamed about Magda's food all these years. You know it was the only thing I was truly sad about when REVOLUTION! broke up!"

I throw a pillow at him and Martin chuckles. "Well, the money and fame were pretty cool, too." He looks at his watch. "All right, time to hit the hay, missy. Morning comes quickly."

I glance at my phone. "Martin, it's 10:30. I don't think I've gone to sleep this early since I was eleven."

Martin walks toward the stairs. "I know it's early, but you had a big day and, trust me, tomorrow will be hard. Up at 6:00, breakfast, workout at the gym. Then we have a strategy meeting with Jenner."

"For what?"

Martin counts on his fingers as we climb the stairs. "To discuss songs, songwriters, dance and vocal coaches, musicians, rehearsal schedules, estimated show dates, publicity..." Martin waves at the air with his hand, "...the list goes on."

I'm confused. "Wait, I only just got here today. It seems way too early to be talking about show dates or publicity. I don't even have any songs yet."

We reach the top of the stairs and make our way toward our rooms. "Honey, the moment Jenner offered you that contract, he jumped into action. He probably knows when and where you'll debut and do your first interview, and he might even have a selection of songs to choose from. I wasn't kidding when I said the train had left the station. Jenner is very serious about making you a star. He has a formula for success, and he knows everything he needs to make it happen."

I exhale heavily. "Wow. I guess didn't realize how quickly this is happening. I keep thinking it's all going to end, that I'm going to wake up and it will all have been a great dream."

We're standing outside of my room, and I flick on the lights. Martin shakes his head and puts a hand on my shoulder. "Sorry, honey, it's not a dream. It's *your* life. We've got a lot to accomplish in a short time, but we're all working together to make you a success. You can do this."

I nod, leaning against the door jamb. "Thanks, Martin. Can I call Lauren and Sean and let them know how the move went?"

Martin smiles and nods. "Of course, you can, honey. Just don't stay up too late." He gives me a quick hug before disappearing down the hall.

I hit the button that turns on the fireplace, turn out the lights and flop onto the couch. I watch the firelight flicker on the chandelier crystals, casting dazzling light around the room. I smile and dial Lauren first, saving Sean for last. She picks up on the first ring.

"Tell me everything! I can't believe the photos you sent. By the way, can I tell you that I love that you *finally* have a cell phone now? So, what was it like when your family left, how do you like the compound and do you really have a fireplace in your bedroom?"

I laugh as Lauren keeps spewing questions. I text her a photo of the fireplace. "Yeah, check it out! God, I miss you already, Laur. Hey, I listened to your CD today while I was unpacking. It kept me from losing it!" I groan and fill her in on every moment from the awkward drive to Malibu, the tour, the awkward family goodbye and the rest of my day.

Lauren sighs. "OK, how is it that you're living every teenager's dream and still most of your story is talking about your freaky family. Dani, you've got to start appreciating what's happening and stop letting them get to you."

I roll my eyes. "Did you and Martin have some sort of conference call today? He said the same thing after my family left."

"The only crazy thing is that you're not thinking it too! This is too big an opportunity to blow it by getting upset because your mom is, what, just being herself ?"

I sigh. "You and Martin are right, as usual." I take a deep breath and exhale. "OK, all stressful family thoughts have been purged. I am now very Zen and appreciating where I am at this moment in my life. We have our first big meeting tomorrow. Martin said Jenner is already talking about when I will have my first performance."

"What? But you haven't even recorded a song yet. How's that possible?"

I shrug and pick at a thread on the couch cushion. "I don't know. Martin said that Jenner's been working on everything from the moment he signed me and that all this stuff just falls into a formula or something."

"So, you're like some pre-packed pop act or something?"

"Eww, gosh I hope not. When you put it that way, it makes me sound like some god-awful Hungry Man TV dinner." I wrinkle my nose. "I hope he doesn't have anything like that planned for me. I don't want to be like every other auto-tuned pop act."

"Look, Martin is there to watch out for you. Just make sure they know how you feel. They can't make you do something you don't want to do, can they?"

I shrug. "Um, I don't know, Laur. I mean, I signed a contract. I don't know if that means if I have a vote in anything. I guess I'd better find out."

"Can you go ask Martin now? It's better to know where you stand so you can be prepared, right?"

I stare at the door and shake my head. "No, he's already asleep. I'm supposed to be asleep too, only I told him I wanted to call you and Sean first."

"Aww, now that's a true friend. Giving up beauty sleep so we can chat on the phone! I knew there was a reason I loved you."

I smile. "I love you too, Laur."

"Look, I didn't mean to freak you out. Martin has your back. I'm sure everything will be fine. Stop worrying. It'll give you wrinkles."

"Ha! OK, yeah, I'll talk to Martin first thing. Thanks, Lauren."

"Good luck tomorrow. I can't wait to hear all about it."

I smile. "I'll call you tomorrow night. 'Bye."

"'Bye."

I hang up and gaze at the fire again, mulling over what Lauren said. I hope Jenner has a good plan for me. I don't want to be some lame pop singer who's big for a summer, but everyone gets tired of by the time school rolls around. I have talent. I just hope I'm given a chance to use it.

Before my worrying kicks into overdrive my phone rings. I smile and pick up the call.

"Hey, D. Is it a bad time to call?" Sean speaks quietly, which I love because it makes it seem like he's whispering in my ear, not miles away from me.

I snuggle deeper into the couch cushions. "It's a perfect time. I was just going to call you. It's been a crazy day."

Sean chuckles. "I'll bet! I can't believe where you're staying. It's a total mansion! And I love that you have our photo on your night-stand."

"Now it's the first thing I'll see in the morning and the last thing I'll see at night. Best going-away gift ever."

"How'd it go today?"

I giggle, "Can you believe I'm lying on a sofa in front of a fireplace in my room? This place is beyond crazy!" I fill him in on the day. "OK, enough about me. How was your day? How was practice? Will you guys be ready for the game on Thursday?" Sean tells me about his day. He is just starting to tell me about his basketball practice when I yawn uncontrollably.

"Oh wow! I didn't realize it was so late. What time do you have to get up tomorrow?"

I answer through another yawn. "6:00, but I really want to hear about practice. Did coach say if he was going to have you start?" As I yawn through the word "start," Sean cuts me off.

"Yes, I'm starting on Thursday, but you've got a big day tomorrow. Let's catch up tomorrow."

I yelp with excitement. "I'm so happy for you, Sean! I wish I could be there to see you play."

Sean sighs. "Me too. I'm sure my mom will take video, and I'll send you the highlights, OK? Now seriously, get to bed. It's past midnight."

I groan. "Crap! You're right. Night."

"Night."

I sigh happily as I hang up. I'm so excited for Sean. He's been dreaming about starting since freshman year. I'm just bummed I'm going to miss it. I'm grateful that I showered before dinner because I know I'll be too tired to take one in the morning. I turn off the fire-place, set my alarm and fall into bed. I don't move until morning.

30

Six a.m. comes all too fast, the alarm jolting me awake. Out of habit, I reach to turn off my alarm. But since I'm sleeping in a king-size bed as opposed to my twin bed at home, I just slap the pillow next to me. Disoriented and half asleep, I sit up, the alarm still blaring, and look around, confused. It takes me a few seconds to realize where I am. Martin barges in, all smiles, dressed in his workout gear and turns off the alarm for me.

"Rise and shine, sunshine! It's time to get to work!" I stare at him blankly, still disoriented. Martin laughs. "Remember, we're here at the compound...in Malibu...so you can be a big star."

He smiles as I rub my eyes and nod. "Yup, it's all coming back. I got to sleep later than I expected and I'm..." I stop mid-sentence as I look at Martin, who's standing next to me in skintight, striped work-out leggings. "Oh God, Martin, it's way too early for you to be in those pants." I hold up a hand and cover my eyes. "I just can't."

Surprised, Martin looks down, smoothing his deep-cut, neon-green string tank top over his belly, "What, too much? You're not the only one working out today. I'm taking full advantage of the personal trainer, dietitian and in-house chef." Martin looks up regally, takes a deep breath and exhales. "You might not have noticed, but I've gained a pound or two since my REVOLUTION! days. So, I figured that while you're in boot camp, I might as well be, too." He lifts a finger and strikes a pose. "I'm going to REVOLUTIONIZE! my body!"

I laugh. "You sound like an infomercial! But good for you, Martin. I'm glad you're going to be training with me. I like helping the elderly."

He picks up a pillow and whacks me with it as I giggle. "Old jokes, huh? We'll see, Missy. I bet that by the time you go on tour, I'll dance circles around you."

I laugh as I get out of bed. "You're on, Gramps!" We shake on it.

"Now get washed up and be downstairs in ten minutes. The trainer will be here at 7:00."

I turn around on my way to the bathroom and salute. "Yes, sir. And you change into something more...uh...well, just something with more fabric. Remember, I'm an impressionable minor." The pillow hits the bathroom door just as I close it.

Fifteen minutes later, we're both changed and sitting at the huge kitchen island. Magda has served up egg whites, spinach, quinoa and sliced grapefruit. A pot of green tea sits between us.

"I've eaten egg whites for years, but I've never enjoyed them until this moment. Magda, you're a genius," I gush, shoveling another heaping forkful into my mouth.

Magda, who's cleaning the frying pan, smiles. "Breakfast is most important meal of day. You cannot work hard on empty stomach."

"Didn't I tell you Magda was the best cook ever?" Martin starts to heap more egg whites onto his plate as Magda and I watch. He notices, puts back the spoon and raises his hands. "You're right. If I'm going to REVOLUTIONIZE! my body, I need to stop eating so much." He helps himself to some more green tea instead. "Thanks for looking out for me, ladies."

I clink my mug with Martin's. "No problem! We're in this together."

We finish up, grab our workout bags and walk down to the gym. As we enter the gym bungalow, Martin snaps on the lights, and I set my workout bag down on a wooden bench.

The gym is enormous. One wall of windows faces the ocean, and mirrors cover the other three walls. Spin bikes, elliptical machines, stair climbers and rowing machines stand along one of the mirrored walls. There are several wooden machines with padded benches and cables that look like medieval torture devices; I have no idea what those are for. Weight racks are along one mirrored wall and nautilus equipment stands in the center of the room.

Martin turns on some music, and we hop on bikes to warm up while we wait for the trainer. After a few moments, the glass door opens and in walks an impeccably coifed man of about 5'10" with bike shorts covering his tanned, muscled legs. He smiles and drops his bag next to the bench. "Good morning!"

Martin smiles and says under his breath, "Good morning, indeed!" I can't help but giggle at Martin's reaction to the trainer as he sits on his bike and straightens his tank top.

"I'm Brett Foster. You must be Dani and Martin!" He heartily shakes our hands. "Great to meet you both!" He claps his hands loudly, making both myself and Martin jump. "Be ready in a sec."

I don't know what to make of Brett as he walks toward the bench. He has a closely trimmed beard and an impeccable gentleman's haircut that I don't associate with the image of a trainer. But when he unzips his track jacket, I see how chiseled his body is and figure he must know what he's doing. He seems very high-energy, which could be good or totally annoying.

Brett claps his hands loudly again, grabs a clipboard and heads over. I'm glad he's holding something so he can stop that ridiculous clapping. "OK, let's get started."

I point to the strange machines in the corner. "What are those things?"

He slaps his clipboard on his hand, making me and Martin jump again. "Excellent question, Dani! In fact, why don't we start with these today?" Brett walks over to the machines.

I look at Martin and he gives me a dirty look right back and angrily mouths, "Thanks."

Brett waves us over. "Best way to learn about the Reformer is to use it!"

I give what I hope is an enthusiastic smile as I dismount my bike. Martin follows me, all smiles now that he's talking to Brett, "The Reformer? That sounds scary. Maybe I'll sit this one out."

Brett laughs. "I know, it sounds scary. But the Reformer is great for teaching muscle control, precision, stamina and a host of other good things. Trust me, by the end of the week you're going to be begging me to use it every day."

Martin rolls his eyes at me while Brett bends down to take off his shoes. I give Martin a push as we kick off our shoes. "Come on, Martin. Time to start the REVOLUTION!"

***

Forty-five minutes later, limp as noodles and covered in sweat, Martin and I sit on the floor mats, stretching our shaking legs. Brett bustles around, wiping down equipment and putting things away.

"Words cannot describe the pain I'm in." Martin speaks each word quietly, slowly, as if the effort to talk is too much. "I'd strangle you if I could move my arms." Martin pulls a face and says in a falsetto voice, "Gee, Brett, what are those things?"

I slowly shake my head and glance at the clock hanging across the room. "How is it only 8:00 a.m. and I'm already exhausted? Do we have time for a nap before we meet with Jenner?"

Martin musters the strength to shake his head once. "Nope, we've got just enough time to head up to the house, shower, change and get down to the studio." Martin's entire body sags. "How am I gonna drag my bones up to the house?" He turns to me. "Do I smell that bad?"

I laugh. "Yes, you do."

We're interrupted by another sharp clap from Brett. "All right, you two. I'm off. Finish your stretches and be sure to drink plenty of water. I took the liberty of calling the house. Magda's sending Anatoli down to fetch you in the golf cart."

We smile gratefully and thank Brett. He grabs his things and heads toward the door. "Don't worry, it'll get easier every day. See you tomorrow."

We give half-hearted waves as Brett leaves. Seconds later, Anatoli pulls up and comes inside. "Mama said you might want a ride back to the house." He grabs our bags and places them in the cart while Martin and I contemplate standing up. Anatoli returns and offers me a helping hand. It takes a bit more effort to get Martin upright, but eventually, we're all in the golf cart, driving up to the house.

"Thanks a million, Anatoli. I would never have left that gym if it weren't for you." Martin leans his head back against the seat, utterly devoid of energy.

Anatoli laughs. "In a few weeks, you'll be running up to the house after your workout. You're just out of practice."

After he parks outside the house, Anatoli hands the cart keys to Martin. "Why don't you keep these and use the cart while you're here? Just remember to park it in the garage at night so I can charge it."

Martin smiles. "Thanks, Anatoli. I appreciate it." Martin heaves himself out of the golf cart.

He turns to grab his bag, but Anatoli already has both bags. "I'll just run these up for you two. Use the butler's elevator in the kitchen—save your legs." Anatoli winks and runs up the steps.

"God, my legs hurt just watching him!" Martin groans and I laugh.

"I can't wait to see you dance circles around me in a few months," I retort playfully.

That does it! Martin straightens up and starts to painfully mount the steps. "Oh yeah? What if this is all an act I cooked up to give you a false sense of security? And don't think I don't see you limping too, you little brat. I know you're hurting just as much as me." I give him a sidelong look and he laughs. "OK, well, maybe not as much as me. But I don't see you sprinting up those stairs, either. Come on, let's go. We've got an hour to get down to the studio. And it's going to take me forty-five minutes just to get up these damn steps!" I laugh as I put my arm around Martin's waist, and we hobble up the stairs together.

31

Too soon, we're back in the golf cart and driving toward the studio. Long showers have relieved much of our pain as have a couple of ibuprofens for Martin. We munch on homemade trail mix from a cooler Magda shoved in our hands before we left. It's stocked with enough healthy snacks for ten people, along with two customized *Pedazo de Cielo* S'Well® water bottles.

I marvel, "Jenner doesn't miss a beat! Personalized water bottles, snack bags, post-workout golf carts—he thinks of everything, huh?"

Martin nods, concentrating on navigating the narrow pathway while trying to move his arms as little as possible. "He believes that the solution to half the world's problems is preparation. There's never been a problem I can remember that started because Jenner forgot to do something. When he's got a project, he spends hours calculating, speculating and preparing for every possible contingency and issue that might arise. Some might say he's a controlling tyrant, but to me, he's always been a bit of an evil genius."

I take a sip of water. "God, this must all cost a lot of money. I mean the staff, the house, water bottles, etc." I reach out to pluck a flower from a passing hibiscus.

"Yup, last time I checked Jenner was the only one who walked away from *our* little project a millionaire." He exhales as I look up from the flower. "That's why I was so specific about your contract." He nudges me with his elbow. "That's also why it's important for you to write as many songs as you can. If you can pen a hit or two, that's the way you're going to make some real money."

Martin is quiet for a moment. "Most people at this stage of the game would retire to a private island with their trophy wife and kids. I don't think Jenner has to work another day in his life, but some people just have that drive to succeed, regardless of the money. I think

Jenner has something to prove, and he knows he can do it through you."

We reach the studio and park our golf cart next to a gold one. Martin checks his watch. "Looks like Jenner's already here."

Inside, we walk past an elegantly furnished waiting area, down a hallway lined with gold and platinum albums and into a large conference room. A gray wooden table with seating for ten people gleams in the center of the room. A glass wall overlooks a furnished outdoor stone patio and the deep blue sea. A buffet runs along one wall, containing a platter filled with fruit and hummus in addition to tea, coffee and water. At one end of the room is a sitting area with leather couches that surround a rectangular modern fireplace built into the wall, flames flickering over blue glass. A flat-screen TV is mounted above the fireplace, replaying the Redman Enterprises logo on a loop. At the opposite end of the room, a piano, an acoustic guitar and a stereo system sit, waiting to be used.

Jenner stands to greet us. He's wearing a white linen shirt, jeans, loafers and tinted glasses. Sitting on his left is an impossibly skinny man of indeterminate age, dressed like an Andy Warhol stunt double. His black asymmetrical haircut flops over one eye and the gray ascot tied at his throat seems to be tied uncomfortably tight. He remains seated and stares at the ocean.

Jenner walks over to give us a warm hug. "Good morning! I heard from Brett that he put you through your paces. I hope you're not too tired because we have a lot to get through today."

Jenner walks back to his chair, indicating we should sit. "Dani, Martin, I'd like you to meet Terrance Flemming. Terrance, this is Dani Truehart and Martin Fox."

Martin leans over the table with great effort and holds out his hand. "It's an honor to meet you, Terrance. Your writing is truly unique and timeless."

Martin's hand hangs awkwardly in the air until Terrance waves his hands ineffectually and murmurs, "Yes, of course," as he looks to Jenner for help.

Jenner smiles brightly and says, "Terrance doesn't believe in shaking hands or having much physical contact with strangers. He prefers to keep his exposure to germs at a minimum."

"Especially when working with children," he murmurs again, nodding toward me with mild disdain.

I do a double-take, shocked. Jenner reaches over and pats my hand. "Don't mind Terrance, Dani. We all know you're healthy and far from being a child. You'll find the more time you spend in this business that sometimes the creative world is populated by people with many different..."–Jenner searches for the right word–"...idiosyncrasies. But we're all working toward the same goal, namely, making you a huge success, and I believe Terrance has the talent to achieve that goal."

Terrance, whose eyes remain downcast during this exchange, merely nods his head as if what Jenner said wasn't completely insulting.

"Now, Dani, I've played a recording of your audition for Terrance, but he'd like to hear you sing in person."

I look at Martin, who nods encouragingly. I suck up how irked I am and smile graciously instead. "Of course."

He turns to Jenner and Terrance. "It's been a few days since she's practiced, what with the move and all, but she's a natural, and she can certainly sing for you now."

Martin gets up, pulling out my chair, and I try to shake off my anger as we walk toward the piano. He whispers, "You've got this." Martin asks Jenner, "Anything in particular you'd like to hear?"

Jenner rocks back in his chair and contemplates. "Well, we want to hear a bit of a range. Let's try that Ariana Grande ballad and the newest Gaga song. You know those, right Dani?"

I nod. Jenner smiles. "Good. Martin, you'll find the music on the bench. Just let us know when you're ready."

Jenner turns to Terrance and they have a whispered conversation while Martin and I go over the music. After a few minutes, Martin clears his throat. "OK, Jenner, we're all set." Martin looks at me and nods. "Ready?" I nod, exhaling, and Martin winks.

Normally, my stomach is tied in knots before I perform, but I'm so annoyed by this guy that all I can focus on is showing him how well I can sing. As soon as Martin plays the first few notes, I concentrate only on the music. I belt out the ballad as if I'm on stage, my voice filling the entire room. The music and words are all that exist for me. The only reason I don't close my eyes and lose myself entirely in the music is that I'm scared I'll mess up the lyrics if I'm not looking at them, and I don't want this guy to have the satisfaction of seeing me screw up. But no one else seems to notice any hesitation in my performance.

I sneak a glance and see Terrance sitting forward in his chair. He seems to be entranced, a look of pleasant surprise transforming his face. Martin bangs away on the keys, the entire atmosphere of the room changing in a few short minutes. When the song ends, I feel giddy with the energy of a good performance, my anger gone. I beam at Martin who smiles encouragingly before turning to prepare the music for the next number.

Terrance nods to Jenner as he sits back in his chair. Jenner smiles at me. "Terrific, Dani. You can start the next one any time you're ready." I glance at Martin who gives me a small shrug. I take a deep breath and give Martin a nod to start.

The second song is a fast-paced pop song that is next to impossible to replicate with only a piano. With no thumping bass or drums to keep the tempo, I have no idea how this will work. But I tap my foot where I know the drum belongs and plow into the song as if there's a full band behind me. Shaking my head and snapping my fingers, I work myself up into the music, closing my eyes and pretending I'm singing along in the car with Lauren. I'm surprised to hear thumping on the table and open my eyes to see Terrance drumming in time to the music, bouncing his head. I glance at Jenner, who has a huge smile on his face and gives me an approving wink.

The song ends and Jenner claps his hands loudly. Terrance doesn't display quite as much emotion, seeming almost embarrassed by his enthusiasm moments earlier. He splays his hands on the table as if to smooth out any wrinkles and nods emphatically. "You have a nice voice, Dani," he says quietly. "I definitely think we can work together." He nods to himself, almost confirming what he just said out loud. "Yes, I think we can."

I smile as Martin gives me a high-five. We start back toward the chairs, but Terrance holds up a hand. "I'd like to run through some exercises, so I can see the range and agility of your voice."

I look at Martin who shrugs and says, "Sure."

For the next two hours, we run through various scales, vocal exercises and songs. Terrance takes fastidious notes in a small leather notebook, expressing no opinion and speaking only to give directions. I sing so much I start having trouble hitting some of the higher notes, and my voice is tired.

Finally, Jenner glances at his watch and clears his throat. "Well, Terrance, do you think you have what you need to get started on something for Dani? I'd like to give her voice a rest."

Terrance, furiously writing in his notebook, reluctantly looks up. "Yes, I suppose I have enough to get started." He frowns. "You will make sure she continues practicing? I don't like to hear that she hasn't practiced daily. I can hear it in her voice. I need her to be at one hundred percent at all times."

Before Jenner can respond, Martin chimes in. "Yes, as I mentioned earlier, the only reason Dani *didn't* practice for the past few days was because she had to leave her family to move here. That is the longest break she has had in years."

Terrance turns his chair to face Martin at the piano. "Yes, well, from now on there will be no breaks unless required by a doctor. We have much to do in a short time. I will leave you a practice schedule for Dani. I will email you daily lesson plans that I expect you to go through."

Terrance whips out several sheets of music and thrusts them in Martin's direction. "Here is the first lesson for today."

Martin takes a deep breath, trying to contain himself. Jenner places a hand on Terrance's arm, causing him to jump. "Tomorrow, Terrance. We don't want to wear her out before we get started." Terrance stares at Jenner's hand on his leather jacket and Jenner gives his arm a pat before removing his hand.

I'm very uncomfortable watching this subtle power struggle. Jenner and Terrance stare at each other for a moment. Finally, Terrance exhales loudly, clearly put out. "If you insist. But it is not what I would advise."

Jenner smiles, his eyes hidden behind his smoky lenses. "I understand, and I take full responsibility. I'm sure that this won't put Dani too far behind." Jenner taps the table once. "Now Terrance, can I interest you in some lunch? You know my Magda is an expert in macrobiotic cuisine."

Terrance sniffs, clearly still put out by their little tête-à-tête. "That's kind of you, Jenner, but I really must be going. I have much to do."

Jenner nods. "I understand. When do you think you'll have something to show us?" Jenner rocks in his chair, eager for an answer.

Terrance packs away his notebook in his black messenger bag. "I don't think I will have anything I'd consider showing you before two weeks. But if we're lucky, I will have a couple of songs, not just one. I had some ideas when I came in here, but now that I've met the girl and heard her range, I have a better idea of what direction to go in."

Now that he's met me? I think. *He barely said a word to me.* I'm pissed as hell that they're all talking about me as if I'm not in the room. "Um, excuse me, Terrance? Is there anything you might want to know about me? Like, personally? My hobbies, my family or school? I mean, if you're writing songs for me, don't you want to know something about *me*?"

Jenner opens his mouth to speak, but Terrance beats him to it, shaking his head as he stands up. "No, there is nothing I need to know. Teenage girls are all the same." He gives me the briefest of looks. He heads toward the door, stopping to face us.

"I am not writing songs about you, Dani, but for the masses of adolescent teens around the world who are misunderstood by their parents, teachers and boyfriends, caught between childhood and womanhood, looking to make their mark on the world, to be noticed or to fall in love. I am not writing songs for *one* girl, but for a world of girls, all facing different shades of similar issues, most of which are timeless." Utterly ignoring me, he continues. "That is what I am writing. If you have a burning passion to sing a personal song, I suggest you put pen to paper and write it yourself. Good afternoon." With a nod, Terrance sweeps out of the room.

Martin scowls with rage and my jaw hangs open. Jenner's raucous laughter shocks us both. "Well, that's what you get for questioning his genius, Dani!" Jenner continues to laugh as he gets up and puts his arms around Martin and me. "Oh, come on, lighten up. I said you had to deal with some weird people in this business, Dani, and you just met one of the weirdest."

He lets Martin go and faces me. "You can't let that guy get under your skin. He has a job to do and so do you. He's hired to write you a platinum record, and that's exactly what he's going to do. And, like most anything in this business, the key to success is plugging in the right formula. Terrance has more Grammys than anyone I know. You want a love song, you talk to your boyfriend. You want a *hit*, you talk to Terrance."

Jenner pats my back. "Lunch is ready for you two up at the house. I've got a meeting in town." He grabs a folder from the table and hands it to Martin. "Here's Dani's schedule for the rest of the day. Get some rest. We'll meet again tomorrow. Good work!" Jenner calls as he leaves the conference room. His pep talk has done nothing to improve our moods.

"Are you kidding me?" I fume. "That guy barely looked at me the entire time he was in the room. He acted like I was either an incoherent toddler or a prized cow! What the hell! Is this normal?"

Martin takes a deep breath. "Well, I haven't experienced someone like that in a while. But yeah, there are people in this business who treat the talent like a coffee table, especially young talent. It's a hard line to walk. I can stand up to Terrance for you, but then we run the risk of his walking out. As much as it galls me to say it, we've got to give that little freak a chance. Everything he writes is pure platinum, Dani. Including the two songs you just sang."

My jaw drops again. "No *way*. You mean I sang his songs back to him?"

Martin nods, resigned. "Yup, and I'm pretty sure he was impressed by what you did. So, if we have to swallow a little pride and pretend we don't exist, I think we should if we want him on our team."

I shake my head. "Holy crap. I guess I don't have a choice." I pause and look at Martin. "This kinda sucks."

Martin pats me on the back and gives me a light-hearted smile. "Congratulations, honey. You've just made your first compromise! Sometimes you have to do things in this business that you don't want to do to get where you want to go. The tricky part is making compromises that don't alter your principles. While Terrance might be rude, he isn't a bad person. So, this is a relatively small compromise that just involves your ego taking a backseat."

He puts his arm around me as we leave the room. "The key is to avoid compromises that make you do things you know are wrong or that don't really represent you. Hopefully, we won't have to cross that bridge for a while. Or ever, if we're lucky. Come on, let's see what Magda's got cooking for lunch."

32

I pore over the afternoon schedule as Martin drives back to the house. I'm ecstatic to see there's an hour nap scheduled after lunch before my dance rehearsal. Normally I'd be enraged to be treated like a baby, but I honestly don't know how I'll make it through the day otherwise.

After a healthy lunch of salmon and grilled veggies, Martin and I flee to our rooms for naptime. I thought I'd take a few minutes to text Sean and Lauren when I lie down, but I nod off before I even finish typing.

It seems like only a few minutes later when Martin shakes me awake. "Rise and shine, sunshine. If it feels like we've done this before, well, we have." An enormous yawn escapes Martin's lips as I struggle to open my eyes.

"Magda has tea waiting downstairs. It's into dancewear for our afternoon session. Then we get off easy today and watch research videos: 'Jenner's Famous Do's and Don'ts for Pop Stars.' I know it sounds lame, but you won't believe what you can learn from video footage." Martin slowly stretches and winces while I continue to lie still, eyes half open. Martin nudges me with his hand.

"You alive? Girl, please don't make me call your mama and tell her we killed you on Day One."

This makes me snort, and I sit up, smiling.

"I'm alive, barely. You weren't kidding with this schedule stuff, were you?"

Martin crosses his arms. "I tried to warn you, but you don't really get it 'til you're in it, you know? But you'll get used to it. It takes time to get used to everyone focusing on you. It can be a lot of pressure at first."

I nod slowly. "Is that it? I've felt mild panic all day, and I haven't been able to figure out why."

Martin continues, "The more you get used to being the center of attention, the easier it'll be to deal with the pressure. Just have to give it some time." He squeezes my hand and hops off the bed.

"OK, third outfit of the day, Dani. Come downstairs when you're ready. Let's get dancing!"

***

After changing and downing more green tea, we're back in the golf cart and cruising down the hill toward the dance studio. I glance at my schedule. "Who's this dance instructor 'S' we're working with?"

Martin holds out a hand, and I hand him the schedule. He makes a face and hands it back. "No clue. 'S' could be their name or a code—Jenner loves all that cloak-and-dagger crap. I think if managing hadn't panned out for him, he'd have been an amazing spy. I'm sure he or she is topnotch, though, so just be quiet and do whatever they say. You never know what these geniuses are like, as illustrated this morning by Terrance. We don't want to offend them as soon as we step in the door."

We arrive at the dance studio, grab our bags and go inside. The studio has maple sprung flooring with mirrors and ballet barres on the two long walls. Arched floor-to-ceiling windows dominate the two smaller walls, flooding the studio with natural light. High-beamed ceilings soar over the dance space and a glittering chandelier hangs down in the middle. Brown leather straight-back chairs are lined up against one of the mirrors. A small but luxurious conversation area is set up in the corner of one of the window walls, with plush, oversized armchairs and a furry rug. A massive stereo system stands in another corner, enclosed in a custom-built cabinet.

In the center of it all stands a barefoot, willowy woman dressed in a maroon leotard, loose gray pants and a light-pink cotton cardigan. Her skin is luminous, and her short brown hair falls carelessly over her forehead. Simply standing there, she emanates beauty, elegance, strength and some other quality I can't quite name. I feel as if I'm in a fairy tale and about to meet a very magical and important character. I stand there, transfixed. After a few moments, the woman smiles.

"You must be Dani. My name is Serena." Her voice is mellow and deep. She speaks slowly and clearly, a faint accent coloring her words. Serena walks over, hand extended, while I just continue to stare. Martin gives me a nudge, snapping me back to reality.

"Sorry. Hi. It's nice to meet you. I, uh…" Serena gazes at me, giving me time to complete my thought. Seconds pass slowly, and now I feel like an idiot. I can feel a blush creep across my face. "Sorry, I don't know how to explain it. Seeing you there, I just got this overwhelming feeling like we know each other, like I knew who you were, but we've never met."

A mischievous grin breaks out on Serena's face and she giggles. "That, my girl, is what I am going to teach you!" She pats me on the back and reaches across to extend a hand to Martin. "Hello, Martin. I'm Serena."

Martin chuckles and shakes Serena's hand. "What a way to start your lesson! Serena, I'm honored to meet you. I've been following your career since I can remember. I had no idea we would be working with someone as groundbreaking as you. You're an icon!"

She smiles. "Thank you, Martin, that's kind of you to say. Can I assume that this one," she indicates to me with a nod, "has learned a thing or two from you about my methods, then?"

We both nod silently in unison and Serena smiles. "Good! Now we can begin."

Martin and I change into our dance shoes as Serena takes off her flowy cardigan. Together, we run through several warmup exercises. Grabbing a sip of water, Serena turns to Martin. "You have some routines already rehearsed, yes?"

Martin nods. "I brought the music just in case you wanted to see them."

"That's fine. Let's see them all." Serena looks at me. "If that's OK with you. I want to see how you move, see your skill level and how comfortable you are in your body, so I know where we stand. No point in asking Baryshnikov to do hip-hop, you know?" She winks and nods at the stereo as she walks toward a chair. "Any time you're ready."

Martin and I huddle to discuss the order of the routines. I'm overcome with stress. For the second time today, I'm expected to perform without warning for an industry legend. "At least when I sang for Terrance, I had no idea who he was until afterward, and I was so angry with him, I didn't have time to be nervous. Now I'm supposed to perform for the woman whom you've based all your teachings on who is like, I don't know, a goddess, and I'm just supposed to be all, 'Sure, no big deal. I've got this.'" I start breathing too fast and begin to feel dizzy. Martin steps in front of me to block Serena's view and puts his hands on my shoulders.

"Stop talking, now. Deep breaths through your nose." Martin breathes with me and stares into my eyes. My heartbeat begins to slow. I feel less panicky. Martin nods and slowly takes his hands away as if I'm a bomb. "OK?" I nod back, slightly unsure. "This is nothing new to you. You've performed a million times in shows and pageants. Don't look at her, just focus on me. As soon as you hear that music, your body is going to do what it needs to do because that is what we've been training for. Get your mind out of the way and let your instincts take over."

Serena calls over, concerned. "Is everything OK?"

Still looking at me, Martin answers. "Yup, we're all set." Martin gives me a wink. "Oh, and we're starting with your modern piece. It's high time someone other than me saw what you can do." Not waiting for a reply, he sends me off to the center of the room with a little shove and puts the CD into the stereo.

I look everywhere but at Serena, trying to avoid another panic attack. I can feel Serena staring at me and know it'll be odd if I don't at least acknowledge her, so I flick her a glance and a shaky smile before settling into my game face. I strike a pose and wait for the song to begin.

As soon as the first notes hit the studio, I'm swept up in the music. Martin was right; this routine is so well-rehearsed that it's a logical progression from one move to the next, and I flow effortlessly through the dance. This is a special treat for me since it's the first piece I've choreographed on my own. It's purely a movement routine, not a song-and-dance number like I usually perform. I don't have to worry about running out of breath to sing or forgetting words while remembering what steps come next. I feel myself smile as I perform a *chainés* straight into a hitch-kick. I completely forget about Serena and feel like I'm back in Martin's studio. All my nerves are forgotten. I throw myself into the dance, feeling my confidence come off me in waves.

When the piece ends, Martin and Serena are smiling. But neither has a bigger smile than I do because I finally feel confident for the first time since I entered the compound. I blaze through the next few routines without missing a step. I'm drenched in sweat when Serena stands up and approaches me.

"I'm so pleased! You and Martin have done a great job on your technique and timing. I definitely think we can get a lot accomplished in the short time we have together." She turns to Martin. "Thank you for teaching Dani so thoroughly. Teachers like you keep the art alive."

Martin smiles shyly. "Thank you. That's high praise coming from you."

Serena grabs a towel and hands it to me. "While there are a few things I want to polish, I think we're in great shape. Let's face it," Serena says, shrugging, "you're not joining the National Ballet Company. You'll be singing pop or rock to thousands of excited fans. They want to see you move, have fun and..."—Serena searches for a word, grabbing the air with both hands—" ... be in your presence, you know? That's why people go to concerts; to feel all that energy live, see the best *you* there is." She pats me on the back, "And that's what we're going to give them."

Serena turns thoughtfully away, walking toward the mirror. "So how do we make all these people's dreams come true when everyone has a different vision of who you are and you are so very young that *you* are still discovering who you are?" Serena turns back, waiting for me to answer.

I'm at a loss. I look at Martin, who gives me a blank look, whispering, "No idea. This was never a part of REVOLUTION!'s boot camp."

I look back at Serena and shrug. "I don't know."

Serena smiles. "Of course, you don't. Your passion is dance and song. Marketing and showmanship are Jenner's passion. That's why he hired me." She walks back to me, talking with her hands as she goes. "I'm going to teach you how to create a stage persona. Someone who is the best version of you while you are performing, but someone you can leave behind on stage at the end of the show. You can't open your heart on stage to thousands of people, night after night, and hope to keep anything for yourself when the lights go out. If you live like that, it will drain you. You will only feel happy if they love you, and you will fall into despair if they don't."

We're face to face now, and she gives me a tender smile. "You have to protect your heart if you want to survive this business. Every successful star understands that you have to have a public and private persona. It is the key to a long career and a happy life."

I try to wrap my mind around what Serena's saying. "But isn't it dishonest to pretend to be someone I'm not?"

Serena nods. "It might feel that way. When you're young, everything seems so black and white—true and untrue, good and bad. But there are many shades to life. Finding the moderate path between these extremes is one of the lessons you have to learn growing up." Serena pauses and turns to Martin. "What do you think? Did you have a stage persona in REVOLUTION!?"

Martin sighs and shakes his head. "Other than pretending to be straight, no. And, truth be told, I honestly think it's the reason why so many of the guys got messed up in the end. We were told to be ourselves; that was what the public wanted to see. For a while, we rode a huge wave of success, feeling great about ourselves every time we read an amazing interview or saw ourselves hyped on TV. But when we started to become less popular, it killed us to hear reporters ridicule our style or our music. They were putting down the very things they had loved about us for years. Being the youngest, I was somehow able to shake it off when everything went bust. Besides, I could finally be open about my sexuality without risking my financial success. I had my mom to go home to, and she helped me out. But the rest of the guys were older, and they were devastated. They started drinking and drugging to escape, and it just went downhill from there."

Martin pauses and nods to himself. "I sure do wish someone told us that we shouldn't give everything to the public. Because we *literally* gave everything we had to our fans, and we had nothing left at the end of it. It was hard enough to recover from our fall from popularity. But having to figure out who we were after such a big public rejection and losing all our money to Jenner, that was damned near impossible." He shakes his head and addresses me. "I'd hate to see you go through that."

I wipe my face with the towel, a shiver running up my spine as the sweat starts to cool on my body. "I never thought about all the consequences of success, let alone failing. I don't want to end up like you guys are saying. But I don't want to come off fake, either."

Serena nods. "I know. Martin and I are going to work with you to find out what kind of persona you feel most comfortable with, and that's what we'll develop." Serena reached out and caressed my cheek in a maternal way. "You will always *be* Dani Truehart. Put forth your most confident, musical self when you're on stage and understand that at the end of the day, this is your job and not who you are. Songs, concerts and fans will come and go. You have to develop a way to enjoy that and not fall apart when it ends, or when a critic pans you. Because in order to live a real life, you have to understand that the popstar lifestyle is never going to last; it is never going to be everything for you. It's just an amazing job you are lucky to have for a while. Does this make sense?"

Is being a singer really as complicated as that? I never got a big head when I won a pageant or a dance competition. I can't imagine chang-

ing that much *if I ever hit it big. But it can't hurt to learn how to handle rejection*...I shrug. "You guys have way more experience, so I'm willing to give it a try. And if it helps me not be so nervous every time I go on stage that can't be a bad thing, right?"

Serena smiles and nods. "Good. We're just trying to protect you. Once you are out there with your first song, it's going to be nonstop for a long time. We want to prepare you for that."

I smile. "Thanks."

Serena gives me a hug. "Our time is almost up. Let me give you your homework for tonight."

33

Hours later, I'm finally back in my room, music softly playing and fireplace quietly flickering. I spent the remainder of my time with Serena looking at myself in the mirror doing what she called "learning my face." I don't get it, and I feel weird staring at myself, but I hope one day to understand what Serena's trying to teach me.

After dinner, Martin and I spent two hours watching Jenner's video clip reel. I couldn't stop laughing at the falls, fashion faux pas and verbal meltdowns of pop stars past, despite Martin's best efforts to get me to see how small mistakes were huge dents in public image. Seeing as I was too tired to absorb anything after such a long day, Martin shut off the video and sent me up to rest.

I'm in the bathroom, staring at my reflection. I have another fifteen minutes of "mirror time" before my homework for Serena is complete. My mind keeps wandering. I can't wait to call Sean. I hope Jenner will relax the "four-week rule" and let me see Sean soon. This first day seems so long already; I don't think I'll last a month without seeing him. I imagine his arms wrapped around me and I smile, noticing a far-away, dreamy look entering my eyes. So *that's what I look like when I think of Sean.* My cell rings. Without taking my eyes off my face, I answer.

"Hello?"

"Hey, how was your first day?" Sean's deep voice sends a thrill over my body. My smile widens, and I see myself blush.

"Amazing and crazy. I'm doing my homework right now."

"Homework? I thought you were taking a break from classes?" It feels so good to hear his voice. It's the first time all day I've felt utterly calm and safe.

"Not that kind of homework. I'm looking in the mirror, trying to 'learn my face.'"

Sean laughs. "Huh? Are you serious?"

I laugh, noticing how my eyes pleasantly crinkle and my teeth flash. "Yup. I've got, uh, ten minutes left. Weird, huh?"

Sean laughs again. "Here I am studying for an algebra test, and there you are getting paid to look at your gorgeous face. I don't think you're doing half as good a job as I'd be doing. Maybe I'd better come over there and do your homework for you. Nothing I'd rather do right now than spend ten minutes staring at you."

I watch a blush creep up from my neck, covering my entire face in red. "I wish you could! But I'd probably fall asleep before you got here."

Sean sighs. "Yeah, I know, it's late. And I have to finish this up so I don't fail tomorrow. I've been so distracted with you leaving that I haven't been able to study. I miss you so much, D."

I start to tear up. "Yeah, I miss you, too. I was so busy today that the one hour I had free—nap time—I tried to text you and fell asleep before I finished."

Sean laughs. "Nap time? What are you, five years old? What else are you doing there besides looking in the mirror and napping? Sandbox? Play-Doh?"

I roll my eyes, noticing my face harden with frustration. "It's not like that. In fact, if they hadn't scheduled a nap, I wouldn't have made it through the rest of the day. I was up at 6:00, I trained at the gym, then I sang for more than two hours for this famous songwriter who was a total jerk, I had dance rehearsal, we studied video clips and now I'm doing homework. I know it all sounds stupid, but I'm busy non-stop."

"I didn't mean to give you a hard time. Your day sounds pretty intense. It's just hard to understand what you're doing all day. I guess I felt a little left out."

I'm totally irked, but I don't want to spend what little time we have on the phone fighting. "Well, it sounds like you need a nap, too, Mr. Crankypants."

Sean laughs. "Yeah, maybe I do. I just miss you, that's all. Guess I'm not handling it very well."

I sigh. "It's OK. I'm sorry I'm putting you through this. How was your day?"

"The usual. Lots of tests this week, so everyone's stressed. Coach ran us ragged in practice. Oh, and you'll love this. Now that you're gone, guess who my new lab partner is? Zoe! She's driving me crazy. She has it in her head we have to enter the state science fair, which would mean a whole lot more work after school and on weekends. I don't want to do it, but she won't leave me alone."

Every muscle in my body tenses up, and I feel like I'm going to be sick. *I've only been gone forty-eight hours and already Zoe is making a move on Sean? What a bitch!* I abandon the mirror and fling myself onto the couch.

"Zoe is your new lab partner? How's that even possible? She's partnered up with one of the minions."

Sean exhales. "I don't know...something about her partner working on a solo project for the state science fair and not needing lab credits. Zoe was now a single and so was I...it just happened. You know it's not a big deal on my end, right?"

"I know you'd never fall for her, but I don't trust her. God, I wish I weren't stuck here!"

"Hey, you're there for a short time for an incredible reason. I'm Team Dani all the way. Don't waste your time worrying about me. I think I can handle spending a little time with Zoe in the lab and remain one hundred percent loyal to my favorite girl, OK?"

I take a deep breath and exhale. "OK. I just love you so much, and I don't know what I'd do without you." I freeze. OMG. *Did I just tell Sean that I love him?* That's a first! I hold my breath and wait.

"Well, I'm glad to hear it. I've been kicking myself ever since you left for not telling you that I love you. You *definitely* have nothing to worry about. Our love can't be harmed by Zoe's little reindeer games."

I'm so happy I'm flying! I sigh, staring at the fire. A few moments pass in silence.

"Dani?" Sean murmurs.

I smile into the phone. "Yes?"

"Just wanted to make sure you're still there. You OK?"

"Absolutely OK now. Just a little tired. It's been a crazy day."

"Well, get some rest. I've got a couple of hours of studying left to do. Will tomorrow be as crazy as today?"

I shrug. "I haven't seen the schedule yet, but I'm guessing every day is going to be intense. My first songs should be ready for recording in a few weeks."

"Wow. I can't wait to hear you on the radio. And I can't wait to start bragging about you to anyone who'll listen. I'm so proud of you, D."

I close my eyes and smile. And I start to drift off. "Thanks, Sean. I love you. And I miss you."

"Love you too, Dani. Sweet dreams."

"Umm, mmm," I mumble, falling asleep.

34

The next morning, Martin gently prods me awake. I slowly open my eyes and realize I'm curled up on the couch, the fireplace still blazing. Martin sets a mug of tea down on the coffee table and shuts off the fireplace.

"You didn't even make it to bed last night. I guess you were pretty worn out." I stretch like a cat and then slowly smile.

"I was doing my homework when Sean called." I give Martin an expectant look and wait a few seconds. "I accidentally told him that I loved him. It just slipped out! And he told me he loved me too! Can you believe it!? I'm so happy."

I sit up and reach for the steaming mug.

Martin smiles. "That's great, honey. I'm happy for you guys."

I grin back. "Yeah, me too." But then I grimace. "Oh God, I forgot to mention that Zoe is now Sean's lab partner. She didn't wait long before making a move on him."

Martin looks confused. "Wait, I thought you two were happy and in love and everything was just peachy. Why are you worried about tired, old Zoe? Even if you're not there, you guys just took the next step by saying, 'I love you.' What am I missing?"

I roll my eyes again. "Only everything! I *know* Sean loves me and he'd never do anything to hurt me. But come on, Martin. Zoe jumped into action the second I was gone. First, they become lab partners, which isn't the end of the world, but she's also pushing him to do a bunch of extra science fair crap. What if something happens?"

Martin holds up a hand. "You just said you know Sean loves you and he would never hurt you. So, no matter what Zoe orchestrates Sean isn't going to fall for it, right? That's how love works."

I shake my head, frustrated. "But what if he gets lonely? And Zoe's always there, everywhere he turns, constantly fawning all over him. Don't you think he's eventually going to give in and take her up on it?"

Martin shakes his head. "Sweetie, if you truly love each other, even Gigi Hadid in a bikini isn't going to distract Sean. Love isn't about physical proximity. It's about no one else in the world being the person you love. Distance, bad moods, weight gain, arguments; *nothing* on the planet will stop you from loving that person. You have to trust that Sean will put you first and foremost above every woman, including Zoe. If not, it doesn't mean he doesn't care for you or have deep feelings for you," Martin pats my knee, "but it's not really love. It's hard to tell the difference when you're so young. Like Serena said, everything is so intense and black and white right now for you. All you can do is trust in what you feel for each other and not worry if or when he is going to get with Zoe. Because if he does get with her, it was never love."

Hurt and anger pulse through me and I jump up, sloshing my tea on the floor. "I'm so *sick* of people treating me like a child. In the past twenty-four hours, I've been treated like a bratty toddler by Terrance and you and Serena have told me I'm too young to see the world as it is because all can see is black and white. My feelings for Sean are *real*. Everyone's so quick to write me off as a kid who knows nothing, but everyone's pretty eager to cash in on what this kid can do. I'm over it already!"

Martin holds up his hands in surrender. "I'm sorry, sweetie. I wasn't implying that your feelings for Sean aren't real. I was trying to give you a little relationship advice, and it very clearly backfired. I'm going to step away. I'll see you downstairs when you're ready."

Martin starts to walk out but turns when he reaches the door. "Just remember that you want this success just as much as we all want it for you. The minute you start seeing us as the enemy, everything will fall apart. Please remember we're all on the same team."

Martin leaves and I burst into tears. *I can't believe I just yelled at Martin! It just pissed me off that he didn't seem to take Sean and my feelings seriously.* But as my anger fades, I'm left with a guilty feeling in the pit of my stomach because I know deep down what he's saying is true. *Only time will tell if what Sean and I have is real. But by saying that, somehow it makes things seem less romantic, less ideal. Because if it is true love, do you have to wait and see if it really is?*

My weeping subsides and I'm disheartened at how drained I feel before the day has even begun. I drag myself into the shower, hoping the stream of water will turn my mood around. I feel somewhat better by the time I'm dressed. My outrage over Martin's words is replaced by regret for yelling at him. I enter the kitchen and sit down at the island next to Martin. Magda places an egg white omelet and mug of tea before me. I give her a shaky smile and look away. "I'm not hungry," I say quietly, pushing the plate away. Magda notes the tension and leaves the kitchen.

Martin shrugs and says in an even voice, "I can't make you eat it, but we've got another packed day ahead. You might find it hard to concentrate on an empty stomach."

I pull my plate closer and begin to pick at it, avoiding looking at Martin. I finally work up the courage to speak. "Martin, I'm sorry I yelled at you. I know you're only trying to help." Tears slide down my cheeks as I continue to look down, talking to my plate. "I'm scared it might not be love for him. Because even though I really can't imagine him ever hurting me, I can still somehow see him doing it. Not out of meanness, but because I'm gone. I'm so scared I'm going to lose him."

Martin picks up my hand and squeezes it. "I wish there was something I could say to make you feel better. I'm here if you need me, honey."

I nod and continue to stare at my plate. Martin continues making notes in his folder. Eventually, he puts it in his bag. "Shall we get started?"

I nod and follow Martin outside to the golf cart. I'm about to more or less relive yesterday.

35

Day Two rolls into Days Three, Four and beyond, blending into a blur of routine. Up early, training sessions, voice lessons, dance, and stage-presence lessons, endless video clip watching interspersed with healthy meals, snacks, and naps. Before I know it, three weeks have passed.

I try my best to text or call Sean, Lauren, and Geena as much as I can, but in the end, exhaustion usually wins out. More often than not, I fall asleep on the phone or in mid-text. I feel disconnected from the people I love. I'm plagued with anxiety about Sean, agonizing whether something is happening between him and Zoe, my worries easing only on the rare occasion that we're able to talk. I try my best to keep my fears to myself because I don't want to waste the short time we get to talk nagging Sean.

Lauren is a lifesaver. She keeps me updated on what's happening at school and talks me off the ledge when my worries get the best of me. Lauren feels Zoe isn't a threat at all, and that Sean's being a picture-perfect, loyal boyfriend.

Geena keeps me posted on things at home and reports that Mom has lightened up a bit since I left. The fire seems to have gone out of Mom. She and Dad fight a lot less and spend more time running errands together and watching TV on the couch. I'm sorry I had to leave home for my parents to get along. Geena also helps coordinate my calls home so I'm able to leave a voicemail rather than having to talk to my parents. *I know. I'm the worst. I should just stop being a chicken and call my parents.* While I really miss my dad, I just don't have the energy to deal with my mom these days, even if she might have changed for the better.

The biggest surprise is a photo Geena texts of her posing with our grandmother, both with their thumbs up and big grins. Geena's been keeping her up to date on what I'm doing here at the compound. I'd hoped we would have talked on the phone by now, but it's such a huge call to make, and I just haven't had the time. And maybe, if I'm totally honest, I've been avoiding it, too. I feel awful for not realizing that my mom was keeping us apart, and I have no excuse for not reaching out to her before now. But putting it off isn't making me feel any better, so sooner or later, I'm just going to have to bite the bullet and make that call. *Ugh!*

My relationship with Martin was strained for a couple of days after my blowup. But as the weeks pass and we concentrate on our packed daily schedule, things soon return to normal.

Saturday morning rolls around and I'm up early, staring at the ceiling when Martin comes in to wake me. He looks up too. "See anything interesting?"

I shake my head. "Nope. But my days have been so hectic lately, any time I can veg out is gold."

Martin nods. "Makes sense."

I sigh and sit up, forcing a smile. "What's today at the compound look like? More video clips, a five-mile run on the beach? High colonic?"

Martin gives me a look. "Aren't we cynical so early in the morning? Has it gotten to you already?"

I shake my head. "Sorry, I guess I'm going a little stir crazy. Doing the same thing every day...it's a lot."

Martin nods. "I know. But we're going to be mixing it up soon. Once Terrance finishes your songs, it's into the studio to record, choreograph your dance routines and decide on costumes, makeup and hair. And then the fun begins, with live performances, interviews and travel. Enjoy the monotony now because soon every day will be a crazy train of unpredictability, and you'll be craving a little mundane repetition."

I shake my head again and smile. "Promises, promises...seriously, what's scheduled for today?"

Martin pretends to clean his nails. "You know I had planned a little surprise for you for today, but you're being so squirrelly that I just don't know if you deserve it."

My curiosity is piqued. "What surprise?"

Martin pauses, relishing the moment. "Well, I thought you might want to see Lauren, Geena and, uh, what's that guy's name? John, Ron..."

I jump on the bed. "*Sean!* Sean's coming here? *Today?*"

Martin laughs. "Yeah, I called your sister earlier this week. They're all driving out to spend the day with you. They'll be here around eleven."

I hug Martin, practically knocking him over. He smiles. "So, I take it that's OK with you?"

I nod vigorously. "Oh, thank you, thank you, thank you! I can't thank you enough. I really need this."

"I know you do, honey. I hate to see you get so down. I know it's hard to miss out on things at home, but it's a small price to pay for what you're going to get. So, no schedule or diet today. Magda's making her deluxe BBQ spread, complete with her world-famous chocolate layer cake. Let's get a quick workout in before they get here, and then you are off duty for the next forty-eight hours."

I let out a whoop as I jump off the bed. "Come on! I want to be ready when they get here."

Martin laughs. "We've got five hours, so I think we'll be fine, but I love your enthusiasm. See you downstairs."

36

I'm sitting on the top step, watching the driveway. I have gulped down my breakfast, raced through my workout, showered and rushed outside to wait for my friends. I'm beside myself with excitement. I tried to thank Jenner for giving me the day off, but I've barely seen him all week. He's been hunkered down in his office, planning everything down to the last detail.

I hear the gate open and leap up. Sean's car doesn't even come to a full stop before Lauren hops out of the backseat and tackles me. We jump up and down, screaming like crazy. Even normally reserved Geena runs over and joins in the melee, squeezing me tight.

"It's so good to see you, sis! Home just isn't the same without you. Though living here," she nods toward the mansion, "I don't think I'd ever move back."

I beam at Geena, "I'm so happy you're here. Thanks for coming. And for not bringing Mom. I feel kinda bad saying that, but I just really want to enjoy my day, stress-free."

"Believe it or not, when Martin suggested that it should just be us kids, Mom didn't put up a fight. I'm telling you, it's downright strange. I can't decide if she's lost her will to live or if she is just conserving her energy for some diabolical scheme." Geena shrugs. "Doesn't matter today, though." She puts her hand to her ear, "I hear the pool calling my name."

Sean has finished parking the car and comes over just as Geena leaves to get her bag. He sweeps me up in a hug and spins me around. I bury my face in his neck and inhale his scent so deeply it makes me dizzy. He's just what I've been missing, and I feel so happy I just might burst. He puts me down and gives me a deep kiss. We stay locked in an embrace until Geena slams the car door. Startled, we separate and giggle.

Geena smiles. "Now I know you're all excited to see each other, but can you wait for a bit before you maul each other? Lauren and I plan on sitting out by the pool so you lovebirds can have a little time alone later."

I laugh and nod. "Sure. It just feels like it's been such a long time since I've seen you guys."

Geena laughs. "It has, but I'll pass on a greeting like that."

***

We decamp to the pool. Magda has a spread of fruit, salads and iced teas on one of the shaded tables, and she's warming up the grill. Music pumps from the speakers and Anatoli is placing a few large pool floats in the water. Jenner's locked away in his office working and Martin's gone back to the gym to get in some more reps with Brett. We have the whole place to ourselves.

They look around, amazed. "I can't believe you get to live here every day," Lauren marvels. "You are so damned lucky, girl! If you weren't my best friend, I'd be so jelly!"

I shrug. "It's not like I'm laying out every day. Martin and Jenner keep me on a pretty tight schedule. I'm just grateful we can share it together. Almost makes being apart worth it."

Sean grabs my hand and gives it a squeeze. "Almost," he whispers, giving me goosebumps.

Meanwhile, Geena strips down to her bathing suit and takes a running leap into the pool. "Cannonball!" We take off our coverups and shirts and follow her in.

I'm positively giddy. We play Marco Polo, have chicken fights, sing along with the music and float in the pool. Geena drifts over to me, her big, pink, unicorn float bumping into my swan. "Do you think this is what it feels like to be an adult?"

I smile. "Umm, if you're a millionaire maybe."

Geena concedes. "Yeah, the mansion, servants, etc. Of course, that's all cool. But I meant just the four of us, hanging out on a Saturday, no one micromanaging us. I feel so free, you know?" Geena marvels. "I'm doing a horrible job describing what I mean...I don't think I'll ever forget this day."

I grab my sister's hand. "Me either. I'm so happy you're here. It's been really lonely, and everything's changed so much. I miss you guys, school, Dad..."

Geena chimes in, "Mom?"

I think. "Um, maybe a little. Not the nagging or fighting, but she's Mom. It's kinda scary when you leave all that and you're out on your own. Liberating, but scary."

Geena squeezes my hand. "Sis, you're living a whole new life. I'm so proud of you. Just try to enjoy the ride and don't worry too much about what's happening at home. We're all fine. Grandma, too. She sends her love and wants to set up that call soon."

I grimace. "I know, I need to call her. It just seems so huge, you know? I don't even know what to say." I shake my head, frustrated, "I just keep putting it off."

Geena gives me a level stare and says nothing, which makes me squirm.

Finally, I cave. "OK! Call me next time you're together." I give her a sheepish smile and turn my attention to watch Sean and Lauren hit a volleyball back and forth. Geena catches me. "How's it going being away from Sean?"

I shake my head and groan. "It's awful. I miss him so much. I'm so worried about the whole Zoe thing. I know Sean would never do any-thing with her, but still...if she keeps flinging herself at him and I'm not there, who knows what can happen in a moment of weakness? It's all I can think about sometimes. It's making me crazy."

Geena thinks for a few moments. "Honest answer: If you could go home right now, leave all this behind and just be with Sean, would you give it up?"

I don't even think about my answer—it just flies out of my mouth. "*God, no!* I've been working for this my whole life. There's no way."

Geena shrugs. "That's your answer then. You have to live your life and he has to live his. I know it's not easy for him to have you here and not be able to talk to you or know what you're doing. Heck, at least you know all the characters he's hanging around with. Who knows who's coming to this mansion to hang out with you?"

I almost fall off my floatie, shocked. "No one!"

Geena waves her hand. "*You* know there's no one, but *he* doesn't. And when he doesn't hear from you every day, trust me, his imagination can be just as active as yours. Just remember why you're here…not to be Sean's girlfriend but to chase your dream. I'm not saying you can't do both. But one shouldn't prevent you from doing the other."

I frown, mulling over Geena's words.

"You're not mad at me for saying that, are you, sis? I just want to make sure you're appreciating what's happening here, and that you aren't getting distracted by things at home."

I finally nod slowly. "I'm just so scared everything's going to change. I love him so much. He's everything to me."

Geena reaches for my hand and gives it another squeeze. "If he was everything to you, D, you wouldn't be here."

I stare at Geena, my eyes filling with tears. She continues, "It doesn't mean you can't have both, but please don't give up on what Jenner's doing for you because of Sean. It's too important. You're too close."

Geena gives my hand a final squeeze and slips into the water. My head starts to spin. First Martin and now Geena. But unlike Martin, who called into question the sincerity of our feelings, Geena simply described reality. I'm not willing to leave here to be with Sean, so what does that ultimately say about *my* feelings? *Is it really love after all?* I stare at the water, unseeing, as thoughts swirl in my head. Lost in thought, I don't see Sean swim up.

"Hey, you." He gives my leg a playful nudge. "You OK?" I snap out of my thoughts and stare at Sean, my heart aching. *What's wrong with me? Why isn't he enough?* I nod quietly and smile.

"Magda said burgers are on. Race you to the table." He flashes me a gorgeous smile and I grab his face, kissing him deeply. We separate and he smiles. "Love you."

"Love you, too," I whisper hoarsely as I slide off my float and race Sean to lunch.

37

We scarf down everything in sight, including the decadent cake. Lauren and Geena nap in the sun while Sean and I steal up to my room to be alone. Snuggling on the sofa, we make up for three weeks of being apart. Music plays softly in the background as we lose track of time, exploring each other's bodies and whispering how much we've missed each other.

It feels so good I don't want to stop but, in the back of my mind, I know I'm not prepared to go any further with Sean. I want to keep going—my entire body is vibrating like crazy—though I know I won't be able to handle the emotions once he's gone. I pull away and shake my head, trying to catch my breath.

"Can we just slow down for a sec?" I stare at Sean, worried. He's never pushed me to do anything that I didn't want to do. Then again, we've never been alone for this long before, partially undressed, with no parental supervision in sight.

He closes his eyes and takes a deep breath, shuddering. "Yeah, of course. Sorry if I got a little carried away. You OK?"

He caresses my shoulder as I lay my head on his chest, nodding, relieved. "Yeah, I'm fine. I just don't want to go too far right now, you know?"

I feel Sean nod back. "Yeah, I know. It'd be hard if we kept going then couldn't see each other for another few weeks. It'd really mess with my head." Sean plays with my hair and quietly kisses the top of my head.

I'm thinking of the conversation I had earlier with Geena as I run my finger along his chest, tracing his tanned muscles. We lie in silence for a while. Sean squeezes my shoulder. "Are you *sure* you're OK? You're awfully quiet."

I shrug. "I don't know...I had a conversation with Geena that kind of made me sad." I sit up and face Sean. "She said that if I really wanted to be with you, I'd come home and the fact that I'm choosing to stay here says a lot about how I feel about you. She's concerned that I'm spending too much time missing you or worrying about Zoe and not enough time focusing on my training. She doesn't want me to blow my chance." I look up at Sean tearfully. "I really want to do this, you know? But it doesn't mean I don't love you. I'm worried that you're going to get tired of waiting for me, and that stupid Zoe is going to catch you in a moment of weakness."

I hide my face in my hands and start to bawl. Sean leans over and pulls me into his arms, shushing me and stroking my hair. "You've been dealing with this the whole time and you never said anything? Come on, Dani, you know you can tell me anything. I love you!"

My crying starts to subside. Sean grabs his shirt off the floor and wipes my eyes. "You're not the only one feeling insecure. I'm living the same boring life. You know exactly where I am most of the time and what I'm doing without even talking to me. You're going to live this amazing celebrity life while I'm still stuck at home. I didn't say anything because I didn't want to be the jealous high school idiot holding you back. Hell yeah, I miss you! School and my whole life sucks without you. But I'm not that desperate that I'd replace you with Zoe, no matter how hard she tries."

Scared, I look up and Sean nods. "And yes, Zoe has tried. Repeatedly. I didn't want to worry you, but maybe not talking about it has made it worse." Sean shakes his head, annoyed. "She's always hovering and trying to insert herself into my life, but like I've said before: I'm not stupid and I'm not going to fall for her." He shrugs. "I miss you like crazy, D. I cannot wait for this to be over so we can see each other more."

We sit in silence, taking it all in. "So, what do we do now?" I ask. Sean crosses his arms and thinks for a few moments. "Well, first off, we're not waiting three weeks to see each other again. We'll call and text, too. Even knowing the other person might not be able to pick up. We just have to try harder."

I nod. "But what about when I go away? I'm scheduled to travel soon. I could be gone for months."

Sean shrugs. "By that time, you should be able to demand some time to call or see me. I'll do what I can on my end, though I don't have much money to travel. We'll figure it out."

I bite my lip hesitantly, scared to ask the obvious question. "Do you think we can make it?"

Sean looks at me and gives me a sad smile, caressing my damp cheek. "If I didn't think we could make it, I wouldn't be here. You mean the world to me."

I wrap arms around him and give him a hug. Sean laughs. "You know, I can't carry a tune, but I've got some killer dance moves."

I smile. "Done. You're my first backup dancer hire." I lean in for a kiss and whisper, "I feel better, but I'm still worried."

Sean nods. "Me too." He sighs, "I guess that's just because we love each other so much."

We sit quietly for a few minutes when the intercom buzzes. Lauren's voice bursts into the room, "OK, you two. Get dressed and meet us down here for a bonfire and s'mores."

We share one last, long kiss before we change our clothes and head downstairs.

38

I go for a long walk with Lauren while Sean and Geena help Anatoli get the bonfire going. We fall into our old rhythm of talking, finishing each other's sentences. I tell her about my talks with Geena and Sean. Like the best friend she is, she just listens, knowing I'm maxed out on deep conversations for one day.

Later, we eat hot dogs and s'mores while we gaze at the stars and talk about everything and nothing, just like we used to. They all encourage me to see my parents, saying that I'll eventually need to get it over with.

D: Hi! Know it's last-minute, but R U & Mom free 4 brunch tomorrow?

Seconds later my dad pings me back.

Dad: Yes!!! We'd love to see you! We miss you so much. What time should we be there?

His excitement makes me feel awful. I have been a brat for not reaching out sooner.

D: 11?

Dad: Perfect. See you then. Love you, Marie.

My relief at finally reaching out to my parents is mixed with guilt that I've put it off for so long. While my dad seems super excited to see me, I'm worried about how my mom will react. I try to shove all my worries to the back of my mind and enjoy the little time I have left with my friends instead.

The smell of the bonfire still clings to my hair as I snuggle down into bed. It's just past eleven when Sean, Geena and Lauren leave. I'm exhilarated and exhausted. And I'm much less anxious about things back home.

I drift off to sleep feeling happier and more secure than I have in weeks. My worries are still there, but I feel assured that my friends have my back.

On Sunday, it's almost 9:00 a.m. when I wake up and bolt out of bed. My parents are due at eleven, and I haven't told anyone yet. I race downstairs to find Martin and Magda in the kitchen. Before I can begin, Martin hands me a mug of tea. "Morning, sleepyhead! Geena texted me last night, and Magda's already preparing brunch for your parents. So, take a deep breath and have some tea." Relieved, I plunk down next to Martin at the island. He asks, "Did you have fun yesterday?"

I beam and lean over to hug him. "It was the best day ever and exactly what I needed. Thank you so much for planning it! I'm so happy I got to see them. I feel so much better about Sean now. I caught up with everyone, and I just feel like I've got a better grip on things, you know?" I pause to sip my tea. "They made me realize that I need to see my parents. I've probably just been building it up in my head. I just need to get over it and see them already."

Martin laughs and smiles. "I haven't heard you talk this much in a while, so you must be feeling better! Sounds like it was just what you needed to get back on track and get your head back into the game." He reaches over and gives me a quick hug, patting my arm as he sits back.

"And that is definitely where you need to be because we're starting to get serious as of today." Jenner's booming voice takes us by surprise as he enters the kitchen, helping himself to a cup of coffee. It's been at least two weeks since I've seen Jenner in person. He's lost some weight in that short time. He looks tan but tired. "How you doing, darlin'? I hear Martin organized a day of fun for you and your friends. I'm glad to hear it. I'm told you've been working like an ox these past few weeks. You deserved a break." He browses the tray of fruit on the counter as he speaks and, deciding against it, takes a deep sip of his coffee. "I apologize for being so scarce lately, but I've been setting up your schedule. Starting in a few days, you're going to be a very busy young lady."

I nod, taking a deep breath before I smile. Jenner continues. "I spoke with Terrance last night and he's headed over this afternoon with some songs he thinks we'll be very happy with. If all goes well, we'll have you in the studio next week recording your first single."

My jaw drops. "*Next week?* Isn't that kind of fast? I mean, I haven't even heard the songs yet."

Jenner shrugs, unconcerned. "Come now, Dani, you've been singing and performing all your life. Time is money, and every day we're not producing is costing us. Frankly, if you're not ready now, you'll never be ready. We might as well find that out now."

I flinch at Jenner's curt tone. Out of the corner of my eye, I catch Martin giving Jenner a look, making a "slow down" motion with his hands. Jenner takes a deep breath and continues in a gentler tone. "I know it seems fast, but sometimes that's how things work in this business. You have to be ready to go at any time. I suggest you squeeze in some more vocal sessions to boost your confidence and just try to relax. Martin's been through this all before; he'll talk you through it."

Jenner looks at Martin who nods, acknowledging Jenner's effort. Jenner snorts and leaves wordlessly.

The thought of recording stuns me, making my breathing ragged. Martin turns, looking straight into my eyes, but I don't even see him. My heart is racing but beating at a snail's pace all at the same time as panic overtakes me. I feel as if I'm peering over a towering cliff, millimeters from the edge.

"Take a deep breath," Martin orders and I do, slowly regaining control of my breathing. I force myself to focus on his eyes, seeing the love and determination in them.

"I know Jenner can come on strong, but he's got a point. You've been working your whole life for this. You don't need more lessons or more rehearsals. You need to get your butt into the studio. Lay down those tracks, let's get them mixed and polished by the best in the business, then see if people want to buy what you're selling. You've got this, girl; I keep telling you. I wish you'd believe me."

I remain motionless, staring at Martin, still panicked.

"When are *you* going to start believing in you, Dani? If you don't start fighting for yourself, we're all going to lose out on this golden opportunity. You're going to regret it for the rest of your life if you don't."

That is the word that makes me snap out of it. "Regret." I picture my mother: bitter, nagging and always clawing for the chances she feels she never had. *My mother's life is fueled by regret, and that's the thought that turns my blood cold. I will not be like my mother, torturing those I love because I feel I've lost my chance in life.* I nod at Martin. "I'm ready, Martin! I'm ready to start fighting."

"YES!" Martin yells as he slaps the counter with his hand. "Finally! Alright, let's get this brunch going. This afternoon, you and I are going to hear the hits Terrance has created for you. Let's get this done!"

39

I'm pulling a brush through my hair when the doorbell rings. I say a silent prayer and head downstairs. My dad sweeps me up in a crushing hug before my foot even reaches the last step. I melt into the hug and squeeze him back. I can feel myself smiling when he puts me down.

My dad just stares at me. "It's so good to see you, Marie! I know it's only been a few weeks, but I swear you've grown! It's not the same at home without you there."

I smile. "It's good to see you too, Dad. I'm glad you came." My mom stands by the door, clutching the strap of her purse with all her might. She seems so tightly wound. "Hi Mom, it's nice to see you."

She plasters a plastic smile onto her face. "Hi, honey! You look great."

There's an odd pause, and I walk over and give her a hug. After a few stilted pats, we separate, and Mom turns as Martin appears from the kitchen.

"Jodi, Don! Great to see you. Thanks for making the drive over. I know those canyons are always a mess of traffic on Sundays." He gives my dad a manly, backslapping hug and, reading my mom's standoffish posture, he simply nods and smiles. "I can't imagine how hard it's been on you two not to be in contact with Dani these past few weeks. But she's been putting in tremendous work. I appreciate your letting her focus on her preparations. You'll be happy to know that we head into the studio next week to start recording her first single!" Martin claps his hands for emphasis, and I snort, reminded of Brett. A sly smile spreads across my face and I clap loudly, which startles Martin. Before I can explain the joke, the moment is lost in my parents' excitement as my dad sweeps me up for another hug. My mom grows animated and seems to thaw out at the news.

She childishly hops up and down. "So, basically, this time next year Dani could be a millionaire? If people love her album?"

Martin chuckles and sighs. "Yes, Jodi, Dani will be one very wealthy young lady when her album takes off. And we'll all be happy for her as we watch her trust fund grow with the money she's worked so hard for."

My mom pauses, and we can all follow her train of thought. Her face falls as she remembers that she won't get any money from my success. Anger flashes across my mind, and I feel like we're right back where we were when I moved out.

Before I can open my mouth, Martin gestures toward the terrace and says brightly, "Why don't we have a seat outside and we can celebrate Dani's impending success over lunch. I don't know about you, but I'm starving!"

***

Dad and Martin work to keep up a steady stream of conversation throughout brunch. Martin tries to lure me into the conversation, but I'm struggling with my anger and find it hard to participate. Mom has a hard smile on her face throughout the meal and her comments are limited to "oh" and "how interesting."

As soon as our brunch plates are taken away, Martin hops up from the table. "I'm going to leave you to catch up. I have a few calls to make, and I want to hit the gym before Terrance gets here."

"Hit the gym?" I give Martin a suspicious look. "You've been spending a lot of time in the gym lately. What gives?"

Martin smiles innocently, "I'm taking our challenge seriously. Instead of mooning around over my boyfriend or watching *Friends* in my spare time like someone I know, I'm putting in the sweat equity to win our little dance-off." He gives me a narrow-eyed glare. "Prepare to lose, Truehart."

He chuckles and explains it to my parents. "Dani and I have a little friendly bet as to whom can out dance whom before she goes on tour." He points at me. "Youthful confidence just might be your undoing, young lady." To my parents, he adds, "Don, Jodi, thanks again for coming out on such short notice."

Dad gets up to shake Martin's hand. Mom nods and smiles coldly, looking over Martin's shoulder. He continues, "On a more serious note, I hope you both understand that the next two weeks are very important for Dani. I'm going to ask that you let her focus on recording and wait to call her until she's finished. Would that be OK?"

Martin looks at them expectantly. Mom shrugs while Dad nods. "Well, it sure is hard not being able to talk to our little girl every day. But we know how close she is, and we don't want to stand in her way, do we, honey?"

Dad turns to Mom; Martin and I look her way, too. Mom pulls her eyes from the horizon and nods in agreement. "Of course not," she says dully, smiling at the end for emphasis. Martin smiles and leaves.

I stand up and go hug my dad. "Thank you. I'm sorry I didn't do a better job of staying in touch. I'll make more of an effort in the future. I just..."

Mom stands up so quickly, she practically knocks over her chair. "Is there a bathroom around here? I've had to go ever since we arrived. In all the excitement of seeing you, I forgot to ask." She smiles expectantly.

I shake my head. "Yeah, sure, Mom. It's to the left of the front door; you can't miss it."

She leaves and I shake my head again and stare at the ground. My dad puts his arm around me. "What I was trying to say was that I didn't call you back more these past few weeks because I..." I take a deep breath. "I guess I didn't know what to say."

Dad wells up, hugging me close. He gives me a kiss on top of my head. "I know, sugar. I thought about what you said. I understand how you might think that I didn't care very much, letting your mom run the show all these years. I'm sorry, I thought I was doing the right thing. You might think it was easy for me to let you go, but can you imagine what things would be like at home if I stood in the way of this opportunity? Believe me, when this whole popstar thing started, it never crossed my mind that I'd have to give up guardianship of my daughter. I hope one day you'll know that you would have been angry with me no matter what I'd done. Sometimes there are no good decisions, and I feel this was one of those times. At the very least, I wanted you to follow your dreams to the end and, hopefully, succeed."

I nod. "I never thought about it that way before." After a few minutes, I laugh. "Can you imagine how pissed Mom would have been if you hadn't signed those papers?"

Dad chuckles. "Oh, we'd have been in the news for sure over that." He sighs. "Well, darlin', just know we love you to bits. Even though she might not say it, your mom is very proud of you. She misses you like crazy. She just sits in your room, looking at all your things, cleaning and dusting just in case you stop by."

"I can't even imagine that." I tilt my head down the hall. "I mean, she runs out of the room at the first hint of me talking about my feelings. The only time she seemed remotely happy to see me today was when she thought I'd be rich soon. So, no, I can't imagine her missing me like you say she does."

"She's a tough nut to crack, your mom. I think she has a rough time seeing all the opportunities you have and knowing she never had a chance at the life you're going to have. Our getting pregnant so young really changed the paths our lives took."

I throw up my hands. "But it's not my fault she got pregnant! And I never asked to do all this in the first place. I was just a little kid who wanted to take tap. This was all her idea!" I shove my hands in my pockets. "I just wish she loved me for who I am. That's all I've ever wanted."

My dad stares down at me, listening and chewing his lip. "I know it'd mean more coming from her, but she does love you very much. I'm sorry she doesn't express it as well as she should, but you and Geena mean the world to her. Maybe if I let her know how you're feeling..."

"No! Dad, please don't. It'll only make things worse. You know every time someone says something that isn't positive, she takes it personally and gets all upset. Then she'll somehow turn it into something to be mad at me for, like I was bad mouthing her or something. You can't say anything to her. Promise me?" I stare at my dad, waiting.

He sighs, "All right, I promise. I won't say anything now, but if things don't improve between you two, I might have to step in. Can we agree on that?"

It's not what I want, but I know it's the best I'm going to get. I nod. "OK. Thanks, Dad."

Mom still hasn't returned, so we go to look for her. We find her just leaving the bathroom. "Oh, there you are," I say. "All finished?"

We nod and she gives us a strained smile. "Well, we should hit the road. I know you had a late night with your friends. I think you should probably get some rest before this afternoon."

"Your mom's right, Marie. You need your rest before you hear those new songs." He gives me a squeeze. "Should we say goodbye to Martin before we go?"

"He said he had a few calls to make, so I don't think we should disturb him," Mom chimes in. "Dani, you'll tell him goodbye and thank him for us? And Jenner, too. We didn't get a chance to see him today."

I nod. "Sure. And don't feel bad about Jenner. I've barely seen him lately."

She gives me a quick hug and says, "I guess this is goodbye for now. Give us a call when things calm down."

"Sounds good, Mom."

My dad sweeps me up again. "Love you, Marie." He gives me an extra squeeze and sets me down.

My heart is heavy as I watch them go. I love my dad so much; it's such an easy relationship. I want that same thing with my mother. I wonder if we'll ever get there. I sigh and pull out my phone. I don't have the energy to find Martin, so I text him that I'll be in my room until it's time to go to the studio. I trudge upstairs, my mind spinning from all the visitors I've had in the past forty-eight hours. I lie on my bed and fall asleep instantly.

40

I sleep hard for a couple of hours before Martin shakes me awake. I'm struggling to perk up, and I keep yawning every few minutes as we hop into the golf cart.

Martin hands me a travel mug of tea with one hand as he starts the cart with the other. "Drink up, little lady. I don't want you yawning your way through this first session. We don't want Terrance storming out because you're snoozing through his masterpieces."

I take a sip. "I know. I don't want to insult him any more than I already do just by being 'a child.'" I make air quotes around my travel mug and shake my head, annoyed. "How is it that I've met that guy one time and he already dislikes me so much?"

"That's just Terrance. You're going to meet a ton of people like him throughout your career. Don't take it personally. When you're very good at what you do, you'd be surprised at what people let you get away with. I'm sure once, long ago, Terrance was polite to strangers. Now he's so famous, he doesn't need to be polite anymore." Martin points a finger at me. "Just make sure that never happens to you. Everyone deserves respect. From the hotel maid to the sound engineer to the biggest producer—be respectful to all, and you won't have anything to worry about."

We pull into the studio just as I finish my tea. The caffeine starts kicking in, and I feel more alert.

"OK!" Martin claps his hands loudly. "Sermon over, let's get this started."

I stare at Martin and hold up a hand. "Wait just one minute. Are we not going to address the fact that you've picked up that annoying clapping habit from Brett? We used to roll every time he did it like he was some uptight schoolteacher. Now, all of a sudden, you're clapping all over the place like some psychotic audience member. And you're spending a ton of extra hours in the gym. That can't all be for our bet. What gives?"

Martin looks at me, surprised. "What, can't a guy clap for emphasis every once in a while?"

I raise my eyebrows and wait.

Martin shakes his head, caught. "Well, all right, maybe I do have the tiniest crush on Brett. I mean he's the only eligible man here... And we *might* have been spending a lot of time together in the gym where I *might* be going for some extra reps after hours."

I punch Martin in the arm. "Extra reps! My eye! You're only getting into such good shape to hang out with Brett." Then I cross my arms and lean in conspiratorially. "Really? Brett?"

I consider it. Ridiculously groomed hair and chipper attitude aside, I can see how Martin might go for Brett. He does have great energy and he can be quite funny when he isn't ordering us around the gym. I smile. "OK, I guess I can see it." I get serious and hold up a warning finger. "But don't let the wedding interfere with the tour. I'd hate to miss out on being a bridesmaid."

I laugh, grabbing my bag and Martin rolls his eyes. "You're not too old for me to put you over my knee and spank you; remember that. I *am* your guardian after all. I'm sure no judge would blame me for keeping your sass in line." Martin gives me the eye and bursts out laughing. "We can talk about my love life later. Let's get inside."

***

I've only been in the recording studio once, during the tour on my first day at the compound. It had been dark and closed up. Now, it's quietly buzzing with activity. Jenner is in the control room with a technician, having an intense conversation, their heads bent over the console. They look up when the door opens, daylight flashing over them through the glass partition. Jenner smiles and waves.

"They're recording this?" I ask. "I thought I was just running through the material today."

Martin nods. "Yeah, Jenner always likes to record the first pass at new songs. He'll give you a demo to listen to so you can learn the songs inside and out. Plus, he and Terrance will use it for reference to decide how they want the songs to be sung, what production they want on the final track, stuff like that. No biggie."

We see Terrance through a window, making notes while he plays a baby grand piano inside the live room where we'll record later. He nods at us briefly and returns to what he's doing. We stand around awkwardly, waiting for someone to make a move.

The studio seems much more inviting than the people in it. The lighting is dim, accented by coconut-and-vanilla-scented candles that are scattered about. A gas fire flickers in the waiting area where Martin and I stand among the oversized sofa and chairs and a fluffy throw rug. Two closed doors stand across from the fireplace, one leading to the booth and the other to the studio. Moody blue-and-purple lighting shines in the recording area where Terrance is working, making it appear like a stage waiting for a show to begin. The wood-and-stone-walled recording booth is illuminated with a warmer light, just bright enough for the engineer to see his board. The waiting room is lit from above by rope lighting that is hidden behind the molding near the ceiling and by a couple of lamps that cast an inviting glow.

The soundproof door to the control booth opens and Jenner comes out, his energy filling the small waiting room. "Excited, Dani? This is one of many big moments you're going to have over the next few months. Hearing your debut single for the first time is an amazing feeling. Just ask Martin." Jenner looks at Martin expectantly, his eyes piercing behind amber-tinted glasses.

Martin nods and smiles. "It's a great feeling. The beginning of the rollercoaster ride."

Jenner smiles. "Exactly! Let's get you inside so Terrance can walk you through the songs. After a while, we'll lay down a few demos so you can practice. Sound good? Any questions?"

I don't have any questions, but Jenner's already turning away before I can even nod.

We follow Jenner into the studio. The walls are lined with black acoustic tiles and the floors have a couple of intricately patterned rugs scattered about. The decorations are minimal, with the colored lights giving the small room most of its atmosphere. A large microphone stand and a wooden stool are next to the piano.

Terrance looks up as we enter the room. "Ready to get started?"

Jenner answers before I can open my mouth. "Yes. Ryan and I just worked out the levels based on what you played earlier. Why don't you play it a couple of times for Dani, then let's go over any questions before we record."

Jenner looks around. "All right?" Jenner and Martin turn to leave. My stomach clenches.

I grab Martin's wrist and whisper, "Where are you going? I thought you'd be in here with me."

Martin shakes his head. "No, honey. Jenner has a rule that no one aside from the person performing can be in the studio during a recording. I'll be in the booth if you need me, right on the other side of that window. I'll be able to talk to you on the intercom, OK?"

I glance at the booth and back at Martin, who gives me an encouraging squeeze. "You've got this, girl. Just listen to Terrance. He won't steer you wrong." Martin hurries out.

"Hello, Dani." Terrance finally acknowledges me. "I've brought several options for you today. This one's a ballad." Terrance hands me several sheets of music without making eye contact. "I'm still tweaking it a bit, but it is ninety percent finished. I need to hear how you sing it before we can know for sure if this is the final version. Take a few minutes to look it over."

The song is called "Without You" and, as I read through it, the raw words and musical phrasing give me goosebumps. I can't decide if it's a song about a broken heart, loneliness or loss, but the feeling of emotional devastation is clear throughout the song and hits me at my core. I look up from the pages and find Terrance intently staring at me.

Terrance nods and almost smiles. "You get it. I can tell you get the emotion of what I'm saying."

I slowly nod. "It's incredible, but is it about a relationship that's over or someone dying? I can't really tell."

Now Terrance really smiles. "And that, Dani, is what makes a good song. It's about whatever you need it to be about. Death, loss, heartbreak—all of those emotions that can tear apart your heart and your world, leaving you broken. If you make a song too specific, then not everyone can relate to it. But a song based on pure emotion, well, more people can feel it. So, if you've just broken up with your boyfriend, your wife died, you lost a dog or didn't make the cheer squad, this song will move you all the same."

Terrance beams talking about the writing process, and I see him in a new light. "I always thought songs were about something specific. How do you even come up with something like this?"

Terrance shrugs. "Most songs are about definite things which do well with certain groups at certain times. But it's the songs that *haunt* you or the songs that fire you up no matter what...those are the ones that last. That's what we're going for. Staying power. And I'll never tell you how I do it, or I'd be out of a job."

He plays a quick chord on the piano. "OK, let's run through it. Music first, then you, Dani. Let's see what you've got. Ready, Jenner?"

With a thumbs-up from the booth, Terrance begins to play.

4I

My nerves fade as Terrance plays through the song for the first time, and I watch his usually sour and pinched face relax into a more peaceful expression. I'm swept up by the vibration of the piano and the arrangement of notes. Reading the words as Terrance plays, I feel the song settle around me as if I'm becoming a part of it. I feel my way through the song at first, singing quietly. The more I hear the song, the bolder I sing. I gather up all my anger, insecurity and guilt of the past few weeks and shove them deep into the music, releasing every negative emotion I've been saddled with since I found out I'd be auditioning for Jenner. I feel empowered, finding the lyrics pouring out of me as Terrance plays the tune. I connect with the music on such a level I feel there is no age or experience difference between myself and Terrance. We're just two people in the music together.

Jenner lets us go over the song several times, snapping a few pictures with his phone before he jumps on the intercom and gives us a few notes. Everyone seems to have changed during the first few run-throughs: voices are quieter, people speak more kindly—almost afraid to break the spell that has fallen over the studio.

We have just finished the last round of "Without You" when the main studio door opens, revealing Magda and Anatoli entering with trays of food. Jenner glances at his watch and stands up, flicking on the intercom switch. "Seven o'clock already! Time flies when you're making hits! Let's take a quick break and be ready to work in thirty minutes. Sound good?"

Terrance and I bound into the reception area where we are greeted with the aroma of grilled steak, roasted potatoes, warm bread and steamed vegetables. We grab our plates and I glance at the booth as I sit, seeing Martin and Jenner smiling. I can hear them talking indistinctly over the intercom. I grimace when I smell the musty tofu-

and-fish concoction that Terrance uncovers. "Oh my God, Terrance, did something die on your plate?"

He sticks out his tongue and flicks his chopsticks at my steak and potatoes. "Laugh all you want, Missy! You keep eating steak and potatoes, you'll pay the price in the end." He snaps his linen napkin open and spreads it onto his lap. "I subscribe to the philosophy of..." Terrance's lecture is interrupted by Martin's enraged voice blaring over the intercom. "...and don't you think for a second that I won't go to the press and revive all the crap you did to us if this album doesn't take off. There's been some progress in recent years regarding breach of contract, taking advantage of underage stars, etc. I'd only be too happy to bring that all back to court to see if I can't get a better outcome this time around."

I'm stunned. I have *never* heard Martin yell at anyone like that. Terrance shoots up. "What in the hell?" He races to the booth as Jenner jumps up.

"Martin, you're right, and I'm sorry. The way I managed REVOLUTION! and all my groups in the past was unacceptable. But it *will* be different this time, I hope you see that already..."

Jenner is interrupted as Terrance slams into the booth and leaps over the console, turning off the intercom switch. I can see Martin's chest heaving wildly like he's just run five miles, and Jenner's face pales when he sees how upset I am watching them argue. Terrance kicks the door closed and drops the blinds covering the booth window with a crash.

This is worse than seeing my parents fight! If those two can't get along, what does it mean for me? If Martin decides he can't work with Jenner, is this all over?

About ten minutes later, Terrance comes out and calmly sits back down. He nods to my plate. "Don't let that cow have died in vain. Eat up."

I stay still, staring at the closed blinds in the booth. "Are we going to ignore what just happened?"

Terrance glances over and nods, stabbing a peapod with a chopstick. "Pretty much."

"Are you serious?"

Terrance looks up. "Yes." He waves his chopsticks at the booth. "That has nothing to do with you. Martin was just clearing the air on some old stuff that happened a long time ago. They'll be fine."

I continue to stare at Terrance. He shrugs. "They're both professionals who have a job to do. Martin knew what he was getting into when he called Jenner. And Jenner certainly knew what Martin was feeling when he signed you. If they want to make you a star, they're going to have to get over their feelings and work together. Now eat."

42

Unbelievably, the rest of the session flies by as if nothing has happened. Fueled by the first successful recording, we tackle a fast-paced party anthem song, "My Place," that has everyone in the studio tapping their feet and moving.

"Wait 'til you hear it with the full band! Horns, drums, bass. You're going to lose your mind!" Terrance has completely transformed from dour, old man to excited hipster in the span of a few hours. I'm delighted at the transformation, and happy that we can connect on a musical level.

We end the night with, of all things, a few classic Christmas carols. Jenner and Terrance agree that having a few holiday tracks on the EP, or extended-play album, will ensure that I'll make appearances throughout the most profitable season of the year. With an EP, we can get away with only four or five songs and get me on the scene sooner. If we wait for Terrance to compose twelve or more songs for a full-blown album, it could be months before the album is released.

It's past two when we decide to call it a night.

"OK, folks, that's a wrap. Just give me a few minutes and I'll have jump drives for you to take home." I close my eyes and stretch. I've been singing since 3:00 p.m. I'm completely drained. But I feel so happy with what we've accomplished that I can't stop smiling. I see Terrance watching me as he packs up his bag and smiles.

"Just wait until we start recording the EP. You won't notice that you've been stuck in here for twenty-four hours. Once you finally leave, you'll be so excited you won't be able to fall asleep. It's the best feeling ever."

I smile wider. "I can't wait! This was more amazing than I ever thought it could be. You know, I was pretty scared of you before today."

Terrance laughs. "Um, yeah, I noticed. No offense, but you didn't hide it that well. And to be honest, I prefer it that way until I get to know someone."

I frown and Terrance waves his hand. "I meet so many wannabes with pushy stage moms and producer dads who are convinced their little Jade or Nomad is going to be the next Mariah Carey. More often than not, they can't even carry a tune and we're all wasting precious time indulging this little snowflake in their pointless dream. I just wanted to see if you have what it takes. And you do."

"Thanks. But you could still be polite to people, even if you think their dreams are pointless. You don't need to be rude."

Terrance rolls his eyes and shakes his head. "You just wait, Missy. You get as big as I think you will be, and I want to see how polite you are to every stranger who wants an autograph or a hug. Every time you talk to people, it's like you're giving a little piece of yourself to them. I just like to make sure that the people I give myself to are worthy of it."

I snort. "That doesn't sound snobby or anything."

Terrance raises his eyebrows. "It might sound snobby, but it's the truth. Learned the hard way by a man who has what people want. You wait. You'll see what I mean."

Martin's voice booms. "And on that horrible note, I must make sure my charge gets her beauty sleep. I hope you haven't been filling her head with awful advice like that between takes."

Martin eyes Terrance and then smiles, extending a hand. "Brilliant work, Terrance. You truly are a genius."

Terrance smirks and shakes Martin's hand. "Thank you, Martin. You admit my genius yet doubt my people skills. I'm confused."

"Just because you're a genius doesn't mean..."

"You can't be polite." Terrance finishes for him in a singsong school voice. "I see where she gets it." He smiles. "As much as I love the Kumbaya attitude around here, I have to get some rest." He picked up his bag. "Great work, Dani. Looking forward to the real thing very soon."

Jenner enters the studio as Terrance exits, handing him a jump drive. "And these are for you two," he says, handing us jump drives of our own. "Listen to them as much as you can. We'll set a date for the recording session shortly."

Jenner gives me a warm hug, taking me by surprise. "You did better than I ever imagined, sweetheart. I am so proud of you and all your hard work. Martin, too. You two make a great team." He glances at Martin briefly, who continues to look at me and smile. "Oh, one more thing!" Jenner grabs his phone and punches the screen. "You just made your Instagram debut." Jenner shows stories and photos he posted from the recording session.

"Wow. When did you do that?" I can't stop staring at myself, the moody light making my face almost unrecognizable.

"During the session. I'm getting the buzz started early. You're a beautiful girl, recording new music for an industry legend"—Martin snorts, which Jenner ignores—"...and working with an '80s icon. It's all very mysterious. People are going to want to know more about you. We already have a few hundred likes."

Martin squints at the screen. "What's my name doing there?" Jenner looks a little uncomfortable. "Um, I hope it's OK that I started Instagram accounts for you both. In this day and age, it's crazy that neither of you has any online presence. We need to change that ASAP, so I got started tonight. I sent you the links so you can start sending it out to friends and family. You OK with that, Martin?"

Martin purses his lips to the side like he's sucked a lemon. "Of course you did, and of course I am. I'm willing to do anything for this kid. Next time, I'd appreciate a heads-up."

Jenner nods. "Of course. I meant to tell you during the dinner break, but we got a little sidetracked...and I never had the chance to get to it."

I look from one to the other, waiting for one of them to mention the fight. "Is everything OK?"

They both turn to me and too quickly say, "Everything's fine," at the same time. I stare at them.

Martin speaks up first, holding up a calming hand. "No, seriously, everything's fine. We just had some old business to discuss."

I look at them for a moment and shrug. "I'm too tired to worry. But you two are acting like my parents when they're fighting. So, either stop fighting or get better at covering it up. I don't want to deal with the same stuff here that I have to deal with at home."

They nod. Martin hands me my bag. "Time to go."

Jenner squeezes my shoulder as we leave and says, "Get some rest. We'll talk soon."

43

The next few weeks are a hamster-wheel of activity. I do my best to text and FaceTime friends and family whenever I can. We rarely connect long enough for deep conversations, but the quick "I love yous," bits of gossip and tons of photo updates keep me feeling connected to the people I love. Since Carlton is keeping up my Instagram account, at least they can see how I spend my days.

But I still manage to put off touching base with my grandma, which Geena keeps bugging me about. I just don't think I'm ready and with all the stress I'm under heading into the studio, something has to give, and that's what it is.

With my monotonous schedule of workouts, rehearsals and lessons, I can't thank Magda enough for keeping me fed, caffeinated and clothed. There's always food and green tea standing by whenever I crave it, and a stack of clean laundry when I open my dresser drawers.

It's been five weeks since I entered the compound, though it feels more like six months. At first, it felt weird not to be at school with my friends. But I barely have time to shower, let alone master algebra or history. I'm OK with putting off studying for a while, but I don't want to get so far behind that I can't walk in the graduation ceremony with my friends. Martin assures me that they'll hire a tutor in the spring once we lock down my album and I'm preparing for the tour.

I endlessly play my songs. In the shower, in the kitchen, in the golf cart and at night before I fall asleep. My songs loop over and over on my phone until they became a part of me. I can sing them backward and forward, and I often freestyle with the tune or lyrics just to change it up. Terrance has sent over a few new songs with his voice on the tracks, and I sing along with those, too.

The only place I can't play my music anymore is in the gym. After three days of listening to the songs ninety minutes at a time, Brett banned them. Martin and I are relieved to have a break; we spend as much time as possible working out, just to escape my songs.

I've also started to notice that Martin and Brett really do have a little thing going. They're always professional in front of me, but I notice how Brett hands Martin a towel or lingers a bit longer than necessary when spotting Martin at weights. I'm happy that Martin's found something for himself these days since everything seems to revolve around me, my music and my physical well-being.

We're heading into the studio in a few days to lay down the tracks for the album. My first single will be released shortly after that. A meeting is called after lunch so we can go over the schedule that Jenner's been working on since he signed me. I can't wait to see what he's planned. My pings with a text from my mom as I'm getting ready.

M: *Do you want these or can I throw them out?*

It's a photo of some stuffed animals I left behind at home.

Why would she want to throw those out? I call my mom.

"Oh, Hi, Dani. Do you want these things or not? I can box them up for you and put them in the garage with the other stuff."

"Other stuff? What's going on? Why are you moving my stuff?"

I can hear paper and fabric rustling in the background. "I'm cleaning out your room. Going to convert it into an office for me and your dad. You aren't here and since you're going to have all that money coming in, you won't need it. I've been cleaning this room and keeping everything perfect since you left, which is just stupid. I need to use it for something more productive."

"What?" I screech, "You can't just throw out my stuff and take over my room. That's *my* room!"

My mom sighs, annoyed. "No, it belongs to your dad and me. We pay the mortgage; we own the house. You moved out and according to Martin will be making more than he and I put together. I'm not going to keep this room as a shrine while you're living in a mansion in Malibu. The world moves on, Dani. You're living your life; I need to live mine."

Martin knocks and then opens my door, looking concerned.

I'm so angry that tears start to pour down my face. "You are out of control! Why now? You know I'm about to record my EP. I don't need this right now!"

My mom sighs dramatically. "See? There you go again! I hate to break it to you, darlin', but the world doesn't revolve around you, Dani Truehart. Some of us have ordinary, boring lives and they go on regardless of you having to record an album."

Before I can speak, Martin takes the phone from me. "Hi Jodi, it's Martin."

I pace the room like a tiger, stalking back and forth, furious. I can hear my mom's garbled voice on the phone as she shouts at Martin, who just nods and calmly utters, "Uh-huh" every few minutes.

"Well, I see your point of course. I just wish it had been delivered differently. I'll speak to Dani and please don't get rid of anything." More talking from my mom. "Uh-huh, that's fine. In the garage and we will deal with it in the new year. Fine. Thank you."

Martin shakes his head and hangs up. "Are you fu—"

"Whoa, whoa, whoa! Not OK, Dani! You cannot use that language no matter what your mom just did!"

My anger blurs my vision and I feel like I want to punch something. I scream instead and throw a pillow across the room. I stomp on the ground, my muscles taut and ready to spring. Martin just nods his head at me. "Let it out, Dani. It's OK. You have every right to be upset."

Hearing Martin's calm voice sparks something in me and I sit down hard on the couch and burst into tears. Martin sits down and puts an arm around me.

"I knew something was coming after that brunch with your mom, but I didn't expect this. I'm so sorry, Dani."

I shudder as my tears subside. "I just don't get it. *Why* now? And what does she need an office for? It's so stupid."

Martin sighs and gives me a squeeze. "I think your mom is just jealous, sweetheart. She sees you living in a mansion, starting on a career where you'll earn lots of money and I think she's just plain old jealous. I think she was just lashing out after hearing you're about to lock down your EP. You're going through all these monumental changes and milestones and she's stuck in the same old house with the same old job, and she just got a little bit crazy."

I shake my head, incredulous. "But no one else is treating me this way. Geena, Dad, Lauren?"

"Well, I'm sure at one time or another, everyone feels a little bit jealous about what you're going through. Hell, even I do, and I've already done it." He gives me a sad smile. The thing is that we're all more happy for you than sad that it's not happening to us. I think your mom just has it a little backward. She's more sad for herself than happy for you."

I consider what he says and shake my head. "Yeah, but she's my mom. She's supposed to want these things for me. That's why she did all this for me."

Martin takes a deep breath and exhales slowly. After a long pause, he finally says "Maybe while she was doing all this for you, she was really wishing it were happening for her. It doesn't make her behavior OK, but it explains it."

I slouch down on the couch and groan. "This is messed up on so many levels." I look at Martin. "See, *this* is why I never call home! No good ever comes from it."

Martin nods. "I can't argue with that. Look, forget about the room. I'll reach out to your dad and figure it out. Just get ready for our meeting. We leave in five."

"OK," I muster as Martin leaves. Too drained to call my dad, I text him about what just happened. He pings me back instantly.

Dad: *I'm so sorry Marie. Of course we won't clean out your room. I'll talk to Mom and clear this up. Don't worry about a thing. I promise I won't let you down this time.*

We'll see. I toss my phone on the couch and head to the bathroom to splash some water on my face.

***

As we park in front of the conference bungalow, Martin says, "OK, try and forget about your mom and get focused on this meeting. Be sure to speak up if something doesn't feel right and ask questions if you have them. Jenner's known for setting up murderous schedules. I want to make sure you're on board with everything he's got set up. Nothing is set in stone. We can always make changes, no matter what he says."

I nod. "OK. My dad said he'd make sure my mom doesn't change my room, so I'm feeling hopeful." I pause and ask, "How far in advance has Jenner planned?"

Martin shrugs. "Who knows? My bet is at least twelve months. It all depends on the success of the songs, but Jenner isn't planning on failure, so..."

Martin lets his sentence trail off as he opens the door of the bungalow. Jenner and Carlton are seated at the conference table, and they stand when we enter. Jenner greets us warmly. "Afternoon, Dani and Martin. Help yourself to refreshments." He motions to the buffet that is laden with the usual fruit-and-beverage spread. "Once you're ready, let's get down to business." Jenner indicates to the table.

There are two laptops and notebooks placed in front of two empty chairs. Martin and I each sit down at a computer; mine's pink. "I thought since we were getting our schedules synced, you both could use some updated computers. There's also a paper calendar if that's what you'd prefer."

I bounce in my chair. "Are you serious? I've never had my own computer before. Thank you!"

Martin nods silently and runs his hand over the computer before firing it up. Things are still a bit frosty since that night in the studio. "Nice. Thank you, Jenner. This will definitely make things easier."

Jenner reaches down and puts a box on the table. "And I think Dani will agree with me that it's time you retire that old flip phone. You definitely need one of these to make your job easier."

Martin's eyes bug out as he takes the box and pulls out a black iPhone. He swipes at the screen, amazed. "I don't know what to say. Thank you, Jenner." Martin shrugs. "I don't even know how to use this."

I grab the phone and snap a selfie of us. "I'll catch you up in no time. You're gonna love it. Welcome to the twenty-first century!"

Martin laughs, mugging for another selfie. "All right, I get it, I've got an old phone. Ha ha. Now let's get down to business."

Jenner rubs his hands together as Carlton starts a PowerPoint presentation. "OK, here's what I have in mind."

I shove my computer aside, opting for the colorful kikki.K day planner.

Over the next several hours, Jenner explains his proposed schedule for the next twelve months (*Martin was right!*), starting most importantly with recording tracks for the EP. Jenner and Terrance decided that we would record three original songs and close the album with a Christmas song to be determined at a later date. We'll start the recording process next week, hiring an additional sound engineer to mix the tracks throughout the night so that the entire EP can be finished in three weeks. *Three weeks!*

It's an unforgiving grind of a schedule, demanding that Jenner and Terrance burn the candle at both ends to participate in the daytime recording sessions and graveyard mixing sessions. But this will guarantee that the EP will be released mid-November.

Jenner plans on releasing "My Place" in three weeks. He'll release another song called "Nuthin' 2 Do" immediately after that to ensure enough buzz on the airwaves before hitting the public with the EP. He's convinced that the third song, "Without You," will seal the deal for my success. He's saving that song for the EP drop.

He's already got me booked on several late-night shows and morning news programs in early November, where I'll sing "My Place." On the day of the EP release, I'm scheduled to collect canned goods for the Thanksgiving drive at a local food pantry and sing the national anthem at the Lakers game.

Jenner's left no stone unturned to launch my career. Once the EP is released, I'm scheduled almost daily for an interview, a photo op or a performance. Jenner has dates for *Jingle Ball, Christmas at Rockefeller Center*, the *White House Christmas Tree Ceremony* and *Dick Clark's*

Rockin' New Year's Eve penciled in. He's optimistic that one or all of these can be booked once my songs hit the air.

In the new year, we'll record a proper album and prep for the tour. The full album will drop in May to coincide with my sixteenth birthday, and we'll depart for a world tour by June. After our North American concerts, then it's on to Europe, Japan and wrapping up the tour with South America. Jenner projects us to return to Los Angeles almost a year after we depart.

Martin's fingers fly over the keyboard as he types in dates and details. I try to keep up, scribbling furiously in my calendar, trying to wrap my head around everything Jenner is throwing at me. It is an impossible amount of information to absorb.

At the end, Jenner looks at us. "Well, what do you think?"

Martin finishes tapping at his keyboard and stretches. "It's a lot, but definitely doable. I know you're just painting things with broad strokes because we won't know what we're doing for sure 'til we see how the EP does. But I want to make sure that once the full album is recorded, we've got a tutor lined up for Dani. She wants to walk with her friends at graduation, so she needs to keep up with school once things settle down." Martin turns to me, "Right?"

I nod slowly, overwhelmed, and Martin squeezes my hand. "I know it seems like a lot right now. If you have any questions or concerns, let us know. That's what we're here for."

All the dates and events swirl in my brain—I can't make sense of it all, so I blurt out the first thing that pops into my head. "I don't have a passport."

Jenner bursts out laughing. "Is that your biggest concern? Because we have people to take care of that." He turns to Carlton. "Can you take care of that for Dani?"

Carlton scribbles on his notepad and gives me a creepy smile. "Of course."

Jenner nods his head once. "Good! Now, what else is bothering you? Come on, talk to me."

I look from Jenner to Martin to Carlton. I don't know how to articulate what I'm feeling. *So much depends on something that doesn't even exist yet.* The pressure is enormous. "We haven't even recorded any songs and you've already got me booked around the world for the next year. It's a lot to take in."

Martin starts to speak, but Jenner holds up a hand. "I know it seems like I'm putting the cart before the horse. But I've been through this many times, and if I know one thing, it's that you're *going* to make it. We're on the brink of something very big. We have to be prepared so we can make the most of it. That's what I do—I plan and prepare and get you hooked up with the best people in the business." I see Martin give Jenner an approving nod, and he continues. "I've changed since Martin worked with me. I realize now that I don't have to put as much pressure on the talent as I once thought. Your only job is to sing and be you, Dani. It's my job to put you in the right place at the right time with the right folks. OK?"

I nod, feeling a bit less overwhelmed. "When you put it like that, it's not so bad. I can keep singing."

Jenner knocks on the table. "Good! Now that we've got that settled, on to the fun stuff!" Jenner holds out his hand and Carlton gives him a sheaf of oversized pages. "Let's decide how you want to look."

Jenner spreads out drawings of various costume designs from skimpy showgirl outfits to basic jeans and T-shirts and every look between. "I want to get an idea of what type of look you and Martin are interested in. Then I can have Petra put some pieces together and we can start building your wardrobe. Of course, we'll provide you with jeans, dresses, etc., for all your scheduled appearances. But these are the stage looks we're trying to lock down."

Jenner quietly confers with Carlton while we look over the sketches. The girl in the sketches looks like me. The clothes are out of this world. I'd love to wear every one of the costumes, though I'm not quite sure I can pull off some of the sexier ones. Although I pick a few sequined mini-dresses, I stick mostly to jeans and tops.

Martin adds several sexier looks and showier outfits. "Remember, you're selling an image. I love the girl-next-door look, but you've got to have some fun with your appearance when you're up on that stage. And if you've got it, you might as well flaunt it—age-appropriately, that is," Martin winks at me. "I'm not letting you perform in your underwear, but you don't need to dress like a nun, either."

Jenner interrupts, "I see you've found some looks that you like. Good! I'll have Petra come out next week, and you can try some stuff on in between studio time. We want to make sure you're ready to go ASAP."

Carlton reaches forward, silently gathering the sketches we've selected. It creeps me out how he always tries to blend into the background.

"Well, that's it for now. I know you've got to get back for Serena at 4:00. We'll see you in the studio next week. Obviously, we'll curtail your normal routine while we're recording. Just keep up the great work, you two."

Jenner stands up, indicating the meeting is over. Everyone shakes hands and Jenner leaves the room, Carlton trailing behind him.

Martin and I look at each other, stunned. "See?" Martin says. "Told you he'd scheduled the whole year. You ready for this?"

I widen my eyes. "No!" Then I pause and realize I feel a little more excitement than fear. "And yeah, I'm ready to get out there and have some fun. I think I've earned it, right?"

Martin laughs. "Well, if you haven't earned it by now, you definitely will in the next few weeks."

Truer words were never spoken!

44

"I can't believe you're recording your first song tomorrow! That's awesome, D! I wish I could be there!"

I sigh into the phone. I know I'm going to regret this late-night call with Sean in the morning, but I need to hear his voice more than anything right now.

"Oh my gosh, me too! It'd make me feel so much better if I were there tomorrow. Say, any word from your mom after what happened?"

I groan, "No, thank God! Geena said they had a huge blowout, but that my dad actually stood his ground for once. She sent me a pic and my room looks just like it did when I left. I can't believe my mom. What kind of mother does that?"

Sean exhales, loudly. "I don't know, D. It was messed up for sure. But I'm glad your dad finally came through. That's something anyway."

"Yeah, I guess." I pick at my sweatpants, a gross combination of angry and sadness filling my stomach as we talk about my mom. I shake my head and change the subject. "I miss you so much! I can't believe it's going to be another few weeks before we see each other."

Sean groans into the phone. "I know. It sucks. But hey, by then you'll have all the hard stuff behind you. Hopefully, with your EP finished, you'll have a normal schedule. I mean, I know you'll be making appearances and stuff, but we need to find some time to see each other."

"Definitely! I've already got it scheduled in with Martin. It's all going to be worth it once it's done. I'm just super bummed I'm missing Homecoming."

"Me too. We've all been texting Martin about it; even your dad. But Martin said Jenner won't budge. I get it. He's dropping all this money for your EP, so he doesn't want you too tired to work. But I was really hoping you could make it."

My stomach burns. I know there's no way to make the dance in two weeks, but it *kills* me to be left out once again. I've already missed almost half the basketball season and all of the parties. I pause, my insecurities getting the better of me once again. "Are you taking any-one?" I ask in a quiet voice, hating the jealous edge that creeps out.

Sean answers matter-of-factly, "Zoe, didn't I tell you?"

I catch myself before I lose it. "Uh, you're kidding, right?"

Sean laughs. "Duh, of course I am! There's no way! I'm going over to the Hannon's house that night to hang out with Scott. He's not seeing anyone right now, so we'll probably game and grab a bite to eat later."

There's a knock on the door and Martin pops his head in. "Are you *serious* right now, girl? It is midnight, and you're in the studio tomorrow at 8:00 *a.m.* Tell Romeo you love him and hang up *now*." He crosses his arms and glares at me. "I'll wait."

I quickly say goodnight to Sean and hang up. Martin nods blows me a kiss.

"OK then, good night. Get some rest."

I climb into bed and fall asleep imagining what it would be like to go to the Homecoming dance.

***

Eight hours later, my head's spinning as I enter the recording bun-galow. An impossible number of people are crammed into the wait-ing room...assistants, technicians...some lounging and having coffee, others rushing in and out. I glance at the live stage, and I'm surprised to find it dark.

I poke Martin and point at the stage. "I thought we were starting at 8:00. Where is everyone?"

Martin shakes his head. "We couldn't all fit in there, sweetie. That's just the isolation booth used for rehearsals and recording solos. You're in the main studio." Martin leads me down the hall and opens a door I've never noticed before. I see a space twice the size of the rehearsal space with about twenty people inside. They're busy tuning guitars, testing horns and adjusting mics. A piano, keyboard, guitar amps and backup singer mics are scattered about. A smaller isolation room is behind this space and holds the drum kit and the horn section. The main room has wood-paneled walls beneath a vaulted ceiling with acoustic tiles suspended in an artful display. Blue and purple lights are hidden in the crown molding and light the ceiling, while softer white lights bounce off colorful tapestries on the walls, hiding white acoustic tiles underneath. Rugs and candles are scattered about as in the rehearsal studio. The smaller isolation room with the drums and horns has simple white acoustic tiling and similar lighting.

Jenner, speaking with several musicians, looks up when Martin and I enter and claps his hands loudly. "If I can have everyone's attention for a second. This is Dani Truehart, who we are about to launch into musical orbit. It's her first day in a studio with a live band, so let's give her a warm welcome to the Magic Factory." Jenner leads a booming round of applause.

I smile and wave awkwardly, taking in all the faces of the men and women around me. "Hi. It's nice to meet you." Everyone chuckles while I just keep smiling idiotically.

Martin gives me a side hug. "Let's get you settled. Not to sound like your mom, but don't forget to run to the bathroom. We'll be starting soon. This train stops for no one."

About twenty minutes later, everyone who isn't going to sing or play is crammed into the control booth. I'm happy that Terrance is with me; he'll be playing the piano on all of the tracks.

"OK, settle in." Jenner's voice through the intercom comes across small and tinny. "This is the first time we've all played together with Dani. So, let's just run through "My Place" start to finish, no stopping no matter what happens. By the end of the day, we'll have played it so many times that we can do it with our eyes closed."

Everyone chimes in with agreement. "Dani, don't worry about the musicians. They'll keep pace with you. Just watch Terrance. He's been working with these guys all week, and they've got it together. Any questions?"

I try to smile, but I'm so nervous my lips stick to my teeth, so I just shake my head.

Jenner smiles encouragingly. "Good. Terrance, count us in whenever you're ready."

Over the intercom, Martin says, "Dani, you've got this. Take a sip of water to unstick those lips. Just have some fun, honey."

I follow Martin's instructions, happy for guidance. I'm sweaty and cold at the same time; I just want to crawl back into bed. All of these adults are here, waiting for me to be amazing. A wave of doubt sweeps over me, and I suddenly feel like I just can't do this.

Terrance hands me some sheet music. "Headset on, sweetheart. These will let you hear my piano and your voice. It can be overwhelming with the entire band in the same room. Just sing like you've been singing all week and we're home free, OK?" He taps the sheets. "Here's the music in case you need it."

He gives my arm an encouraging squeeze before stepping away. I feel like an idiot when I put on the bulky headset. Martin gives me a thumbs-up. The closer we get to starting, the more the pressure builds. I keep thinking someone will notice how panicked I am, but no one does. My heart pounds harder and faster and it feels like I'm going to have a heart attack.

Terrance looks at the band. "Here we go, kids, on three. One and a two and a three." On three, Terrance nods his head and I jump when the trumpets blast a sequence that will be the backbone of the song. The drums slam in right behind them, laying down a beat so contagious that I can't help but tap my foot, their beat overtaking my racing heart. I've been listening to this same song all week, but with only piano music and my voice; this full-band live version is blowing my mind. A heavy funky bass line starts up, and the piano plays in. *Thank God I'm watching Terrance!* I'm so lost in the music, I'd have missed my entrance if he hadn't nodded his head at me.

I'm grateful for the headphones that allow me to hear the band, just not at full volume. Once I start singing, I tune them out and focus on Terrance's piano. I close my eyes, belting out the lyrics. It's a lot easier than I thought it would be. I open my eyes when I hear singers chime in at the chorus and nod at them as they sing with me, bolstering my voice. Toward the end of the song, I can't help myself. I start ad-libbing with the music and the backup singers, adding notes and exclamations as the song ends with a flourish of horns.

The silence in the studio is deafening. No one moves. After a brief eternity, I slowly pull off my headset. The booth erupts in cheers and applause. Jenner tears back into the studio and hugs me. "That was amazing!" He spins me around, knocking over my stool. He sets me back down. "You all were incredible! We've gotta hear that back. Ryan, can you cue it up?"

Ryan nods. "In a sec. Let me clean it up first."

My head's buzzing. I can't stop smiling. I'm drenched in sweat and I peel off my sweater. Terrance leaps over the piano bench and gives me a hug. "What did I tell you? You nailed it!"

I squeeze Terrance back. "Ohmigod, I can't even..." I can't finish my sentence because Martin runs in and sweeps me up in a hug. We hop up and down together, squealing.

Jenner laughs. "OK, which one of you is the fifteen-year-old girl? Because I thought I only hired one?"

Jenner heads over to chat with Terrance. Martin playfully gives Jenner the finger when he thinks I'm not looking. "I'm telling you, Dani," he says, "that was perfect. We could put that on the air right now. Pure, solid gold. You're amazing."

Carlton slips over and hands me a bottle of cold water and a towel. "Congratulations, Dani, that was wonderful. Jenner is very pleased." "Uh, thanks, Carlton." I smile. I'm so giddy with relief that even Carlton can't bring me down.

"Creepy," Martin whispers, making grasping fingers at my face. I laugh and almost shoot water out my nose. Martin chuckles. "Keeping it classy, even when you're recording your first gold record. I love it." I laugh and wipe my nose with the towel.

"OK, we're ready, Jenner." Ryan's voice comes over the intercom. "Let's fire it up, folks, and see what we've got."

The entire band piles into the studio. Heads bop, feet tap and smiles grow broad as each person's pride swells at their hard work. Jenner occasionally leans in to whisper to Terrance, who's gazing off into the distance, listening intently and writing notes in his notebook. Martin keeps his arm around me, squeezing me now and then when I've nailed a particularly hard note.

Hearing my voice backed by such outstanding live music is indescribable. But, typical me, I begin to pick out mistakes even as I marvel at the incredible song we've just recorded. *My breath is too loud here, I'm late on a cue there, my voice is flat or I hold a note too long.* I'm sure that I can predict every note Terrance is scribbling. As happy as I am that the song sounds so incredible with the instruments, I'm worried my singing isn't good enough. I shrug off Martin's arm, feeling less celebratory as the song ends. The band bursts into applause and congratulatory handshakes. I drink some water, trying to avoid everyone.

Martin gives me the side-eye. "What gives? You don't seem as excited as a few minutes ago."

I shake my head and chew on a hangnail. "Didn't you hear how flat I was in the first chorus and how late I was with the second verse? I held notes too long or not long enough, and I didn't even give the background singers enough time to vamp during the bridge." I flop down on a small sofa in the corner of the studio.

Martin holds up a hand. "OK. Who are you right now, Quincy Jones? It was a great first run. *First run!* Just enjoy that you made it through without puking. Yes, we have to tweak it, but don't rain on your own parade, OK?"

Martin calls out, "So, Jenner, Terrance, what do you think?" They finish chatting and come over. Terrance sits on the arm of the couch and Jenner stands, too excited to sit.

"I think it was a *fantastic* first pass. Most people record days—weeks—to sound that flawless, and you did it on the first take."

I nod slowly. "Thanks, Jenner. But I heard a lot of errors. I felt so good singing it, but hearing it played back, there was just so much that was off."

Terrance's head snaps up from his writing. "That's ridiculous. Yes"—he waves his notebook at me—"I have a few notes, but I *always* have notes. Minor fixes to turn a great performance into perfection. And this was a great performance, make no mistake about it. The more you sing with a live band, the more accustomed you'll become to timing. This next time around, now that you aren't so swept up in the music, you can concentrate on vocal quality, and the flatness will disappear. Just keeping your eyes open will make some of the changes we need. Don't fret, pet." Terrance winks at me and gets up. "I'm going to give a few notes to the band. We should be ready to go again in about fifteen if that's OK with you."

Jenner looks at his watch. "Absolutely." He pats my arm. "You were wonderful, darlin'. Please don't stress. I saw you enjoying yourself in here. More of that, less worrying. That's my job." He nods at Martin and heads to the booth to speak to Ryan.

Martin gives me an "I told you so" look. "Seriously, girl, stop being crazy." He pulls out his phone and shows me the screen. "I took the liberty of snapping some photos and texting them to your peeps. Check out the responses."

I scroll through messages from my dad, Sean, Lauren and Geena. They all sent photos of them celebrating and cheering, messages of love and support. My entire history class posed with a "Sing It, Dani!" sign on the classroom whiteboard. Lauren even sent a hysterical photo of Zoe furiously looking at the photos Sean was sharing in class. "See, not only are you killing it in the studio today, you're sticking it to that brat, Zoe. Just look how pissed she is, fuming that Sean is still mooning over you and not her. I know it's catty, but I love it."

I feel satisfactorily smug for a few moments until I notice that a message from my mom is glaringly absent. I take a deep breath and try to sound nonchalant, "Nothing from my mom?"

Martin shakes his head and says brightly, "No, not yet, but I'm sure she's at work and can't text at the moment." He elbows me in the rib and says seriously, "You're living the *dream*, girl. Stop worrying about your mom and start enjoying it."

I take a deep breath and silent repeat over and over, "*Martin's right, Martin's right...*"

45

We run through "My Place" for another ten hours, stopping only for a couple of quick meal breaks. We add and subtract instruments and vocals, and tweak timing and pacing so much that we're all sick of the song. Jenner finally calls it a day when the night shift comes in to run the song through post.

As the band packs up, Jenner talks over the intercom. "Great work today, everyone. We'll see where we are on this song tomorrow and decide if we'll keep working on it or move on. See you back here at 8:00 a.m."

I'm completely drained. The boundless energy required to keep up with the pace of the song for a whole day is even too much for my teenage self. My entire body aches as if I've run a marathon. Martin comes up and wraps a baby-blue cashmere scarf around my neck. "From now until tomorrow, no talking, got it?"

"You can't be seri—"

Martin cuts me off by placing his index finger on my lips, which is annoying. I pretend to bite it. "One-hundred-percent serious." You can text Sean tonight, but no speaking. You need to rest your voice."

I scowl. "This is ridiculous! Why didn't you tell me earlier?"

Martin winces. "Seriously, *stop talking!*" He raises his hands in surrender. "My bad, OK? When I was in the group, we didn't sing as much solo work, so Jenner wasn't such a stickler. Frankly, I didn't even think you'd have to do this until Jenner reminded me in the booth." Martin puts a hand over his heart. "Honest to God."

I roll my eyes and mumble to myself, totally irked. Martin narrows his eyes. "I can read lips. I'm disappointed you're using such language. I'm chalking it up to exhaustion and not just plain rudeness." He holds my gaze. "I'm serious, Dani. I know you're peeved, but that's no excuse to start swearing at me. You've only been in the studio for one day, so hold off on the diva attitude for now."

I feel guilty and mouth, "I'm sorry."

Martin nods. "That's better. Now let's get you some dinner and some rest."

***

Martin offers to sit with me during dinner, but I don't see the point since I can't talk. Besides, I've been crammed into a tiny room with an impossible number of people all day, so I'd just prefer to hang out alone in my room.

Magda brings up some delicious homemade chicken soup, hot, crusty bread, salmon and a Caesar salad. I thought I'd be too tired to eat, but I plow through my meal while mindlessly watching TV.

I'm overjoyed about my first day in the studio. My mind and body are so exhausted, but I'm too keyed up to fall asleep, and I can't sit still. All I really want to do is talk to Sean and Lauren and tell them all about my day. But the thought of having to type out an entire conversation seems overwhelming. I settle for a bubble bath, hoping I'll either relax enough to fall asleep or wake up enough to text.

Forty-five minutes later, I'm propped up in bed with tons of pillows, fire blazing in the fireplace across the room. I decide to send a group text to Sean, Lauren and Geena because I'm too tired to text them individually.

D: *Hey Guys! Wanted 2 call but Jenner has me rest my voice after recording. As in, not allowed to talk AT ALL. Can U believe that? Sorry 4 group text.*

G: *Hilarious! How many times have I wished U'd stop talking?? Great photos. How was it??? So proud of U, sis!!*

L: *Bigtiming us already? JK—totally weird U can't talk. Sure, Jenner's not just sick of U already??*

D: *Ha ha. Apparently, this is normal 4 Jenner. 2day was amazing, scary,*

& cool. Wish U were there. Think 1st song is done. How R U?

L: *That's sick! Can't wait 2 hear it. Will we get a sneak peek?*

D: *I'll ask Jenner...maybe, if U R cool enuf?!? LOL*

G: I taught U everything U know about cool so UR welcome. Can't wait 2 hear the song.

D: I'm beat, know where Sean is?

L: Prolly gaming

D: Dang. OK, night. Falling asleep as I type

G: Rest up, sis! I'll tell M&D how 2day went. Showed them pics & mom geek'd out. Posted them everywhere.

L: Gnite!

D: Night

D: Night Sean, wherever U are.

I slip into sleep holding my phone, hoping I'll wake up when Sean texts me, but I sleep soundly through the pinging of my phone hours later.

S: U there? S: ...

S: Damn, guess U R asleep. Sounds like today went great! So happy 4 U. Miss U like crazy. Call U tomorrow. Luv U D.

46

Morning comes in an instant. Martin lets me sleep until 7:00, then rushes me through my shower and breakfast. We walk through the studio door just as the clock ticks 8:00 a.m. Jenner sees us come in and pointedly looks at the clock on the booth wall.

Martin shrugs and calls out, "*Technically*, we're right on time."

Jenner shakes his head and yells through the open booth door. "Don't be cute, Martin! Tomorrow, be here ten minutes early."

"OK," Martin calls brightly, exhaling loudly. I can't help but notice the tension and look at Martin quizzically.

Martin shakes his head, watching Jenner and Terrance in the booth. "I don't know and I'm not going in there to find out. Let's wait here until they tell us what's up." Martin ushers me over to the couch. "Let me get you a..."

Before Martin can finish his thought, Carlton creeps up and hands me a steaming mug of green tea. "Here you go, Dani. Martin, would you like one?" Carlton holds out a second mug of tea like an offering.

"Uh, thanks, Carlton. You are always *right there* waiting to help. Thanks, man."

I smile and mouth, "Thanks," busying myself by blowing on my tea to avoid further conversation with him.

Martin leans into Carlton and tries to whisper, but I'm an expert at eavesdropping. "So, C, why's Jenner in such a mood? Everything OK?"

"Well, Martin, seems like there's a low-level humming somewhere in the system during some of the recordings. It isn't constant, but it can be heard on some of the tracks we laid down at the end of the day. Jenner's pissed that Ryan didn't pick up on it and fix the issue during recording. Ryan swears he didn't hear a thing until the grave-yard tech pointed it out to him this morning. He feels it's faint enough to be mixed out for the master, but Jenner's livid."

A cold flash runs through me and I blurt out "What?" way too loudly, blowing my cover. Martin looks at me, shaking his head and sits down next to me. "How could Ryan miss that? That's like his main job!"

Carlton opens his hands and addresses us both. "To be fair, the hum really only comes through on a few of the tracks. It is so low-level that half of us don't even hear it. Ryan and the graveyard guy are in there now checking all the mics and connections. They're almost finished."

Martin runs his hand over his scalp. "So, do we have to record everything all over again?" I groan at the thought and Martin shushes me.

Carlton shrugs. "We don't know yet. Depends on what Jenner and Terrance decide. Sit tight. I'll let you know when I can. Unless you want to come in and see for yourself..."

Martin shakes his head, practically sloshing his tea out of his mug. "No, I'm good right here."

Carlton gives him a knowing look and scurries away.

Martin sighs and shrugs. "Let's cross our fingers and hope for the best."

We settle in and wait.

An hour later, Jenner comes out of the booth looking wrecked, wearing the same clothes as yesterday. He flops onto an armchair and rubs his face. "Sorry for the delay, guys. Carlton said he filled you in?" We nod.

"Were you able to fix it?" Martin asks.

Jenner takes the mug of coffee Carlton brings out to him. He takes a sip and nods while Carlton slips away. "At least we found the cause. Turns out someone kicked a mic cable on the way to the john during that last break and loosened the connection. Only the recordings after our 5:00 p.m. break are affected. I was more worried we wouldn't find the source and have to scrap the whole damn day today." Jenner sighs. "Ah well, lesson learned. With so many people in the studio, we're going to have to check connections a few times a day and take a few minutes to run back our recordings to make sure they're clean. I was rushing yesterday because I was so excited. I didn't give Ryan the chance to check things out. Stupid mistake. Hopefully, it won't cost us too much."

Martin sighs, relieved. "I'm glad they found it. Can we mix it out of the tracks? If not, can we use one of the recordings from earlier in the day?"

Jenner nods. "We'll have to in order to save time. I have to keep reminding myself that we need to get this EP out ASAP. Stay focused."

Martin nods. "Too true. We'll have more time once we put the real album together."

Jenner shakes his head. "All I want is to get enough down on this EP to get picked up by MEGA. I can't float an entire album on my own." Jenner jumps as soon as the words leave his mouth, all exhaustion disappearing from his face.

Martin freezes as my head snaps toward Jenner. "What?" I exclaim loudly, shocked. My mind races. *What does he mean he's paying for the EP himself? MEGA's backing us. Aren't they? Besides, he's rolling in cash; it's everywhere I look. What's going on?!?*

Jenner realizes he's let the cat out of the bag and sighs. "I'm not the big shot I used to be." He shrugs, "Couple of bad divorces, a few unwise investments and," he looks at Martin, "your career wasn't the only one that got damaged in the fallout from your lawsuit. I managed a few acts after REVOLUTION!, but I never had another success like I had with you boys."

He shakes his head, "I didn't have enough clout to get MEGA to sign you just off my word and your audition demo, Dani. So, I've been footing the bill for the EP. Leveraged everything I own to finance this project. If it fails, I'll be the oldest barista Starbucks has ever trained." He chuckles, and when no one else does he holds up a hand. "But I have a verbal deal with MEGA that if your EP sells a certain number of copies, they'll sign you, repay all costs and fund at least one album, possibly more."

My mouth hangs open. I'm dumbfounded. "So you mean you've

been paying for my training, musicians—" I wave my hands wildly around the room—"all of this by yourself?"

Jenner nods silently.

My mind reels as I try to piece together the situation. My words come out slowly, stumbling like my thoughts, "And if... for some reason, the EP fails... like not enough people buy it or I'm just horrible, you're out *all* that money."

Jenner looks me in the eye and slowly nods again.

Holy crap! If I'm anything less than an instant success, Jenner loses everything? I turn to Martin, my hands raised questioningly. "And you knew about this?"

Martin shakes his head, running his hand over his now sweaty head. "No. When I made a deal with Jenner, he laid everything out with me—contract details, music rights, etc. When I asked what label was backing him, he said before he had convinced MEGA to take you on and he wanted to see you first. I just assumed MEGA was on board." Martin looks up and curses. "This is all my fault. Here I am promising to protect you and your interests, and I fail right out of the gate."

Martin's words are drowned in the swirling tide of thoughts raging in my head. I feel duped and lied to, like a sheltered kid who just follows the adults around her, blindly obeying. *Does this mean we can't finish the EP? What happens if Jenner runs out of money before we finish? If I don't continue with them, do I have to start over—find another guardian and producer? What if the EP flops? How can I ever move back home and live with my mom after this? She'll never let me live this down.*

Jenner raises both hands. "Now, calm down, both of you. Dani, Martin *has* taken care of you and everything I'm doing is above board. I'd be happy to have a lawyer come in and explain my verbal agreement with MEGA. You'll find that everything *is* as we originally stated in the contract. I'll also let you know that no new artist would be getting the financial deal you are. Whether I'm financing the EP or a label is, nothing has changed in our deal. You'll be getting all the money agreed upon once we start earning."

I look from Jenner to Martin then stare off in the distance, my mind in overdrive. In the end, I keep coming back to one thought: *I'm so pissed at being kept in the dark.* I feel manipulated; shades of my mom's past manipulation spurring my anger on. Doubts about Jenner and Martin swirl through my head and I decide to grab onto my anger like a life preserver, letting all the other issues fall away.

Martin reaches out and places a hand on my shoulder. "Dani, I'm so sorry..."

I shrug my shoulder quickly, knocking his hand off abruptly. I catch Martin and Jenner exchanging looks, but I don't care. I throw my hands up in the air. "Look, the bottom line is that I *need* to record this EP. I don't want to leave here and start all over again." My voice unexpectedly rises to a yell and everyone in the studio turns my way. "I just *can't!*"

Jenner looks up and waves his hand at everyone to go back to their work. Embarrassed and feeling out of control, I sigh and lower my voice. "And Martin, if I *don't* go forward with you, who'll be my guardian? *My mom?*" I feel physically sick at the thought. *God, I can't go back to that again. As bad as it is right now...I just can't give my mom that power over me again.* I feel trapped; like there are no good answers. So, I decide on the lesser of two evils.

Martin and Jenner watch me, waiting for me to finish thinking. Finally, I shake my head and sigh, "I know I should probably walk away because things haven't been as honest as you both promised." I shake my head, resigned. "But in all reality, I don't think I have much choice."

Jenner and Martin look at each other, relieved.

Jenner gives me a serious nod. "I think that's a very mature decision, Dani."

My anger flares and I shrug, hating the bitter tone in my voice that reminds me so much of my mother. "See? And I feel like it might be a stupid decision, Jenner, but I really can't see starting over and finding a whole new team. So, I'm stuck with you whether I like it or not."

Martin flinches at my temper and I turn to him and snap. "Hey, I'm not trying to make you feel bad, but you have to admit it's kind of a big thing not to know. In your defense, you've never done this before. But to be fair, that's not really my problem, is it?" The futility of my situation overwhelms me and suddenly my rage evaporates, leaving me drained and exhausted. I sigh heavily. "But I guess now it is."

I look out the glass front door. "I'm going to take a walk to the bluffs and clear my head. I won't be long. I know we're waiting to record. I just need a break before we start."

Jenner stands up. "You've got about half an hour before the techs will be finished."

I stand and nod. "OK."

I rummage through my bag and pull out my phone. Martin opens his mouth and I cut him off. "Seriously? I think after this conversation, I'm allowed to talk as loudly and as often as I want. I'll go back to whispering when I get back."

Martin shuts his mouth and waves goodbye. As I go through the door, I see Jenner and Martin with their heads together, discussing details.

47

I stalk across the lawn and down to the bluffs. I dial Sean, but he doesn't pick up and neither does Lauren. I glance at the clock on my phone and groan, realizing they're in first period. I hopelessly dial Geena, expecting it to go straight to voicemail and am relieved when she picks up.

"Hey, sis, what's happening? Aren't you supposed to be recording right now?"

I moan into the phone. "I am, but it's a total nightmare today. I needed advice. I already called Sean and Lauren, but they're in class. Why aren't you?"

Geena blows her nose loudly into the phone and I groan. "Eww, gross. You sick?"

"Yeah, I *am* sick, Einstein, how could you tell? And good to know I rank third on your list of calls in an emergency."

I roll my eyes. "Sorry. You know it's not like that. I just started dialing..."

Geena laughs throatily and then coughs. "I'm just teasing. I guess this cold has thrown off my comedic timing. What's wrong?"

Words tumble out as I hurriedly describe the recording issues and Jenner's financing confusion.

Geena blows her nose. "Holy crap! What a mess! And here I was feeling sorry for myself having the flu and having to study for my calculus exam...bet you kinda miss school now, don't ya?"

I groan again. "If I wanted sarcasm, I'd have called Mom. Seriously, Geena, I'm freaking out."

"OK, first things first: the recording issue. You can use a recording from earlier in the day, right? You sang that song for what, eight hours before the buzzing started...so, you must have *one* take that's good enough."

I nod. "I think so. It's just that I don't know exactly what the problem is because I haven't heard it."

"Then you march in there and tell Jenner you want to hear the recording. It might not be as bad as he's making it out to be. At least then, you'll know what you're dealing with."

I sit down on a wooden bench overlooking the cliffs, waves crashing in the distance below. I start to calm down. "Geena, that's a great idea. I hope they'll play it for me."

Geena sneezes. "There's no 'hope' about it, D, they *need* to play it for you. Let's face it, after the conversation you just had with these guys, they aren't really in a position to say no."

"I guess you're right."

"Damn right I'm right, sis. Don't let them treat you like a little girl. You might be young, but you're the reason they're all there. You need to step up and start looking out for yourself. Now, I love Martin, but that was a pretty big mistake he made. Just because he's been a pop star, doesn't mean he's an experienced manager. You need to make sure you're aware of every deal he makes as your guardian. If you don't feel comfortable with the job he's doing, you need to speak up."

I bend forward, plucking a tall stalk of grass from the bluff. I let the wind blow the blade around until it's snatched from my hand. "See, that's the thing. While I know Martin isn't a professional manager, it kind of makes me trust him more. I haven't seen anything really bad from Martin, except this label thing. I feel that if I had someone handling things who's been doing this for years, I'd be more suspicious of them. They'd know all the tricks and be so smooth I wouldn't be able to trust them. I guess the bottom line is that I still trust Martin."

I sigh. "So far, Jenner's been working hard, and he seems honest. And now knowing that he's funding this all on his own, it makes me feel that he's especially motivated to make this happen."

Geena blows her nose. "True. He's got everything to lose if this thing fails."

I snort. "Um, ouch!"

Geena laughs, "You know what I mean, sis. *Of course*, I think you'll be a hit. But Jenner's really motivated to *make* you a hit, you know?"

I nod. "Yeah, I know."

"Well then, there you are. Looks like we've solved all your problems. I'll expect a check in the mail for services rendered."

I smile and stretch, feeling relieved. "I'm glad you picked up the phone, Geena! I feel so much better now."

"I'm always here for you. Good luck and let me know how it goes."

"Will do. Feel better."

"I'll shoot Sean and Lauren a text about what happened. I know you're going to be too busy to do that."

"Thanks, sis. Wait, are you going to mention it to Mom and Dad?"

"Ummm..." Geena pauses, thoughtful. "I don't know if that's such a good idea. I mean Dad will be OK. But it might send Mom over the edge. What if she tries to sue Martin for false pretenses or something and tries to regain guardianship?"

I blanch. "*Oh God.* I'm stressed out enough just trying to make it through each day. Martin might not have asked all the right questions, but I'd still rather have him than Mom." In a small voice, I ask, "Would it be awful if I asked you not to mention this to them? Is that too big a lie?"

Geena is quiet for a moment. "Technically, it's an omission, not an outright lie. Unless, of course, Mom straight-up asks me what your label is or if Martin is doing a flawless job as your manager."

"So, you won't tell her about our conversation today?"

Geena sneezes again. "Conversation? Did we talk today? I've had the flu for two days and I've been quite feverish. I can barely remember the last time we spoke..."

I smile. "Thanks, sis. Once again, I owe you big time."

I hang up the phone and trudge up back to the studio, happy to have a plan.

48

Back in the studio, I find Jenner and Martin in the same spot, locked in a discussion. Martin looks up warily, "You OK?"

I shrug and then nod, avoiding eye contact. "Maybe...I don't know." I kick the ground with my shoe. I finally screw up my courage and look up, at first Martin, then Jenner, "I want to hear those tracks. I need to know how bad it is."

Jenner shrugs. "That, I can do." He gets up, "Come on."

Jenner claps his hands loudly. "OK, everyone out! Ryan, Terrance and Martin, in the booth." Everyone else, standby outside the studio and we will be with you shortly."

The musicians grumble and moan as they put down their instruments. Jenner looks at Carlton and snaps his fingers as he walks into the studio. Carlton frantically shoos everyone out, closing the studio door as he follows them.

I flop down into a swivel chair in the studio as Ryan, whispering with Jenner, keys up the first track. Jenner settles himself against a file cabinet, leaning. Martin and Terrance file in and find seats.

"Ready," Ryan says.

Jenner looks at me, "Ready?"

I nod, not knowing what to expect.

We listen through all the compromised tracks first and then compare them to the "clean" tracks from earlier in the day. At first, I can't hear the buzz at all, dazzled as I am by the amazing orchestra and my polished voice killing the lyrics. But after some coaching from Ryan, it's all I can hear, like an annoying fly droning subtly through the recordings. It's irritating as hell.

Jenner folds his arms. "What do you think Dani, now that you've heard everything?"

I shake my head frustrated, kicking the floor. "I hate to say it, but you're right. Since Ryan pointed it out, it's so obviously *there*, I can't ignore it. And those tracks from the end of the day were our best ones. The ones from earlier were *fine*, but not as..." I grasp for the right word. "Oh, I don't know, they just don't seem as finished, you know? We seem so tight and put-together on those last few takes, really jelling together and in the music. Those other ones are too clean; no soul."

Jenner nods his head, a smile creeping across his face. "Exactly, Dani! You get it." He closes his eyes in defeat. "And you get now why we have to record it again."

I groan. "Ugh, yes."

Jenner straightens himself, pulling away from the cabinet he's leaning on. "Get everyone back in here, then. Let's get this over with."

***

It's noon by the time we start recording. We decide to quickly knock out "White Christmas" and then spend the rest of the day re-recording "My Place." While no one's excited about another five hours of the same song, we're more in sync, thanks to our session the day before. The recordings from this latest series prove to be the best of the bunch.

We call it quits around 7:00 p.m. Jenner has been up for almost forty hours and is dead on his feet. I haven't talked to Martin all day; he tried to give me space. As we drive up to the house, I break the silence. "So, about this morning. I'm not *still* mad about the whole label thing. I wish it was something I knew before but, at the end of the day, it doesn't affect our deal, right?"

Martin looks visibly relieved. "No, it doesn't. Our deal is with Jenner, so regardless of what deal he makes with a label, he's contractually obligated to pay us what we agreed upon. Your signing bonus is already in a trust fund, so that's a done deal. If anyone has something to risk, it's Jenner. If the label wants to pay us less than he's agreed to give us in the contract, that comes out of his end, not ours."

I nod. "Good. Look, I know you're upset about this and, to be honest, I'm glad that you are, because it shows me you care about the job you're doing and, well...about me, too. I know you're not a pro at this, and that we're both kinda learning as we go. Just be honest with me. If something like this comes up again, let's deal with it together. I don't want any more surprises. Agreed?"

Martin stops the cart and turns to me, tears in his eyes. "Agreed." We hug it out, and I feel better than I have all day. "Dani, you have no idea how guilty I feel. I thought I'd covered all my bases and asked all the right questions. I'll do my best to make sure something like this doesn't happen again. This morning was the first time I heard about this label thing. I had no idea Jenner was underwriting all costs upfront. I've never once kept a secret from you."

I smile. "I know, Martin. And that's why I still want you here. You really do have my best interests at heart." I squeeze his hand. "Let's go; I'm starving."

Martin claps his hands loudly, which makes me laugh so hard that I almost fall out of the cart as we speed up to the house.

***

To make up for this morning, Martin's arranged a special cheeseburger dinner. We eat downstairs in our sweatpants while we watch *Mean Girls*. I'm even allowed to speak—if I keep my words to a minimum.

"Think they based Regina and the Plastics on Zoe and her minions?" I ask, as I lazily munch on a leftover French fry.

"Absolutely! Too bad you can't come up with your own Kälteen Bar scheme for Zoe. I'm still a big fan of ex-lax brownies. It's an oldie, but a goodie!"

I laugh. "I'd have to be at school so I could enjoy the payoff! I think Zoe is safe from me as long as she keeps her hands off my man. Hey," I check the time on my phone, "I'm gonna give Sean a call before I go to bed."

I start to gather the dishes and Martin waves a hand. "Nope, cleanup is on me tonight. Least I can do. Say hi to Prince Charming for me. Just try not to talk for too long. Remember to rest your voice."

"Will do." I smile before bounding up the stairs.

49

The days blur together as we lock down the EP. Most of the time I feel like a zombie, mindlessly following my repetitive schedule, sending brief texts everyone between recording, eating and sleeping. I've never been more tired in my life.

The only time I truly come alive is when I'm singing. Once I'm in the studio, I forget everything else and throw myself into the music. Terrance and I develop a rhythm during the recording sessions, and I feel like I'm doing what I was born to do. As the days flow past, my confidence grows.

Toward the end of October, the EP is almost complete and Jenner slates the last day to cover "Without You," a song he believes will launch my career into instant stardom.

Exhausted after another grueling day in the studio and too tired to text, I reach for my phone while I wait for dinner and dial Sean. He picks up on the fourth ring. "Hey, how's recording going?"

I smile. "Great! Only one more day, and then we're finished." I can hear rustling in the background. "What are you doing?"

"Oh, sorry. It's Homecoming, remember?"

I jolt up. "Wait, you're *going* to Homecoming? Tonight?"

"Yeah, but only with Scott. The whole basketball team is going. We thought we'd meet up there and then go see a movie. Are you upset?"

I'm completely flustered. "I don't know. I mean, I kind of forgot it was tonight... I feel stupid. You also said you and Scott were just going to hang out and game, but now you're going to the dance. It's just weird; I don't know."

"Hey, it's not like I'm going with another girl. We're just going to say hi, see what's up and then see the new Marvel movie at 10:00. That's it. You've been so busy this week, I didn't think it was important to remind you about the dance since we weren't going together."

I sigh. "Sorry; I just feel really out of it. Go, have a good time. Send pictures."

"Will do, D." The rustling starts in the background. "I feel like a dog, but I have to get going. You sure you're OK?"

I force a smile. "I'm sure. Have fun tonight."

"I will. Get some rest and good luck tomorrow. Love you."

I blow a kiss into the phone, but Sean's already hung up. I toss my phone onto the bed moodily and stomp to the couch, flopping down and groaning loudly. Martin walks in a few minutes later.

"What's with all the noise?" He sits on the coffee table and nudges me playfully with his foot. "What gives, cupcake?"

I scowl. "Nothing. It's just that the Homecoming dance is tonight, and I found out Sean is going."

Martin looks concerned. "Going with who? Not that tramp Zoe?"

"No, just with his friend, Scott, but still. I spend all my time here and my friends are living their lives without me. I feel like I'm missing out."

Martin gives my knee a pat. "I know. It's hard to be here when all your friends are hanging out together. But, hey, at the end of it all, you're going to have this kick-ass EP to show for it. So yeah, missing the dance sucks, but you're going to get a whole bunch more out of this than just a stupid, old corsage. Hang in there. Remember, this is what we signed up for."

I think for a minute and sigh. "Yeah, I know. I'm just feeling sorry for myself."

Martin shrugs. "You're allowed. Look, dinner will be here any minute. I got Thai food; I know that you love pad Thai. Get cleaned up and come down. Maybe we can watch a few episodes of *Friends* while we eat."

I glare at him. "Are you trying to be funny? *Friends*? When I'm just complaining about my lack thereof?"

Martin looks sheepish. "Oops! Sorry, I'm not that much of a jerk. Look, you pick the show. Anything to get you to stop pouting, OK?"

I exhale huffily. "Fine."

After I shower, I pull on my most comfy sweats, pile my hair into a messy bun and imagine Lauren and Geena getting glammed up for the dance. I plod downstairs, grumbling when the doorbell rings. "Can you get that?" Martin calls from the kitchen. "Be out in a sec with the money."

"Fine," I bark sourly, still mumbling to myself in a grouchy way about the dance. I pull open the door, looking down the hall for Martin. "Hi, just be a minute for the..."

I turn to look at the delivery guy and see Sean standing there in a tuxedo, holding a clear plastic box with a corsage. Gobsmacked, my jaw drops open.

"Want to go to Homecoming with me?" A flash blinds me before I can answer, and Lauren pops out from behind Sean, snapping photos with Tom in tow, filming the whole thing.

Tears well up in my eyes. "Are you *kidding* me?!?" I jump into Sean's arms, squealing. I bury my face in Sean's neck.

Martin and Jenner appear in the doorway. "Surprise! Jenner and I thought you've been working so hard these past few weeks that you deserve a reward. We postponed tomorrow's session so you could go to the dance tonight."

I whirl around and hug Martin and Jenner simultaneously. "Thank you so much!!! This is the best surprise ever."

"It was all Martin's idea. I didn't do a thing."

"Except give permission," Martin chimes in, elbowing Jenner in the ribs before calling out to Lauren. "OK, Miss Thing, did you bring it?"

Lauren pushes her way forward with a huge garment bag in her arms. "All set, Martin. Fifteen minutes, and we'll be ready to go." She pushes me upstairs and we disappear in a flurry of giggles and whispers.

"Come on in, gentlemen. We've got refreshments on the terrace." Martin and Jenner lead the boys inside.

50

Thank God I took Martin's advice and showered! I'm on cloud nine when I see the dress Lauren pulls out. It is an aubergine-colored, A-line halter dress with a cutout in the back, beading on the top and a short, tulle, princess skirt. It's just the type of dress I've always imagined I'd wear to my first "big dance"...fun and flirty, with just a hint of sexy. Lauren pulls out matching heels and an adorable sequined clutch.

"Oh my God, where did you get this?" I hold up the dress and twirl in the mirror. "It's just perfect."

Lauren beams. "It is, if I do say so myself. I think my career as a stylist has just begun! Martin told me to pick up an outfit for you with all the accessories and charge it to Jenner. I'm glad you like it! Now about that hair..."

Lauren hangs the dress on the bathroom door as she shoves me into the bathroom. Plunking me down on a stool, Lauren orders me to brush my hair while she grabs her tote bag. While we wait for the curling iron to heat, I do my makeup while Lauren figures out what hairstyle would work best.

Fifteen minutes later, as promised, we walk out onto the terrace to the applause of all the boys. Lauren has curled my hair into beachy waves and put it in a high pony, with tendrils falling around my face. She's added some smoke and shimmer to my simple makeup. I feel like a princess.

Sean's grinning from ear to ear as he walks over to me. "You look beautiful! I want to kiss you, but I don't want to ruin your makeup."

Lauren nudges him into me and laughs. "Go for it, Sean. We've got more lipstick to repair any damage." I giggle and look up at Sean. He stares deeply into my eyes, and I melt. He comes in for a slow long kiss and everyone on the terrace just watches, smiling and snapping photos. After a few moments, Martin clears his throat.

"I don't mean to interrupt, but you'd better get going. Have fun and be safe. Dani, home by midnight, all right?"

Lauren pipes up. "Midnight? But it takes so long to get to school from here that we'll have to practically turn around once we get there."

Jenner laughs nods in agreement. "She's right. How about you leave at midnight. Call us when you're on your way. Does that work?"

Lauren seems about to say something, but Tom grabs her by the arm to escort her out.

I nod, just happy to be going. "Absolutely perfect. And thanks again for letting me go. It's a dream come true. And, Jenner, this dress is amazing. Thank you."

He gives me a hug. "You look like a princess. Enjoy your night with your friends, sweetheart." He calls out goodbye to the rest of the kids as they leave the terrace.

Martin walks me out. "So, you were surprised?" I nod vigorously. "Good! I know you've been missing out on the high school experience these past few weeks. We just wanted to give you a little treat. But you should know that Jenner is having everyone send him photos from tonight, and he'll be posting them as part of your publicity. It's kinda the price of letting you go. You OK with that?"

I grin. "That's a small price to pay for such an amazing surprise. Absolutely. Post away."

We reach the driveway, and I see my friends pile into a black Navigator limousine. My mouth flies open, agog, and I look at Martin. "I convinced Jenner that maybe he shouldn't trust your boys to drive his biggest investment around these twisty canyon roads at night. All I ask is for you to describe Zoe's face when she sees you get out of that limo. It's going to be pure heaven...totally worth the money!"

I laugh and give him a hug as the horn honks. Lauren pops her head out of the moon roof. "Come on, Truehart. You've spent the past two months with Martin. I'm sure he can survive a few hours without you."

I laugh and hop down the stairs and into the limo, snuggling next to Sean. Lauren yelps and pulls her head back inside as the limo pulls out, blaring music.

***

The drive to school is filled with laughter and music, everyone talking over each other. I can't wait to see Geena, who's going with friends from her class and will meet us at the dance.

When we arrive on campus, we fall out of the limo, laughing and causing a scene. Zoe is trudging up the steps to the gym surrounded by her minions when she sees Sean emerge from the car. She starts down the steps to meet him but stops abruptly when she sees me exit the limo. I'm in such a good mood, I don't even register it's Zoe and genuinely smile at her. But as soon as Zoe gives me the finger, I realize who it is. I shrug it off, too excited to let her bring me down. Lauren's giggling, standing next to me and tapping away on her cell phone. "Martin's going to *love* that picture!"

I let the group walk ahead of me as I drink in the moment. I feel so lucky to be here with the people I love on such a special night. I sigh happily as I run to catch up, calling Sean's name.

Having Sean by my side all night, surrounded by our friends, is sheer perfection. We dance, laugh and take a million pictures which we dutifully send to Jenner, who will plaster them all over Instagram.

My circle of friends is small because I often miss school for lessons or competitions. But the buzz of my impending album is a big topic at the dance. Dozens of kids I don't really know come up to congratulate me and take pictures so they can say they "knew me when." I've never felt more of a member of my school than I do at this dance.

The only dark cloud is Zoe, who spends the entire night looking like she wants to murder me. Lauren and Geena find this hysterical and keep snapping photos of Zoe's sour face and sending them to Martin. I'm surprised that I don't enjoy Zoe's misery more. I always thought that, given the chance, I'd love to see Zoe suffer for all the torture she's put me through. But being with Sean is the most important thing to me, and I focus all of my attention on him.

As the dance wraps up, there's a debate on what we should do. Lauren wants to grab some food and Geena thinks we should take a drive to walk on the beach. I'm thrilled when Sean politely overrules them all, saying he needs to spend some alone time with his girl. Everyone rolls their eyes, not wanting the fun to end, but Sean stands firm and asks the driver to drop everyone else off first.

A little before eleven, we're headed back to Malibu. Sean puts up the privacy glass. While I feel awkward at first, worrying about what the driver might think, I soon forget about him as Sean and I make up for weeks apart. It's hard to stay on the seat as the car swerves around the canyon curves, but we can't keep our hands off of each other, and we laugh as we slip and slide around the car. I'm melting, my body buzzing with excitement at Sean's touch. As the limo slows for a red light, Sean looks up to see where we are. "We're almost there."

I sigh. "What time is it?"

Sean smiles. "It's almost midnight. I thought we could go park somewhere until about one."

My eyes widen. "I'm not going to go parking with some random limo driver watching us get it on."

Sean laughs. "Eww, no! I drove myself to Jenner's tonight. So," he says, pulling out his phone, "I'm going to let Martin know we're leaving the dance in fifteen minutes and that buys us about an hour alone."

Once we pull ourselves together, we tell the driver to drop us off outside the compound gates. We hop into Sean's car and drive to a secluded beach. It's too cold to sit on the beach, so we climb into the backseat and pick up where we left off.

It's all we can do to stop ourselves from going all the way. We're saved by the bell when the alarm Sean set on his phone goes off, letting him know it's time to take me home. We both jump at the sound and Sean swipes at his phone, knocking it on the floor of the front seat. He scrambles to find it. I feel my blood beating rhythmically, my heat ebbing as my heart slows.

Sean flops back next to me, frustrated. "God, this is so hard. You feel so good." He turns and nuzzles my cheek, his hands wandering to my thighs, caressing. "Just a few more minutes..." he sighs as the phone buzzes again, as does mine.

Sean groans. "We're late. I don't want to risk Jenner saying 'No' the next time we want to be together. Just give me a minute."

I start to protest, but Sean quickly gets out of the car and walks around for a few minutes, taking some deep breaths. Once I realize he isn't getting back in, I get myself together and climb into the front seat, still a bit shaky. Finally, Sean gets into the car and starts the engine. He gives me a short smile as he backs out of the parking space. I feel bad. "I'm sorry, Sean."

He shakes his head and cuts me off. "Don't even worry, Dani. I'm just happy we had some time together." He looks at me and winks. I feel relieved. I'm suddenly exhausted.

Sean pulls into the gates a few moments later and Martin's waiting at the door. He gives us a sharp look, taps his watch and shuts the door to let us say goodbye.

Sean leans over and gives me a long kiss. "I will never forget tonight."

I smile, drinking in his face. "Me either."

A flash of light as the front door opens again and Sean nods toward the house. "Better get inside. Martin looks pissed."

I sigh and unbuckle my seat belt. "See you soon. I hope."

Sean reaches for my hand and gently squeezes. "Me too."

He honks as he drives off, and I wave. I smile at Martin dreamily. "I know we're late, and I'm sorry. But it was the best night ever. Thank you so much!"

I give Martin a hug and float up the stairs.

51

I'm still asleep when I hear the door creak. I open my eyes and see Martin. "Morning. What time is it?" I mumble through a yawn.

"A little after twelve. Good morning, sleeping beauty." He comes in and sits on the edge of my bed. "How are you feeling?"

I stretch luxuriously, "Mmm, great." Another yawn and I sit up, "I can't believe you guys pulled that off. That was the best night of my life!"

I smile, and he squeezes my hand. "Good. You deserved a special night."

I smile to myself, remembering my time with Sean. "Yeah, it was just what I needed. Sorry about being late. I guess we just were having so much fun, we lost track of time."

Martin nods. "I was surprised you were late, considering Lauren texted me at eleven, saying she left her shawl in the limo and asked me to grab it when you got home."

Martin stares pointedly at me, and my blood freezes. Martin continues. "She said she'd tried texting you and Sean but neither of you were answering. You want to tell me where you were for two hours if you'd dropped everyone off by 11:00?"

I blush uncontrollably and flash hot. "Um, well, Sean and I just wanted to spend a little time alone together, so we, uh, went parking for a bit."

Martin looks horrified, "With some strange limo driver watching you?"

I wave my hands. "Oh God, no. Sean drove his car over here earlier, so we got dropped off at midnight and went to Broad Beach. You know, just to be alone."

Martin looks relieved. "Well, thank God for that. I don't need a cellphone video of you getting frisky in the back seat of a limo dropping the same week as your EP." Martin looks out the window, thinking.

I quietly wait, unsure of how angry Martin is. Finally, he sighs and turns.

"Look, sweetie, it's going to get awkward here for a few minutes, but you're just going to have to deal with it. I didn't think we'd be having a conversation like this because let's face it, I'm not your mom or dad. I have no idea what you've been told or what your experience is, but I feel like I need to say something."

Oh, God! Is he going to say what I think he's going to say? I shake my head. "Martin, I…"

He holds up a hand. "I'm not here to lecture you on sex. That's not my department. I just want to give you a little advice. I know how overwhelmingly strong your feelings are for Sean. Falling in love for the first time is intense. You're dealing with some very big, very real feelings. I remember what that's like at your age. Adding sex to a relationship raises the stakes, and it can mess with your head if you're not ready for it. And I just want to make sure that you keep your focus on the EP. We're almost done. I don't want you getting distracted. OK?"

Phew! Relieved, I slowly nod. "Good. Now there's a lot more I could say about love and sex, waiting, commitment, etc. But I'll leave that alone for now and instead I'll say this: If you get pregnant now," Martin waves his hand around the room, "this all goes away. We cannot put you out there as a rising star if you get pregnant at fifteen. Does that make sense?"

I'm mortified. "Martin! I'm not that stupid!"

Martin holds up a finger. "Stupid has nothing to do with it. No one expects to get pregnant when they're a teenager. You're still learning how your body works—how sex works—and it can happen in a second. It has everything to do with impulsiveness and self-control rather than stupidity and intelligence, you got that?"

I nod uncomfortably. Martin continues. "I will always be here to support you. But Jenner can't be expected to pursue this if you get into trouble with Sean in the next few months. I don't know what you all got up to last night, and I don't want to know." Martin rolls his eyes.

"Unless you need to talk about it, and then, of course, I'm always here for you. But you have to think *all the time* about what your priorities are right now. Think about what's more important... feeling good for fifteen minutes in the back seat of a car, or a career that could set you up for a lifetime of success. It's time to start making smart decisions for yourself, Dani."

I'm appalled and embarrassed by this conversation. *Something so intimate and special like what Sean and I have just experienced is now being discussed like an unwanted stop on a busy concert schedule.* I'm fuming. I cross my arms and stare at the ceiling.

Martin stands up. "Look, I know you think I'm a jerk because I'm talking about something extremely personal and I'm reducing it to a business problem. I'm sorry. I don't mean to trample over your private moments. But as your guardian and friend, I have to be very clear about what any mistakes could mean if you aren't careful with Sean. I love Sean, and you know I'm pulling for you two to make it. But, selfishly, I also want you to make it big as a singer because that's what you should be doing with your talent. Not having babies at fifteen." He pats the foot of the bed and walks out. "Just think about it?"

I continue to stare at the ceiling until I hear the door click. I throw my pillow at the door. I've never been so embarrassed in my whole life. *Does Martin have to get mixed up in every little detail of my life? Is nothing sacred?*

I reach for my phone and dial Lauren, anxious to vent. "Hey, D! How was the drive home?"

"It would have been perfect if someone hadn't texted Martin asking for her lost shawl, telling him we drove back at eleven."

"Wait, what? I tried texting both of you, but you didn't pick up. It's my mom's shawl. She made such a big deal about—"

I cut her off. "I don't care about the stupid shawl. I'm upset because Sean and I went out after the limo dropped us off, and we didn't get in until one. Martin wanted to know what we'd done in the time we were missing. I got this uncomfortable sex/don't-get-pregnant talk from Martin just now. And I'm just so mad because every little thing I do is tracked and watched and commented on by Martin or Jenner. I just want something for myself, *one* little thing. And I can't even have that!"

"Dani, I'm so sorry! I didn't know. I feel like an idiot. Wait..." Lauren takes a deep breath. "Did you say 'sex talk'? Did you two *do it* last night?"

I roll my eyes and flop onto the bed. "No, we didn't *do it* last night, though we came close. It's just weird to have Martin talk to me about the dangers of sex and how all this would end if I got pregnant right now."

"He said that?"

I groan. "Yup, he said all this stuff like sex complicates a relationship and that I need to focus on my career, not Sean, because I'll lose my shot if I get pregnant."

Lauren gasps, "Oh my God, how embarrassing!"

"Tell me about it! Talk about the worst sex talk ever!" I exhale loudly. "Anyway, I'm sorry. I'm not mad at you, Laur. I was just more embarrassed to have Martin talk to me about all this stuff. You didn't know."

"Naw, but I should have figured." Lauren giggles. "So, tell me more about last night!"

***

I start the day by avoiding Martin, but by the time the evening rolls around, I've gotten over my embarrassment and realize he was only trying to help me avoid a major mistake. I'm stretched out on the sofa downstairs watching *Friends* when he plops down on the other sofa.

"Hey," I venture, staring at the TV.

"Hey, yourself. Did you rest up?"

"Yup, I took a nap, biked a bit at the gym and even practiced some scales."

"I'm impressed. I didn't expect any of that."

"Well, I didn't want you to think I don't appreciate what you did yesterday. I want to be ready for tomorrow."

Martin nods. "Thank you."

"I'm sorry I overreacted this morning. I was just really embar-rassed..."

Martin holds up a hand, cutting me off. "Say no more. I appreciate your apology. I'm glad you know I was only coming from a place of love. We won't say another word about it."

I smile. "Deal. Did you have fun with Brett today?"

Martin beams. "Yes, I did. Thank you for asking. We worked out and then went for a picnic on the beach." Martin peeks down his shirt. "I actually have an ab or two hiding around here somewhere. I'm becoming very physically impressive."

I nod. "You look good! Nice job."

"Thank you. I'm in a good place right now with my body, with Brett, with you. I feel very blessed."

I settle back onto the couch and wave my hand around the room. "You know this all goes away if you get pregnant. Just saying." I laugh as a cushion hits me in the head.

52

I wake up the next morning and get ready for my final recording session. I take an extra-long shower while I run scales, warming my voice. If everything goes according to Jenner's plan, my biggest song, "Without You," will be locked down by this evening, and I'll be just weeks away from my world debut. It's hard to imagine that I'm so close to launching my career! I'm excited and nervous.

I shuffle into the kitchen. Martin looks up, relieved. "I was worried I'd have to drag you out of bed. It's 7:30, and we have to leave in fifteen minutes. Jenner's already called the house six times to see how you are doing."

I stand and sip the steaming mug of tea that Magda hands me. Magda gives me a side hug. "We're all so proud of you, Lánv." She kisses me on the cheek and hustles back to the stove. I look questioningly at Martin.

He leans forward and whispers conspiratorially, "It means 'girl' in Hungarian. Quite an honor to get a hug from Magda."

Magda exhales grumpily at Martin. "What? I am very proud of our girl. She has brought life back to this house and Mr. Redman. We are lucky to have her here. I wish her all the success there is."

I beam and put down my mug to hug Magda. "Thank you, Magda. I don't know what I'd do without you."

Magda squeezes back tightly and then shoos me away. "You finish tea, and I get breakfast ready. You eat in the cart."

I look again at Martin. "Magda's making your breakfast to go. Just warning you, Jenner's already stressed to the max, and we haven't even started yet. Be prepared for a total meltdown at some point today."

I frown. "Has something happened?"

Martin shakes his head. "Everything's fine but remember that Jenner's backing this whole rodeo out of his pocket. If we don't lock this down today, we're going to have issues meeting the deadline the recording company set to listen to the EP. If they won't listen to it, they won't back it, and Jenner's left holding a very expensive bag. He doesn't have any extra money to book the engineer for an emergency twenty-four-hour shift. We already lost a day with that buzzing fiasco on Day One. This is crunch time."

I feel the bile rise in my stomach. "You really know how to relax a kid, Martin."

Martin reaches over and squeezes my hand. "No secrets, remember? You wanted us to be upfront about everything. This is what we're up against."

I exhale loudly and nod slowly, trying to calm down, "Right. Let's get down there and get started." Magda places a foil-wrapped burrito on the counter in front of me. I shake my head, pushing it away. "If I eat that, I'm going to be sick."

Martin unwraps the burrito and places it firmly in my hand. "Eat. You'll do us no good if you pass out from stress and malnourishment in two hours. That would *really* set us back."

I nod and bite into the burrito. "Anything for the team," I mumble through my food. "Let's go."

Minutes later we pull up to the studio. We feel the tension as soon as we open the door. Jenner's in the booth, having an intense conversation with Ryan. Carlton bustles in the background, discarding old food wrappers and trying not to eavesdrop too obviously. Martin waves as Jenner glances up.

Martin starts toward the booth. "Let's see where they want you." Terrance pops his head out of the small recording room at the front of the studio. "Morning! In here."

Terrance pushes his bangs away from his eyes, only to have them immediately flop back into place. As we walk in, Terrance grabs a thin, elastic headband from his bag to shove his bangs out of the way. It makes him look like a disheveled teen studying for finals.

Terrance glances at the booth to make sure the intercom light is off and whispers, "I would speak only when spoken to today. Jenner's wound so tightly, he might explode at the least provocation. He's reading Ryan the riot act because he doesn't want any cockups like that first day. I gotta say, Ryan's taking it like a champ. Anyone else would have walked out by now."

Terrance returns his gaze to me and smiles. "Are you ready? Our final day in this tin can before all the fun starts." He rubs his hands together maniacally. "I can't wait to get started. You're going to knock this out of the park."

He spins around to the piano and plops down, playing a couple of chords. "We've got musicians coming at 1:00 p.m. to try it with a full orchestra. But the way I think it's going to play best is with just little old me on piano and you, glorious you, thrilling us with your voice. It's simple, pure and truly the only way this song needs to be played. MEGA gets the final say, but as far as I'm concerned, there's no contest."

Terrance begins to play the ballad, its pure notes filling the small studio. I sit on the bench next to Terrance, and Martin leans against the wall.

As soon as the song ends, Jenner jumps onto the intercom. "Great run-through, Terrance. Let's get started. Dani, do you need to warm up, or are you ready?"

"I'm ready," I say with a nod.

We record the acoustic version of the song until the musicians begin to show up. I look at the clock, my stomach rumbling. "We've been doing this for almost five hours?" I ask, incredulous.

I glance at Terrance who, despite being drenched in sweat, is beaming and nodding his head, exhilarated. "Yup. Time flies when you're locking down perfection." He gets up and gives me a high-five as I laugh.

"Bro, all I can say is that you stink! You'd better take a shower before we start this afternoon!"

Terrance smells his armpit and smiles. "That's the smell of platinum records, Dani. See for yourself." He chases me with his armpit as I scream, running out of the room and right into Jenner, who grabs my shoulders and gives me a bear hug.

"Have I mentioned today how brilliant you are? You're even more brilliant than I suspected, which, of course, makes me a genius for signing you. After today, we all need to buy bigger wallets because we're about to be very rich." He gives me a kiss on top of the head. "Why don't you run up to the house? Magda's got lunch ready for you. Take a break, a shower, whatever you need, and be back here by 2:00. We're going to get the musicians up to speed, and we'll be ready to go by then."

I nod and leave with Martin to eat and freshen up.

***

The second part of the day goes by just as quickly as the first. There are about thirty musicians crammed into the larger recording space, which makes for a very cramped, party-like atmosphere. The music is powerful and the studio pulses with energy. We plug away until 1:00 a.m.

I'm so exhausted that I can't think straight, but I also have such a strange, vibrating energy that falling asleep is impossible. As the musicians pack up, I wander into the booth and sit next to Martin.

"Above and beyond, Dani, that's all I can say. You've just blown us all away. Again."

I grin from ear to ear. "Can I hear both versions? I'm dying to hear how they sound!"

My voice is tired and hoarse. Martin holds up a hand. "Absolutely. Just do me a favor. No talking right now. Your pipes need a rest."

A cup of steaming tea appears at my side. "Chamomile with lemon and honey," Carlton whispers into my ear. I almost slop it out of the mug trying to get my ear away from his warm mouth.

"Thanks," I whisper as he slinks away.

I sip my tea and smile at Martin as Jenner, Terrance and Ryan huddle together, whispering as they listen to the song in their headsets. Just as my eyes start to close, Jenner whips his headsets off and leaps up. "We've got it! Ready to hear your soon-to-be-number-one hit?"

I nod vigorously, sitting back in my chair. Martin leans forward, elbows on his knees, hands covering his mouth.

The booth fills with a wave of strings, piano and woodwinds. I sit entranced as the music I've heard countless times today washes over me as if for the first time, blending with my vocals and transforming the song into a powerful ballad I don't recognize. Chills run down my arms while the violins and piano weave around my voice. I can't believe this is *my* song; this is *my* voice. I have tears in my eyes as the song finishes.

The silence in the booth is deafening. Jenner is the first to speak, boasting, "Dani's reaction says it all for me, Terrance. Get ready to lose. I'm sure my version will beat out yours."

Terrance walks away from the console and drapes himself over a chair, slinging his legs over the arm. He counters, "Of course, she's emotional. She's sleep-deprived. Just wait until she hears my version. There will be no comparison."

I look at Martin, stunned. He grabs my hand and squeezes it. "It's beautiful, sweetheart."

Wordlessly, Terrance leans over and hits a button on the board. Piano music, crisp and clean, fills the room, the notes mournful and deep. The music is the same, but the effect is altogether different. The power and strength of the orchestra are stripped away to reveal the honest and raw emotion of the piano. Rather than weaving around the lyrics, the piano and words work together, voice harmonizing with the chords. When the song finishes, the room is again silent, everyone deep in thought.

Martin throws up his hands and shakes his head. "Well, I'll be damned if I can tell you which one I like better. What a wonderful problem to have! I sure am glad I don't have to decide."

Jenner laughs and scrubs his face with his hands. "It's all up to MEGA now."

We all sit in contented silence, each fantasizing about what will happen next. The only people who don't seem too affected are Ryan and Carlton, neither of whom stand to gain anything from the EP.

They both busy themselves with cleaning up and shutting down the studio.

Finally, Jenner sighs and rubs his eyes. "Well, I've been up for close to twenty-four hours, and I'm beat. Everyone, get some rest. We'll talk tomorrow." He gets up and gives me a hug. "Thank you for giving it everything you have, Dani."

I hug Jenner back, tears coming to my eyes. "Thanks for giving me a chance, Jenner."

He wipes his eyes as he steps back to shake Martin's hand.

"Thank you for giving me another chance. I hope I can eventually make things up to you."

Martin nods and stands, shaking Jenner's hand vigorously. "I appreciate that."

After speaking to Terrance and Ryan, Jenner nods wordlessly and leaves. Carlton scurries after him, grabbing the cart keys and waving goodbye.

"Well, lovelies, it's time to say goodnight." Terrance grabs my hands and holds me at arms' length, gazing at me. "Thank you for surprising me beyond my wildest expectations. I am so excited about your future." He gives me a big hug, then he hugs Martin as well before he sails out the door.

Martin reaches out and grabs my hand, shouldering my bag at the same time. "Come on, superstar. Time to get some rest. It's full throttle from here on out!"

53

Martin wasn't kidding! After taking a day to recover, I'm thrown into EP release prep at a mind-numbing pace. Costume fittings, hair and makeup tests and dance rehearsals fill my days, along with the usual workouts and voice rehearsals.

My favorite activity is working with the dance troupe that will accompany me on my publicity tour. The dancers are a few years older than me. Their confidence and brash humor make me laugh and sometimes blush. But after being isolated from the company of young people for such a long time, I'm happy just to be in their presence and soaking up their energy.

While I love dancing, I'm not used to having twelve older men and women focus their attention on me, acting deferentially and changing their demeanor when I approach. It's slightly embarrassing and stressful that Serena keeps thrusting me to the center of attention during each rehearsal.

The only dancer who seems to treat me normally is Beau. A few months shy of eighteen, he's the youngest dancer of the troupe. He always greets me by name when I enter the studio, while the other dancers only nod or chat among themselves. He tries to include me in conversations and shares his stories about growing up in foster care. He even starts showing up early for rehearsal so we can share a snack, and he often stays for dinner afterward. He isn't being flirty, just friendly. He reminds me more of a classmate than a coworker. I'm grateful for his friendship. He seems to have so much life experience compared to me. I'm glad for his company because Sean and my friends are prepping for midterms and aren't able to visit or chat as often right now.

***

One evening, Jenner enters the kitchen where Martin, Beau and

I are seated at the island, eating dinner. Beau's regaling us with another foster care story.

Jenner clears his throat and it takes some minutes for Beau to notice that Martin and I are staring expectantly at Jenner. Beau seems a bit put out that he's been interrupted, but he stops his story.

"I don't believe we've met..." Jenner looks at Beau pointedly. Beau throws Jenner a nod as he bites into his burger. "I'm Beau. I'm with Dani."

Jenner looks at Martin, who shakes his head. "By 'with Dani,' you mean..."

Beau shrugs. "I'm one of her dancers. Who are you?"

Jenner takes a step forward. "I pay you, so you should *know* who I am. This is my house, and that's my food you're eating." Beau turns white, and he tries to swallow his food.

I jump in and try to clear things up. "I'm sorry, Jenner. I thought you two knew each other. I should have introduced you. This is Beau. He's one of the backup dancers. I invited him up for dinner with us. I hope it's OK."

I must look super worried because Jenner takes a deep breath and decides not to pursue it. "It's fine, Dani. This is your home, too." I heave a sigh of relief. Jenner continues, "Well, Beau, it looks as if you've finished eating. So, if you wouldn't mind leaving, we have some business to discuss."

Beau's far from finished, but he doesn't have much choice. He nods, wipes his mouth and jumps off the stool. He grabs his plate, but Jenner stops him. "We'll take care of that. Let's just walk you out. Anatoli?"

Anatoli appears instantly from the hall, grabs Beau's backpack and escorts a bewildered Beau out.

Martin starts to apologize, but Jenner cuts him off. "We'll discuss *him* later. What I have to say now is *huge*." He pauses, an expectant smile on his face. "I gave MEGA a little sneak preview of your songs and they just offered us a contract! They are buying the EP straight out and want to release three full albums over the next five years.

They're so thrilled with what we've presented that they're bumping your release date to next week. They're also finalizing plans to have you sing in the Macy's Thanksgiving Day Parade. We did it!"

Martin and I scream simultaneously. Jenner lets out a whoop that drowns us both out. He grabs a bottle of Cristal from the fridge and pops the cork. "Dani, I know you're underage, but upon closing your first huge record contract from a major label, at least one sip of champagne is required."

Jenner grabs three delicate crystal flutes from a cabinet and pours. We toast to our hard work and the future. The champagne tastes slightly bitter and the bubbles made my eyes tear up. I quickly put my glass down and grimace.

Jenner laughs. "Wow, turning up her nose at Cristal! She really is a diva, Martin!"

Martin chuckles and reached for my flute. "More for me! They're covering all costs, right? There's no lag in money, so you're not on the hook for anything?"

Jenner starts laughing, and he pours himself more champagne, which quickly overflows from his glass. "No lag in money? Martin, it's a $3-million contract with a $500,000 signing bonus! You're all getting a bonus as soon as we sign the contract tomorrow! It's more than I've ever been offered for an unknown talent." He points at me. "You, my girl, are a gift from heaven."

My head is reeling. "Wait, half-a-million-dollar signing bonus? How much of that goes into my pocket?"

When Jenner explains the breakdown, I fall off my stool and scream again. I can't believe it! "Oh my God! I have to call my sister, Sean, like everyone I know! Jenner, I can't believe you made this happen!"

I jump up and give Jenner a hug, practically knocking him over. He laughs. "No, darlin', it was all you." He looks over at Martin. "And you, Martin. None of this would be happening if it weren't for you, too."

Martin beams and shakes his head. "I don't know if it's the champagne or the thought of all that money that's got my head spinning."

Jenner and I grin at Martin. He shimmies with excitement on his stool. "I don't know who I'm going to call first, Mama or Brett!" Martin pauses and looks at us. "Oh, shut up!" he says, laughing and rolling his eyes. "Yes, I have a boyfriend. Deal with it!"

We all laugh and stand there, smiling like idiots and savoring our first taste of success.

I look from Jenner to Martin. "We make a pretty good team." We look at each other and nod in agreement.

***

Hours later, I'm still on the phone making calls to friends and family. I call Geena first, who screams so loudly my parents rush upstairs, thinking Geena hurt herself, only to find her jumping for joy. I've never heard my mom so happy in all my life. My dad is so emotional he can't even speak on the phone, and my heart practically bursts with love. Geena promises to call my grandmother and share the good news. I feel a small twinge of guilt that I still haven't found time to reach out to her, but it quickly fades away amid all my excitement.

I FaceTime Sean, who's so excited he runs downstairs to share the news with his entire family. Lauren does the same with her family. I'm so touched by how excited everyone is for me. I feel so much love from people I love so much.

I'm *really* on my way!

54

Days later, the contract is signed, and the bonuses are distributed. In addition to dance rehearsals, I prep for radio and television interviews and have photos taken for the EP jacket. Jenner and Martin fine-tune my impending publicity tour schedule. But there is one event that cannot be put off any longer: the dance-off!

The showdown is set for one Friday afternoon, and dance rehearsals are even put on hold for that day! Martin doesn't want me to have any excuse not to be my best. All the dancers are invited as are Terrance, Magda, Anatoli, Serena and Jenner, and they all crowd into the studio, filling the room with a party-like atmosphere.

Beau helps me warm up, and I'm stretching my legs when I hear a ruckus. Martin enters the studio followed by Petra and Pauline in a replica of one of my favorite costumes from his REVOLUTION! days! He's sporting skintight red leather leggings that show off his newly slimmer, muscular legs and a black, skintight wife-beater tank under a flowy, white, silk button-down shirt that has been left open. A white towel hangs around his neck and he's holding it, boxer style, a look of pure intensity plastered on his face.

The *best* part is that Pauline has fitted him with a high-top wig that looks just like his hair back when he was young. The crowd breaks into applause, cheering as Martin sashays around the room, looking triumphant.

I hop up, laughing. "Hey, no fair! I didn't know we could wear costumes."

He tosses his towel onto a chair and shakes his head as he starts to stretch. "That's you're problem, not mine. Dancing isn't just about moves, junior." He makes a flouring gesture with his hand, "It's about *style*. You might be younger, but I've got a lot more experience than you. That's gotta count for something."

A few people snicker, and Martin smiles pointedly at me as he continues to stretch.

I roll my eyes and cross my arms. "More minutes on the clock doesn't make you better, it just makes you older." Snickers in the crowd egg me on. "Grab your Depends and let's get going, grandpa. You've got to finish before Denny's serves the early-bird special."

The room erupts in hoots and hollers. Jenner stands and walks to the center of the room. "Ladies and gentlemen, may I have your attention. We have a challenge to witness. Who is the better dancer? Age?" He indicates to Martin who rolls his eyes at Jenner and then takes a dramatic bow. "Or will it be beauty?" I curtsy and smile sweetly, blowing kisses at everyone.

Jenner claps his hands to quiet everyone. "Best of three wins. Each dancer will do the same routine. One designated by Martin, one by Dani and one by Serena. The audience votes." Jenner pauses theatrically. "Let the dance-off begin!"

We start with a routine I'm doing for my promo tour. Carlton hits the music and "My Place" fills the room. I know this routine like the back of my hand. I spin, kick and flick my way through the moves, confident I've got this victory locked. When I'm finished, everyone breaks into applause and I give Martin a smug smile as I accept a towel and bottle of water from Carlton.

I take my time leaving the dance floor as Martin stands and dusts off his shoulders, looking nonplussed. Everyone eats up Martin's showmanship and he takes his position. Much to my shock, Martin nails my routine! He is spot on with every kick, twist and lunge.

Beau leans in as Martin finishes to thunderous applause. "Looks like the geezer's got some fire in his belly after all."

I grimace at Beau as I step up. Next is a modern piece Serena has been working on. Martin and I practice it almost every day before rehearsals, and it's beautiful. The music starts, new age and soulful, and I flow through the movements slowly, precisely. I'm drenched in sweat by the time the song ends, my muscles singing.

I nod at Martin and wink as he takes the floor. His leather pants present a bit of a challenge for him in this number, not giving him the ability to flow quite so easily in the barrel kicks, but other than that he moves as graceful as a willow despite the constant creaks his leather pants emit.

As I get into position for the last number, I start to get nervous. *Martin is way more in shape than I'd anticipated. While I'm pretty sure I'm winning, I know he won a lot of points for his costume. And we're about to do a routine he's been dancing since he was fourteen. I could be in big trouble.*

The music starts, heavy '80s synthesizer rattling the room as Martin's younger self sings his heart out. While this is far from a traditional dance piece, there's a lot of crazy moves like the Roger Rabbit and the Cabbage Patch, all culminating in a huge jazz split combination that ends in a standing position. I blaze through all the moves, hamming it up for everyone watching, but my foot snags on the wood and I don't stand up from my jazz split as well as I would like.

Martin stands as everyone claps, shaking his head, giving me a fake sad face. "Too bad about that back foot. You were almost flawless."

"Well, see how those old man knees hold up, Martin. I think I've got this locked." I smile more smugly than I feel and sit down.

Carlton starts the music again, and I know from Martin's first move that I've lost. No amount of practice on my part can compare to Martin's long history with these moves. Coupled with his new confidence in his trim physique and his on-point costume, I don't stand a chance. Martin whips off his white shirt, flings it at Magda as he gyrates across the floor, shaking his body so much that his wig slips to the side. He nails his jazz split and scissors his legs together, seeming to rise magically to standing position, victorious in his crooked wig. Everyone jumps up and cheers, including me.

Jenner laughs and steps forward, clapping. "I think we can all agree on who won this challenge." Jenner looks at me and bows respectfully as he pulls a large fake gold medal from his pocket. "I'm sorry, Dani, but I have to award this one to Martin Fox! Who should win alone for wearing that wig!"

Martin punches the air and removes his wig as Jenner places the medal around his neck. I hug Martin.

"You win! Congratulations!"

Martin admires his medal. "Thank you, darlin'. Sure love gold accessories! This will spruce up every outfit."

Brett walks over and gives Martin a warm pat on the back. "You were amazing!" Martin smiles shyly, "Thanks." They continue to gaze at each other, and I start to feel like a third wheel.

"Guess I'll go grab a shower. See you, twinkle toes!" Martin smiles at me but never takes his eyes off of Brett.

***

Finally, the day comes for my first song to drop. It's Wednesday in early November. I wake up to "My Place" blaring on the speakers throughout the house. I leap out of bed as pajama-clad Martin and Jenner storm into my room, and we all start dancing. Soon we're joined by a jubilant Magda and Anatoli, who dance into the room to celebrate with us. *I can't believe my song is finally on the radio.* After it finishes playing, Ryan Seacrest says it's his new favorite tune, and we all scream.

Jenner grabs my phone and quickly punches in some numbers. He mumbles into the receiver, turns down the speakers then hands me the phone. Before I know it, I'm on the air, *talking to Ryan Seacrest in my pajamas!* My first major radio interview! I'm on the air for the better part of an hour, chatting between songs and commercials.

As if starting my day by talking to Ryan Seacrest isn't enough, later that day after volunteering at a food drive and taking publicity photos, we head to the Staples Center. Jenner has arranged for me to sing the national anthem at a Lakers game, which sounds awesome, but really just scares the crap out of me. I'm almost too freaked out to sing before an entire arena full of people—it's my biggest audience ever! I've only ever sung at pageants or in the studio before now. But Martin talks me through it, and I nail all the high notes and I'm on a high for the rest of the night. The best part is that after I sing, I get to sit courtside with my dad! I think seeing my dad's smile as he watches the game and gets a high-five from LeBron James is worth all the nerves. We could *never* afford courtside seats on our own.

Over the next several days, my song plays on every pop radio and satellite station around the country. It's everywhere, and my phone blows up with videos and texts from friends every time they hear it. One morning after a particularly tough workout, Martin drives me to Starbucks for a treat. When we walk inside, "My Place" just happens to be playing over the bustle of customers ordering and milk being steamed. *That's my song!* I can't help but jump up and down and scream. People look at me like I'm crazy—they probably think I'm having some sort of attack. But Martin laughs and explains to everyone that it's my song playing on the radio. Soon everyone in the shop crowds around for autographs and selfies, and of course, we get free coffee. It's the coolest thing ever, and I grin like an idiot the entire time I'm there. It's *the first time I feel like I've made it!*

The surreal experiences don't stop after my second song drops, and I have to pinch myself several times a day to make sure that *this is my life.* Jenner books appearances on morning news shows, late-night shows and at sporting events. The first time I sit at a news desk, I feel like I'll just about die. I don't have a clue what to say even though Jenner and Martin have drilled me with fake interview questions for weeks. But then I realize I've watched this show since I was a kid and feel like I'd grown up with these people, though we'd never even met before. The newscaster is very nice, and I'm so excited to talk about my songs that the interview passes in a flash. They even ask me to stay, and I get to do the weather! It's crazy to watch television your whole life and then one day appear on the shows and meet the people you've followed for years.

The perks of all this publicity I have to do are pretty amazing. Petra gives me a new outfit for each public appearance, and I take a limo or a fancy car to almost every event. I guess Jenner must be pretty relieved that big bonus from MEGA came through, or I don't know how he would have afforded all of this. Oh, and the coolest thing I get to do is get to walk the carpet at a movie premiere when

Jenner gets a last-minute call from an old producer friend needing some extra publicity for his movie. *Me! Providing extra publicity for a movie—that's insane!*

Jenner manages my appearances and interviews to the smallest detail. Although it was scary the first couple of times I was interviewed, I find myself enjoying it more and more. It's wild how much people seem to like my songs, and I have to admit, it's thrilling to see them get excited to see me or hear me talk.

I'm packing my bags late one night before I fly to New York to perform in the Macy's Thanksgiving Parade. I'm excited that my family and friends are making the trip with me. We'll have a chance to spend a few days together between appearances before I make the rounds on the Christmas-show circuit.

My phone buzzes as I zip my carry-on bag. I answer and start talking a mile a minute.

"Hey, Sean, I just finished packing. I can't wait to see you tomorrow. When do you get in?" There's a pause, and I know something's up. "What's wrong? Are you OK?"

Sean sobs and I sit down hard on the bed. "What's wrong?"

Sean finds his voice. "It's my grandfather. He had a stroke. I'm on my way to the hospital right now."

"Oh my God, Sean, I'm so sorry! I'll meet you there."

"N-no, you've got to leave tomorrow. I don't even think you can come in to see him. You'd just be in the waiting room with a bunch of strangers."

"I don't care. Let me come and just be there for you."

He hiccups. "Thanks, Dani. I need you. We're going to St. John's. His name is Walter McEvans."

"I'm leaving right now. I love you."

"Love you too."

I run down the hall and bang Martin's door open. "I need you to drive me to St. John's hospital. Sean's grandpa had a stroke."

Martin jumps up from the bed. "Oh my God. Yeah, of course. Let me get dressed."

I race down the hall. I throw on some clothes, grab my coat and race downstairs. I run into Jenner.

"Martin told me what happened. Go. We'll figure things out later. We can push back the flight 'til Wednesday if we have to."

I nod. "My bag's already packed. If someone can take care of my interview and parade clothes, I'm all set to go."

"Done. And, here, take this." He hands me a few hundred dollars in cash. "The car's out front."

I pound down the steps and hear Martin thundering after me. We hop into the waiting black Mercedes that Anatoli has left running and speed to the hospital.

Hours later, I finally get to see Sean, who's been in the ICU with his grandfather. Sean says they're stabilizing him and that he needs surgery before they'll know the prognosis. I hold Sean as he cries. I feel completely unprepared to deal with this. I wish I could do more to comfort him. I have no idea what to say.

Around 5:00 a.m., Sean falls asleep against me. I do my best to stay still as a mouse so as not to disturb him. As the lobby starts to fill with people, Sean's dad, Pete, comes downstairs. He gently wakes Sean and sits down with us.

"Let's go home, son. Mom wants you to rest for a few hours. You can come back later today. There's nothing we can do right this minute but pray and wait."

Sean nods. His dad rubs his back.

I look at Sean. "I'll be here with you."

Sean shakes his head. "You can't stay. We don't even know when he'll have the surgery. You can't miss the parade. It's the start of everything for you."

Pete leans forward. "I don't mean to butt in, but Sean's right. You're missing the parade won't help Walter get better. We'd all feel awful if you missed it. Go. Sing your heart out and, when we watch, we'll know you're doing it for us." Pete reaches out and squeezes my hand. "I mean that one-hundred percent."

I nod as tears trickle down my face. "It just doesn't feel right."

Pete gives me a small smile. "Trust me. It's the right thing to do. It'll give us something to look forward to." He pats Sean on the back. "Let's go home."

We stand up and Martin, who's been hovering off to the side, comes over. "Everything OK?"

I nod and Martin gives Sean a hug. "We're praying for your grandfather, Sean." Martin shakes Pete's hand. "You've got a wonderful son here."

Pete nods and looks at Sean proudly. "Thank you. We're pretty proud of him."

We say goodbye; my heart sinks as I watch Sean and his dad walk out. Martin puts his arm around me. "I'm glad you were able to be here for Sean. What do you want to do now?"

I shrug. "Sean and his dad want me to go to New York. They say there's nothing I can do here, and they want me to sing for them."

Martin nods. "They're right. There's nothing we can do right now but pray."

I shake my head. "It just doesn't feel right leaving."

"I know, honey."

I sigh.

Martin stands by quietly for a few minutes, letting me collect my thoughts. Finally, he nudges my foot. "What do you want to do, honey? I'll back you either way."

My eyes well up with more tears and I sigh deeply. "It doesn't feel right, but I guess I should go."

Martin nods. "OK."

I shake my head and straighten up. "What time is it?"

"Quarter to 7:00."

I sigh. "Guess we'd better leave."

55

"What's this?" I pick up a stuffed puppy on the front seat of the car.
"Oh, yeah, I forgot. Beau dropped that by early this morning."

"What was he doing there?"

Martin shrugs. "Jenner put the crew on notice that plans might change for New York. Beau texted me to see if you were OK and asked if he could bring you something. He thought you could use something to make you smile."

I look at the puppy and hug it. It *does* make me smile. I catch Martin watching me out of the corner of his eye. "What? It's sweet of him. It doesn't mean anything. He's just a friend."

Martin looks doubtful. "Mmm, hmm. Just a friend. And I'm assuming you have lots of male friends bringing you stuffed animals when you're consoling your boyfriend at the hospital?" He snorts. "That kid's up to something."

"You're paranoid, Martin. Sean knows about Beau, and he isn't worried a bit."

"Maybe he should be," Martin says under his breath.

"I heard that."

Martin speeds out of the hospital and heads north on the 405. As tired as I am, I know he's heading in the wrong direction for the airport. "Um, Martin, you're headed the wrong way."

"We're not leaving out of LAX, honey. Got a little surprise for you."

I'm so tired I can't even imagine what he's talking about. I close my eyes for a minute. I'm surprised when Martin shakes me awake.

"We're here, sweetie. Open your eyes and check it out."

I yawn and look out the window and discover we're parked right on the tarmac in front of a gleaming Bombardier Challenger 850 Learjet, the very same model Beyoncé bought for Jay-Z. The stairway is lowered so I can see a luxurious wood-and-leather interior peeking through the cabin door. An elegantly dressed stewardess smiles warmly at me from the top of the stairway.

"Surprise, Dani! You're about to ride on your first private jet. First of many, I hope!" Martin claps his hands.

All of my exhaustion and anxiety fall away as I look at the magnificent plane before me. Jenner descends the steps, arms outstretched, with a smile as big as the wingspan of the plane. He reels it in, though, as he walks down the steps. I get out of the car, stunned.

"I had hoped to surprise you under better circumstances. How did everything go? Is Sean's grandfather OK?" He opens his arms.

I pull my eyes off the plane and step into Jenner's hug. "It'll be a few days before they know anything."

Jenner nods solemnly. "We're keeping him in our prayers. I sent flowers to the hospital and arranged for meals for his family for the next week."

I'm taken by surprise. "You did that? Thank you." I give him a hug.

Jenner shrugs. "It's the least we can do. I know how much you want to be there with them. Martin told me you decided to go. You still OK with that?"

I pause, then nod. "Yup, I think so." Jenner gives me a look and waits.

I nod. "I mean, yeah, I'm ready to go."

"Good girl. MEGA arranged for Macy's to send a jet for you. I'd hate for you to have missed out on such a special treat. There's nothing quite like your first ride in a private jet."

Martin comes up next to us, a smartly dressed steward taking the bags in his hands. "All set?"

Jenner nods. "We are. First stop, New York; next stop, the stars! It's going to be a wild ride straight through 'til New Year's. Just got a call that Rocking New Year's Eve wants you to sing live right before the midnight countdown. It doesn't get much bigger than that in your first month of fame, does it?"

I shake my head. "It sure doesn't. Let's go!"

I clamber up the stairs, trailed by Martin and Jenner. As the plane door closes and we lift off, I can't shake the feeling that my life will never be the same.

TO BE CONTINUED IN BOOK TWO:
BURNING BRIGHT